Teresa Smith

and the

Queen's Revenge

Part 2

Teresa Smith
and the
Queen's Revenge

Part 2

wilf morgan

88TALES PRESS
Southwell, Nottinghamshire,
United Kingdom
www.88tales.com

First published in Great Britain
in 2021 by 88Tales Alpha
an imprint of 88Tales Press

First Edition, First Printing
This printing published 2021

A catalogue record for this book is
available from the British Library

ISBN 978-1-9997590-8-7

www.88tales.com
www.arilon-chronicles.com

Dedicated to absolutely everyone for doing their best to get through a global pandemic and through to the other side

Especially dedicated to all those who emerged from the other side only as cherished memories

Acknowledgements

Thanks to Bea, Josh and Eva, my fantastic team of dedicated test readers who gave their time and enthusiasm to provide me with feedback, suggestions and point out all the full stops I forgot to put in!

The Arilon Timeline

When the Queen arrived in Arilon, she declared that moment as Year Zero of the Royal Era.

RE : Royal Era
BRE : Before Royal Era

1170 BRE	Fall of the Primacy
1100 BRE	Idea Wars begin
1000 BRE	Idea Wars end
0 RE	The Queen arrives in Arilon
24 RE	*"Trust Me, I'm a Thief"*
25 RE	*"Arthur Ness and the Secret of Waterwhistle"* The Battle of Eris Island Arilon Civil War begins
27 RE	*"Teresa Smith and the Queen's Revenge"*

List of Arilon Islands

A list of some of Arilon's islands and their corresponding Idea.

ISLAND	IDEA
Autela	Caution
Boricia	Building & Construction
Cassinus	Adventure
Catura	Trade
Civita	Community
Doctrina	Education
Duseeya	Self-reliance
Elysium	Paradise
Eria	Relaxing
Excidia	Catastrophe
Exita	Lost Endings
Felis	Happiness
Fess	Business
Fortis	Heroes
Gravisus	Singing, Rejoicing
Imperia	Order
Impilus	Simplicity
Labos / Graft	Hard work
Lamen	Sadness, Despair
Laytans	Joyfulness
Malefic	Viciousness, Wrong-doing
Morior	Loss, Sorrow

Narrato	Histories
Novatis	New Ideas
Oblivia	Forgotten Things
Ofisora	Duty
Pavidus	Fearlessness
Phobos	Fear
Quiess	Silence
Raptor	Thieves
Rustika	Farming
Sapia	Wisdom
Savis	Kindness
Sedita	Mutiny
Segriis	Isolation
Skruto	Travel, Exploration
Tego	Hidden Things
Terminus	Frontier
Toria	Strategy, Planning
Tricium	Aristocracy
Ultima	Endings
Valia	Bravery
Vindictum	Revenge

"If I cannot inspire love, I will cause fear…"
- Frankenstein's Monster
Frankenstein, Mary Shelley, 1818

CHAPTER ZERO
THE UNSTOPPABLE AND THE IMMOVABLE

The Twilight Palace
One hour after the Fall of Titanium

The Queen's life is a giant loop, and it's a loop she needs to break.

She stands in the forest that grows from the deck of her ship. Silver trees, chrome branches and iridescent, gossamer-thin wires hanging down like leaves. The dark figure of the Queen of Arilon stands silhouetted against the Arthur Ness Forest as it catches the light from the blinding white Arilon sun.

The Twilight Palace races away from Titanium. Damaged in a collision with the pirate vessel, *The Galloping Snake*, it returns to Phobos for repairs. Other royal vessels have been sent to take its place at Titanium - they will complete the job of exterminating the insurgents before they can escape their ruined base. In this moment, the Queen has more personal concerns. She must consider her life. Her destiny. Her death. And her birth.

She stands in the place where her communion with the Threads is easiest. The silver forest, spun from the remains of her brother's life energy. His power as a Seer magnifies her own ability to peer into the Threads and see the past, present and - occasionally – the future.

The Queen stares out into the NothingSpace. All of Arilon is out there. Every island. Every citizen. She cares for them all, truly and deeply. She needs to protect them from the chaos all around and the chaos within themselves. The chaos that threatens to destroy them. But before she can do any of that, before she can complete her long-held plans, she must solve the riddle of her existence.

She must break the loop.

Titanium
One minute after the Fall of Titanium

Teresa could barely string two thoughts together. None of it made any sense.

She was the Queen.

She was the Queen.

She was the Queen.

Her eyes were still fixed on the spot outside the hangar deck where *The Twilight Palace* had been a few seconds ago. The Queen's ship. *Teresa's* ship..?

This was crazy. She couldn't believe it. Surely it was all lies, designed to unsettle her. Telling Teresa that she would kill her own brother, steal his power and use it to destroy the Queen. And that this act would lead to her eventually *becoming* the Queen.

None of it made sense. If Teresa became the Queen, that would be in the future, not the past. Also, what could possibly make her destroy Arthur? What event could make her so angry, so desperately insane?

None of it made any sense.

She was the Queen.

The Twilight Palace
One hour after the Fall of Titanium

A loop has no beginning or end, of course. Nevertheless, the Queen can see there is one clear point where the loop is weakest. A point where - if she applies enough pressure - she will surely be able to break it.

The point where Teresa kills her.

The monarch has always been aware of this loop, this cycle that has her trapped in a web of destiny like a fly. Yet her knowledge of the actual details has always been frustratingly minimal.

What does she actually remember?

She knows she does something terrible... something that so enrages Teresa that the girl, in a bid to destroy the Queen, absorbs all Arthur's power, killing him in the process. She turns all that power on the Queen and eradicates her.

Distraught, Teresa goes away and, somehow, over the course of years, becomes the Queen.

She formulates her plan to save Arilon and begins building the Agency Engine.

She marches on Arilon (somehow twenty-seven years in the past) and conquers it.

She rules for a quarter of a century, pruning the Travel Lines, altering the minds and hearts of everyone in Arilon, preparing them for the moment when the Agency Engine is finally ready. Only the infernal Cat offers continuous resistance.

Arthur Ness and Teresa Smith arrive in Arilon. They slow her plans down but cannot stop them entirely.

But then the Queen does something terrible... something that so enrages Teresa that the girl, in a bid to destroy the Queen, absorbs all Arthur's power, killing him in the process. She turns all that power on the Queen and eradicates her.

And round and round everyone goes, like a fairground carousel.

The memories of her past life are like fragments of a shattered mirror. Sharp pieces of glass strewn across the mud

13

of her mind. Everything after she becomes the Queen, she can remember. Everything before is a blur. Simply put, without her memories, she will wander headlong into the moment of her death. However, there is hope. Something the Queen realised only after her first meeting with Teresa and Arthur in Waterwhistle.

After retrieving her mirror and the defeated Lady Eris, the Queen had returned to Arilon and had almost immediately begun to experience tiny flashes of her old mind. Random memories, long forgotten. A cloud in a blue sky. The taste of liquorice. The creak of a playground swing.

Despite initial bemusement, the Queen had eventually suspected the recall had been triggered by her proximity to Teresa. If that were true, it meant that if the monarch could somehow get close to Teresa for long enough, her memories would *repair themselves*.

What a discovery! Finally, she had an opportunity to recover her memories and remember the circumstances leading to her demise. Her goal was clear – capture Teresa Smith.

The sudden explosion of war had delayed her plans for too long but eventually, she had been able to peer through the Threads and learn the girl's whereabouts – the island of Oblivia.

The Queen had intercepted the children there and ended up being incarcerated with Teresa. She found to her joy that her suspicions had been correct. Sitting in the cell next to her younger self, a crucial memory returned to her – the location of the Resistance headquarters. Moreover, the memory featured herself as Teresa standing in the ruins of the base and the Queen revealing they were the same person.

Eager to cause Teresa pain and make this memory come true, the Queen had left the girl on Oblivia, knowing they would meet again soon. When they did, she would capture the girl, keep her imprisoned and reclaim every single lost memory.

Unfortunately, the encounter hadn't ended as planned and Teresa had evaded her grasp. Although it had been General Kingsley and the ever-infernal Cat that had forced the Queen's retreat, they hadn't been the actual reason for her failure. The architect of Teresa's resistance had been clearly visible in the girl's eyes. Her bond with her brother.

The true obstacle to the Queen's victory was the boy.

Arthur Ness.

Titanium
One minute after the Fall of Titanium
"Tee?"

Arthur's voice snapped Teresa back into her surroundings. She saw her friends in front of her, groaning with the pain inflicted by the Queen moments earlier. They were crawling slowly and gingerly to their feet.

She turned and saw her brother stumbling toward her across the battered, wrecked remains of the hangar deck. Arthur's face was a flood of emotions that Teresa struggled to read. That's when she saw the Queen's treasure box in his hand, hanging open. In his other hand were the contents. The paint brushes that Arthur had given to Teresa for her birthday. So *that* was the prized possession that the Queen was willing to destroy entire cities to recover.

The last thing that Arthur had ever given her before she killed him.

Teresa looked back up at her brother's pained face - his expression now made sense.

15

He knew.

Suddenly, she couldn't look at him. What kind of monster was she? To be able to do that to the one person who had always been there for her. Her immovable anchor. Her rock.

The Twilight Palace
One hour after the Fall of Titanium

Arthur Ness is the real problem.

All along, the Queen has despised Teresa. Despised her weakness. Despised her for falling to whatever forces had resulted in her killing her brother and becoming the Queen. She'd hated her younger self so much that revealing her true identity and watching her face fall and spirit break... it had felt like a sweet revenge, justly served.

But a revenge for what?

For becoming the Queen? For evolving into the most powerful being in Arilon? For grasping her destiny as the one who would eventually end all conflict, pain and misery everywhere for everyone? She shouldn't have despised Teresa, she should have celebrated with her!

No, the Queen now realises her scorn for her younger self was misplaced. It only happened because of the lingering influence of Arthur Ness in her mind. Even now, there is some tiny shred of the Queen that longs for him to be at her side once again – when, in reality, he is the one who deserves her anger.

He constantly does his best to hold Teresa back, convincing her that becoming the Queen is a bad thing. In doing this, not only does he keep his sister from becoming her true self, he foils the Queen's plans as well. Neither Teresa nor the Queen can reach their full potential while his malicious, interfering influence permeates the air. He is the needle that is unpicking the tapestry of both Teresa and the Queen's minds.

The presence of Teresa repairs the Queen – but the presence of Arthur destroys her.

She thinks, now, about the item that had been so cruelly stolen from her by that pathetic band of thieves, the Rogue's Run Trio. Her precious treasure - the paintbrushes that had been Arthur Ness' final gift to her. Even as she'd left her old life behind after Arthur's death, something deep inside couldn't let go. She had kept the brushes in a box but she'd placed an impenetrable sheath of Threads around it to keep it tightly locked shut. Nobody – not even the Queen herself – would ever open it and look upon her one weakness. She had destroyed entire cities in her quest to recover it from the thieves, yet she would never actually dare look upon it.

However, now she can see that Arthur is in fact her true foe, the contents of that small, wooden box no longer hold any power over her. Let the cretins have it. It means nothing to her now.

On Oblivia, the Queen had seen the siblings' bond up close and realised how unbelievably strong it was. But she also saw that it was not perfect. There were cracks. Tiny spaces of uncertainty into which she has already jammed the dagger of doubt.

What began as an act of malice, the Queen now realises is her ultimate strategy for victory. Free Teresa from the pernicious influence of her brother. Enable her to reach her true potential. Help her to transform from the grubby caterpillar she is into the powerful, beautiful being of power that will save Arilon.

The Queen knows she must return to the immovable focus she wielded at the start of her journey.

In the beginning, her power had been absolute.

Ultima Island

Twenty-seven years before the Fall of Titanium

Sam and May dived behind a row of wooden shop-crates as the Queen unleashed a volley of lightning at the King of Ends powerful enough to destroy a building. The two titans hurled entire storms at each other and the two humans knew they were too insignificant to be noticed. Unfortunately, being unnoticed was no protection against being disintegrated.

"Well, this is fun!" Sam yelled over the noise. He hoped making a joke would somehow lessen the terror he felt. It didn't.

"We need to get out of here!" May yelled over the noise of the island burning around them.

We need to find the secret we came for, the Guide said into Sam's mind.

"We need to find the secret we came for," Sam repeated for May.

"Tell the Guide I don't care about that right now," May shouted back. "If we don't get out of here, we're done for, then it won't matter *what* the secret is. Ever hear the phrase 'live to fight another day'?"

The secret must be here somewhere. This day is the Queen's first appearance in Arilon, said the Guide into Sam's brain. *This is the moment she ascends to power. Remember what I told you about the Pillars.*

"Remember the Pillars of Arilon?" Sam shouted as the pair huddled down.

"The four beings that created Arilon, yes, of course, the Guide told us all about them," May shouted. "Do you really think now is the time for a history lesson?!"

"Right before coming to this island, the Queen dealt with three of them. The Ender is the last one! This is the moment we've come all this way for! The clue that's going to help us destroy the Queen is about to reveal itself! It has to!"

It was no secret that the trio had *really* wanted to be out of here before the Queen dropped by.

The Guide couldn't read the Threads like a proper Weaver, but from the tiny glimpses she was able to get, she had been able to make certain calculations and deductions. And it was those deductions she'd taken to Sam months ago to inform him that a vital clue on how to destroy the Queen had briefly appeared on Ender island on this day in history. The trio's months-long odyssey had finally brought them here but the exact moment and nature of the clue was still a mystery. After several fruitless hours spent searching the streets, shops and people of the island, Sam and May were still empty handed. Now the moment they'd hoped to avoid had arrived and here they were, still none the wiser.

But despite the initial shock of the Guide's first appearance all those months ago, Sam felt she had earned his and May's trust. He had complete faith in her predictions. If she said the clue was here, then it was here. They'd come too far to abandon the mission now.

"Your power is failing," the Queen said.

Sam was suddenly aware that the deafening noise of the apocalypse had paused. Now, all they could hear was the roar of the flames and the cries of the few people who hadn't yet managed to escape the island.

"I have all the power I need to end you, stranger," the King growled, his voice dangerous and deep like thunder rolling over hills. "I'm just a bit behind on my yoga, that's all. Give me a minute, to catch my breath."

"You cannot defeat me, Ender," the Queen said with a quiet calm that was terrifying. "The Beginner is dead. The Disruptor and Thinker are mine. You are the only Pillar left. You are alone."

"He is never alone," said another deep growl but not the King's. Sam and May poked their heads up over the edge of the wooden crates and saw the Queen of Ends, as magnificent as she had been a few hours ago, during the procession. And with her, two slightly smaller versions of her and the King. A prince and princess? The Cat's children, Sam realised with a start.

"He will never be alone as long as his family stand beside him," the Queen of Ends warned through gritted fangs the size of Sam's forearm. The three newcomers lined up next to the King, facing off against this strange invader.

"Neema, what are you doing?" the King said out of the corner of his mouth, his eyes still on the Queen. "I told you and the children to stay in the castle."

"You appeared to be having problems defeating this stranger," said his wife. "I warned you to keep up with your yoga."

"One of you, four of you, it makes no difference to me," said the Queen slowly. She flexed her fingers and black lightning ran between them. "My destiny is set. Whatever happens will always and eventually be in my favour. Come then, family of Ender. Let us see what power you possess."

Titanium

Teresa looked around. Her friends, even injured by her future self, were concerned for her. As always, the Cat was first in line to check on her.

"You okay, Smithy? Did she hurt you?"

Teresa's eyes flitted over the small, black cat and filled with tears.

She thought she was a good person. But all she could remember now was the Cat telling her that the Queen had taken his family.

Ender Island

The Queen pulled a storm of daggers and fire out of nowhere and rained them down on the four creatures in front of her. The blaze was awash with the dark lightning and it congealed specifically around the King's wife and children. The feline monarch saw what was happening and tried to block the torrent but the lightning strikes kept beating him back. Sam watched in horror as the Queen's black fire sank its teeth into the three creatures. Bright, multi-coloured points of light flowed out of them and into the Queen. Sparkling reds and greens and yellows shot out of the three writhing figures - *emptying* them it seemed to Sam. The Queen, on the other hand, was enveloped in the colours, glowing almost too bright to see. Moment by moment, they soaked into her like watercolours soaking into paper. Seconds later, there she stood, illuminated by multiple pinpoints of light glittering from gems that were now embedded all over her body.

The Queen of Ends and her children were gone.

The Twilight Palace

The Queen knows she has done terrible things over the years. From the day she conquered Arilon right up to the present moment. Death, destruction and misery have resulted from many of her actions. This is undeniable. But it is also necessary.

Improvement is change. To change means to lose some things. Losing things often hurts. But in the end, you have less weight. Less baggage. You are more powerful. You are improved.

Since the beginning, Arilon has been presided over by the Four Pillars - the Thinker, the Disruptor, the Beginner and the Ender - and their ridiculous idea of Balance. Good, evil, order, chaos, creation, destruction all resting against each other in just the right amounts to allow peaceful life to exist? What a preposterous and horrifying plan.

Her way will be better.

But for Arilon to improve, it will have to lose some things.

The war is finally coming to an end. The last few drops of fear will be squeezed from the people of Arilon to complete the fuelling of the Agency Engine. In the meantime, the Queen will work on recovering her memories and breaking the circle.

Dispose of Arthur.

Join with Teresa.

Break the cycle.

Activate the Engine.

Cake.

The Queen creases her brow in confusion. Cake? Where did that come from? What did it mean?

She dismisses it. The Threads often throw up random, meaningless images, impossible to fathom.

Now, as she relaxes her mind into the silver and shadow of the Arthur Ness Forest, the Threads provide her with new clues – and unlike 'cake', she can tell these are most definitely important. The clarity and significance of these images hits her mind like a train. They are clues from her near future.

A narrow corridor. A metal door. A hospital.

And one more - the Queen gasps in awe at this final revelation...

Teresa will come willingly to her on the island of Terminus.

The Queen is overjoyed. The seeds of distrust she has already planted between Teresa and Arthur have begun to blossom. But the Queen knows that the future, even foretold, doesn't simply happen of its own accord. It will only come about through choices and actions. So, the Queen will continue to make choices and carry out actions, nurturing those seeds of distrust until they bloom into an entire forest of beautiful tragedy. She will ensure Teresa comes to her on Terminus. And instead of the Queen's demise, perhaps a new path can be forged. Perhaps they will both be able to place their hands on the loop and break it together.

She will prevail, in the end. The Queen knows this.

She is the ultimate power in Arilon. An immovable object.

Titanium

Arthur was just a few steps away, now. The Cat and the others surrounded Teresa, but it was only Arthur that she saw. Carrying those gifts he gave her for her birthday, proof of her terrible crimes. Surely this would finally be the thing that broke them. The thing that ended the dream team. There would be no coming back from this.

"Arthur, I-" Teresa began but had to stop as Arthur flung his arms around her.

"It's not going to happen," he whispered into her ear. "We're not going to let it."

Teresa squeezed her eyes shut, feelings of hope shooting through her.

He was always there. He would never give up on her. He would never let her give up on herself.

In that moment, she vowed to fight.

"It's not going to happen," she repeated back to Arthur.

This was her goal now. Not to give in to this supposed destiny but to fight it. To fight the Queen. It was her plan all along, why stop now?

When she put her mind to it, Teresa knew deep down that she could be an unstoppable force.

Teresa Smith

and the

Queen's Revenge

Part 2 of 3

THREAD THREE

OPERATION HAMMER

CHAPTER ONE
ENDER'S END

- SAM -

"You murdered them!" the King of Ends roared at the top of his voice. The mountains around them shook in fear. He leaped at the Queen but it would be the last act the King of Ends would ever do.

With a swipe of her hand, the Queen once again sent her black lightning into the charging creature - only this time, the energy was laced with the colours of the gems that now littered the evil monarch's body. The blasts held the king in place, his powerful piston-like legs pounding the ground, pushing him against the torrent... but unable to move him forward, even an inch.

"They are not dead," said the Queen over the noise of the onslaught, "they live on in me, giving their power to me. To a greater cause. One that will save Arilon. Not destroy it, as you and your fellow Pillars would eventually have done. One day, Arilon will thank them for their sacrifice."

Sam put his hand across his eyes. The light from the battle was so bright, the noise so deafening, it was like the end of the world.

"Look!" May cried, pointing. She was shouting at the top of her lungs but the battle was so loud that Sam, right next to her, could barely hear her. "Look at the Cat! He's... he's..."

Shrinking was the word. Sam couldn't believe it. The Cat was shrinking.

Bits of his massive body were being blown away, like an oak tree losing leaves, twigs and branches in a storm. The trunk held firm but even that had to eventually yield to the forces of nature being smashed against it. Perhaps if the King had run away, he could have kept his strength, his power, to fight another day. Insead, he stubbornly continued to try and force his way forward, through the storm and towards the Queen. And through his efforts, all he accomplished was to see his power, moment by moment, stripped away from him.

Shards of lightning peeled off dangerously in various directions, flashing and dying away. Whatever they hit exploded in vicious showers of sparks.

I am beginning to think... the Guide's voice came into Sam's head, uncharacteristically afraid, *I am beginning to think that I have made a mist-*

The last thing Sam felt was one of the stray lightning flashes hitting him square in the chest.

Then nothing.

Years passed.

Suddenly, his eyes flickered open and they were full of tears.

"Sam!" May was shaking him, terrified, panicked. "Sam, I thought you were…"

Sam? Where did you go? I felt you disappear for a minute. Now you are back, your brain is… different.

Memories were flooding back into Sam's head like recalling a dream after waking. Memories of the years and years and absolute years of events he had just witnessed in the last couple of minutes. But it wasn't a dream, his brain reminded him. Those things had really happened.

"Oh, no…" he croaked. "… oh, no… Teresa…"

"Sam, what are you talking about?" May cried. He was about to speak when she cut him off. "It doesn't matter, tell me later. We need to get out of here, right now."

"Where's Ter… where's the Queen?" Sam stammered. He suddenly noticed how deathly quiet it was.

"She's gone! All that's left of the king is… well, the Cat," May gestured to the tiny, unmoving black shape lying on the ground in the distance. "The Queen looked really exhausted and went back to her ship and took off. And we need to do the same *right now!*"

Sam's head was spinning. Why was May getting so panicked? The Queen was gone. Surely now they could relax. They'd survived. They'd-

The landscape.

Sam suddenly noticed that all around them, the island's landscape still boasted many of its hills. And the port. And quite a lot of houses, shops and buildings. None of which were around in the time they'd originally come from. Which meant the real destruction was yet to come.

All around them, shadows started to fall across the landscape. Sam and May both looked up to see the Arilon sun slowly get covered over by… something. Something dark and malevolent. Something with an abundance of long, spindly, spiny legs, slowly waving back and forth like long blades of grass in the wind.

"The Rainhand," Sam whispered.

Get to a boat! Get to a boat, NOW! The Guide all but screamed into Sam's brain.

May helped Sam to his feet, his brain still only half in control of his body. He glanced over to see the tiny, black form of the Cat, lying still and alone where the mighty King of Ends

31

had once stood. It felt bad to leave him there with what was about to happen, but they knew the Cat would survive the imminent destruction. That much was already set by history. There was no such guarantee for them.

But even with destruction just moments away, Sam couldn't stop thinking about Teresa.

With May's arm around Sam's waist, supporting him, the pair scrambled as fast as they could over the rubble and remains of shops they had been walking around inside of just a few hours earlier. As the sky darkened, they found a small, wooden boat, scrambled aboard, released the moorings and sped away as fast as they could.

The very moment the Travel Line took them away from the island, the destruction started. There seemed to be nothing visible above the island but every few seconds, the silhouette of a black claw, descending from above with blinding speed, could be seen flashing past the hills and slamming into the ground. The deafening *boom* of each strike was accompanied by a shockwave that literally shook the entire island, vibrating the Travel Line their little boat was riding on. With every incredible blow, chunks of land flew off and scattered into the darkness, swallowed up by the NothingSpace. The island was literally being ripped apart right in front of them.

Eventually, the little boat made enough distance from the island that the darkness of the NothingSpace mercifully swallowed up the sight, sound and vibrations of the destruction. They didn't need to see anymore. They already knew how much smaller the island would be by the time the creature was finished.

From the first moment of the Rainhand's attack, Sam had been staring but his eyes hadn't really been seeing the devastation. They'd been reliving the scenes of Teresa killing

Arthur, killing the Queen and then spending years and years becoming the Queen in a far away place, in a long ago time.

"I saw it," his mouth said, softly into the silence and darkness. "The thing we came for. The clue. I know how to stop her."

May turned to him. He could see the logical part of her brain trying its best to beat back the terror of what she'd just seen. "Stop her? The Queen?"

Sam turned to May. "That lightning flash that hit me, it connected me somehow to the Queen. And my... I don't know, my Timeline abilities let my brain fly backward along her timestream, witnessing everything that had happened to bring her to this point. I saw how she came into being. I followed her around for years. So, yes, I know how to stop the her."

"Okay, stop keeping us in suspense! How?" May asked, glad to be able to focus on something other than the image of evil claws raining down from the dark. "What do we do? Where do we head to next?"

"Guide..?" Sam held up the mirror on his forearm, still intact after their ordeal. The tall, thin woman appeared. Being visible in a mirror meant both children could hear her speaking at once.

"Yes, Sam, what do you need?" she asked.

"Can you please plot us a return course back to our time?" Sam took a deep breath. "We need to get to Terminus."

CHAPTER TWO
AFTERMATH

- TERESA -

Teresa didn't stand with the others on the deck of the *Galloping Snake* to watch Titanium disappear into the darkness. To all those resistance fighters, the ancient place had been a symbol of their struggle against an evil tyrant. To Teresa, it was the place where she had learned that the evil tyrant was one day going to be *her*.

Instead, she had gone below decks to find some peace and quiet. Not only because of how she was feeling but also to recover from the effort of helping Arthur get the *Snake* and several other ships onto the Travel Lines so they could escape.

The attack had collapsed many of the base's walls and ceilings but the ships themselves were mostly in good shape – they were just trapped on Travel Lines that were covered in rubble. Arthur and Teresa had used their abilities to 'hop' the ships over any blockages and onto the unobstructed portions of the Lines, giving them freedom to escape from the base. They'd even managed to salvage the damaged *Galloping Snake*. After colliding with the *Twilight Palace*, Thrace said it was hanging together with spit and wishful thinking. However, a supreme effort and focussed concentration from Teresa and Arthur coaxed the faithful ship onto an escape path.

Neither Teresa nor Arthur had exactly been in the relaxed state of mind they needed to make ships fly - but knowing a second wave of royal vessels were almost certainly on their way definitely helped with motivation.

As Teresa padded slowly along the ship's narrow corridors, she recalled with fondness the time when she'd had this entire thing to herself. Newly escaped from Lady Eris' dungeons and getting the hang of sailing it on her own. It had been a strange and frightening time, of course. Everyone back home was still under the tyranny of Lady Eris and the Yarnbulls. But, despite that, it had also been a joyful and liberating couple of days. To swing through the Black, just her and her ship.

Back then, she had been full of enthusiasm and energy (and she'd also been a Needleman but, hey, nobody's perfect). Now, though, she drifted aimlessly about like an unsettled ghost.

Her head had no particular destination but it seemed that her feet did, because before she knew it, she had arrived at a very particular cabin.

The cabin where they had laid Bamboo's remains to rest.

Nobody had even realised Bamboo was still on the base. He'd attended a meeting with the General earlier in the day but was supposed to have left immediately after. It wasn't until the young boy, Bamboo's spokesperson, came stumbling into the docking bay as they worked on *The Galloping Snake*, a bag of broken sticks in his hand, that it had become clear that the day's losses were even higher than anyone had realised.

Through his tears and grief, the boy uttered just one word.

"...Graves..."

Eventually, the boy had calmed down enough to recount what had happened.

Bamboo had delayed their leaving because he had wanted to meditate. After a few hours communing with the Threads, the pair had finally been on their way to the docks

35

and their waiting ship. Unfortunately, it was at that moment that the Queen's fleet had arrived.

In the initial onslaught, the boy had become pinned by a falling stone archway and Bamboo had clattered to the ground, landing a few tantalising inches beyond the boy's grasp. Before he could free himself, the boy watched in horror as a huge, ebony-armoured knight had come lumbering out of the smoke and flames.

Instantly recognising the bamboo doll, Graves had lurched forward, snatched up the cloth-wrapped bundle and - ignoring the desperate pleas of the trapped boy - crushed the entire thing in his massive, black-gauntleted hands. Soon the doll was just splintered fragments of wood, scattered all over the floor. Task accomplished, Lord Graves had disappeared into the flames from whence he'd come.

Eventually, the distraught boy had forced himself free of the rubble and, broken remains in hand, had wandered the burning base until fate delivered him to the last ship just before it left.

Teresa looked down on what was left of Bamboo, spread out with care on the bed. Kingsley herself had lain them here with care and affection, even though the boy said there was no point in keeping the splintered sticks. 'Bamboo is not here anymore', the boy had said eventually. 'He is elsewhere. I do not know where, nor do I know if we will ever see him again.'

As Teresa looked down at the shattered branches of bamboo - which Kingsley had arranged back into Bamboo's likeness - she remembered the first time she and Arthur had seen them. Propped up on a chair, they hadn't looked alive at all. Strangely, they looked more alive now than they did then.

The doll stared accusingly at Teresa. Another casualty of her evil, future self.

Future self?

How much of this could she keep putting down to some, as yet non-existent version of herself? Surely the seeds of the Queen were inside her right now. The Queen had said Teresa was twelve when she'd killed Arthur so it was due to happen soon. No, this was no evil future version. The evil was already here. However, that didn't mean she was just going to let it win. Giving up wasn't really her style.

With a start, Teresa suddenly realised what this spare cabin actually was - it was the one she had slept in after being rescued from Needlemen island. And if that was the case...

Ignoring the grisly scene on top of the bed, Teresa knelt down and reached into the darkness underneath the bunk, sweeping her hand left and right, feeling for-

There it was!

Her fingers closed on the object and she brought it back out of its resting place, into the light.

Her bow.

It had been her constant companion in the terrible ice forest. A trusted friend that had saved her life many times. After the two Teresas had melded together, the new version of herself had been confused and uncertain. She had two personalities, two sets of memories... there had been parts of her own mind that had suddenly felt completely alien to her. The harsh, lone survivor who had briefly abandoned Arthur to go and look after the Sleepers was definitely a part of herself that Teresa had wanted to get rid of. Symbolically, she had thrown the bow under the bed, hoping that part of herself would disappear with it.

And yet, as she held the wooden bow in her hands now, just days later, she felt differently. As Teresa softly rubbed the strong vines that she'd wrapped around the handle to make the grip, she found that the harsh, lone survivor was still inside, calling to her – and she welcomed it.

I can protect them, the voice said. *With every fibre of my body. Nothing will stand in my way.*

"Teresa?"

She looked up to see Arthur step quietly into the room. He smiled encouragingly at her and then his eyes fell onto the scene on the bed.

"Sad, isn't it?" Teresa said.

Arthur nodded. "Remember when we first saw him? We thought everyone was playing a joke on us! Either that or everyone in the room was completely bonkers."

"Well," Teresa said, sadly, "I'm the only bonkers one in the room now."

"Totally bonkers, I'm afraid," Arthur bobbed his head, shrugging.

"Hey!" Teresa laughed, mock-punching him in the arm. "You're not supposed to agree!"

"Oh, cool, you found your bow," Arthur noticed the weapon in Teresa's hand. "Don't forget your quiver and arrows."

"Thanks, Tarzan," Teresa giggled, teasing her city-raised brother. "What would I do without your bush survival instincts?"

"Yeah, nature really isn't my strong point," Arthur admitted. "If I ever get trapped in a forest, I'd only last as long as it took to realise there was nothing to read. Then, that would be me finished." Teresa laughed as her brother continued. "I'd try making a bow out of some skinny branch and it'd snap the first time I tried to use it."

"Oh my gosh, what would you eat? You'd starve!"

"Unless they had a cake shop."

"Ha! I bet you'd try and make a spoon."

"Nah, that's one thing I'd be fine without - I'd just put the cake on the ground and throw my face into it."

The pair laughed and Teresa was grateful for the moment of silliness. Despite being the most sensible of the Smith siblings, Arthur definitely had a playful streak too.

"Listen, I was thinking..." Arthur said.

"Did it hurt?"

"Shut up. Do you remember when the Queen attacked us above Oblivia?"

The smile fell from her face. "Great way to kill the mood, Arthur."

"No, this is a good thing," he reassured her. "Do you remember that weird feeling that came over us part way through? Like everything was... I don't know how to describe it... sharper?"

Teresa's eyes widened. "More vivid! Like you could feel every moment passing, every molecule floating by..."

"Exactly!" Arthur said, excited. "So you did feel it!"

"I thought it was my imagination...!"

"No, the Queen did that," Arthur said. "I know because I think I've done it before, too. By accident, but... it was when I was back home in London during the air raid."

"Oh, you mean after Labyrinth when you totally abandoned me?" Teresa teased.

"Yeah, alright, for the million and tenth time, I'm really sorry about that..."

"Accepted. Continue."

"So, as one of the bombs exploded and my window cracked, everything just sort of slowed down. And then it skipped a track, like my way of experiencing the world shifted somehow. It all felt really different. Sharper. More immediate. Just like on the boat."

"So…" Teresa tried to figure out exactly what Arthur was getting at. "What does all that mean?"

"However it is that the Queen does that, I have that power too," Arthur said.

Teresa nodded, slowly and turned away, her gaze falling back towards the bed. For a moment, she had almost forgotten it was in the room.

"Don't you see?" Arthur said, excitedly. "She's no more powerful than us. We have the same abilities, her and us. Okay, we're not as experienced at using them… but there's two of us. I reckon, one way or another, we have the power to beat her. And when we do, we can save you and Arilon all at the same time."

This was typical of Arthur, Teresa thought. Seeing the upside. To Teresa, all it meant was a reminder that the Queen had stolen Arthur's abilities.

Arthur put his hand on Teresa's shoulder but she felt no warmth from it. He knew she was the Queen but he didn't know his sister was going to disintegrate him. How could she tell him that part?

"You and her, Tee," Arthur said, softly, "you're not the same person."

That was also typical of Arthur. Always trying to say the nice things, even when it made no sense.

"Don't worry," she said, turning round to face her brother. "I know we'll beat her. Nothing has changed. I won't let her hurt you or anyone. I'm going to protect you with every fibre of my body. Nothing is going to get in my way."

She gripped the bow and it felt strong and tough in her hand.

CHAPTER THREE
THE MOST IMPORTANT LEAF

- THE CAT -

The Cat sat in the middle of the turbulent activity on deck and closed his eyes.

Whenever I don't know where you are, his wife used to say, *I just look for the biggest crowd of people. I know you will be at the centre.*

He had often been accused of enjoying being at the heart of things. The list of people who had so accused him was long varied and it included (but was not limited to) Lady Taranteen, Big Sally, Little Sally, Karl Frogham, The Queen of Ends, Lady Aerie, Bamboo, Teresa Smith, the Queen, Montgomery Avis and Lady Eris. And every single one of them had been one hundred percent correct.

It wasn't his fault. Pillars were supposed to be in the middle of things. How else could they hold everything up?

Of course, many of the people in that list had accused the Cat of being so big-headed that he actually believed he was the Ender. One of the four Pillars of Arilon, the original creators of the world. Very few people on that list knew for a fact that it wasn't just a joke. And one of those people now actually wore his power on their body like jewellery.

Right now, there were two things that gave the impression to everyone that the Cat was asleep. Number one - his eyes were closed. Number two - he had announced to everyone that he was going to sleep. The announcement, however, like so many things he said, was a lie.

He wasn't sleeping, he was listening. Listening to life aboard *The Galloping Snake*. Listening to the sailors up in the rigging, listening to the gunners checking the cannons in case they were needed for action, listening to orders being given and orders being carried out. He soaked the sounds into himself and became one with all his surroundings.

He *was* a Pillar of Arion, a part of the very fabric of this world. There was no separation between where he stopped and Arilon began. A threat to Arilon was a threat to him. And that was the reason why, even in moments like this where he appeared to be relaxing, his mind was always racing. Questions flew in and out of his brain like leaves being whipped around by the wind. But one leaf, unlike the others, stubbornly kept its place, refusing to be blown away.

How are we going to locate the Agency Engine before it activates?

How many lives do I have left, exactly?

How are we going to locate the Agency Engine before it activates?

How are we going to handle the next step in this war?

How are we going to locate the Agency Engine before it activates?

How am I going to retrieve my family from within the Queen's veins, assuming they're even still alive?

How are we going to locate the Agency Engine before it activates?

How are we going to locate the Agency Engine before it activates?

How are we going to locate the Agency Engine before it activates?

In the end, everything came down to this most important leaf. Even those other crucial questions were just second fiddle to this one.

The Agency Engine, the Queen's ultimate goal, was quite simply, the end of Arilon. But it wasn't the kind of 'end' that was healthy. Countless aeons ago, when Arilon was still unmade and the Pillars had come into being, they each had a task. The Thinker came up with the ideas. The Disruptor came up with opposing ideas. The Beginner brought things to life. The Ender brought that life to a close when its time was up. But even the task of ending life was only there to allow more life to come into existence. He was like a person at the end of a conveyor belt, picking items off as they reached the end. He only did that so more things could be put on at the beginning. This was the process of the universe, the process of Arilon. But the Queen wanted to end that process. She wanted to turn off the conveyor belt.

Exactly how or why, the Cat couldn't figure out. But he knew in his bones that this was her intention - and the Agency Engine was at the heart of that.

Yes, the Cat had personal reasons for stopping the Queen. But even getting his family back came second to locating the Agency Engine. Everything else - even the war itself - was like arguing over what colour to paint a burning house.

As Bamboo had once said, the machine had grown and extended until it was now plugged into every man, woman and child in Arilon (and, he suspected, at least some people in the Human World). So the plan was simple - if the machine is plugged into everyone, then he just had to follow those plugs back to their source.

Fortunately, some progress had been made. With the help of certain allies, he was on the verge of pinpointing the machine's location. A lot had been sacrificed to enable this to happen, but because of that sacrifice, the location of the machine's heart was tantalisingly close to being uncovered. It was hiding in the darkness - but now, only just out of reach. So very soon, the Cat knew he would be able to reach out and pluck that most important leaf from the tree.

"Cat."

The General's voice broke the tranquility inside the Cat's head.

"Dear General, what perfect timing as always" he said, opening his eyes. Kingsley was approaching him, flanked by two soldiers - Maiz and Isaac.

"Have we arrived at Boricia yet? There's a little bakery on Manvers Street that does an excellent quiche."

"You're under arrest for treason," Kingsley said. "And if found guilty, you will be executed right here and now on this ship, before we ever arrive at Boricia."

The Cat blinked slowly. "So...no quiche?"

CHAPTER FOUR
COURT MARTIAL

- ARTHUR -

The Galloping Snake's deck was so crowded with people, Arthur was convinced Cary Grant or Lauren Bacall or some other movie star must have come aboard. From the hold to the crow's nest, from the bowsprit to the rudder, everyone had come and gathered around the main mast in the centre of the deck to witness this intriguing spectacle.

The court-martial of the Cat.

"Wow," said Teresa, "I didn't think we'd left Titanium with this many people - did we pick up extras along the way, or something?" she joked.

"No-one wants to miss this," Arthur replied, gazing at the gathered crowd. "Once in a lifetime event, clearly."

"Once in a lifetime?" Teresa raised her eyebrows, "You know how much the Cat loves breaking rules. It's a wonder he isn't being court-martialed every other week."

Arthur couldn't argue with that. However, watching Kingsley's expression and body language, this felt different. It wasn't the standard opera of Kinsgley being generally annoyed by the Cat's flippancy. Something very serious was happening.

The siblings had a good vantage point, sitting on top of some barrels of salted meat. From there, the two of them could clearly see the drama unfold. The crowd was pushing inwards, everyone jostling to get a good view. Yet even as they pressed in, the centre of the throng was a circle of clear space - like an invisible barrier holding everyone back. And in the middle of the space was the tiny shape of the Cat, sitting calmly on an overturned barrel. Despite the commotion and all the people literally hanging from the rigging to get a look, the Cat himself seemed perfectly at ease. It was as if Teresa was right and this happened so often, he was almost bored of it.

Next to the Cat's perching place stood General Kingsley - his accuser, judge and jury all rolled into one. Probably willing to be the executioner too, Arthur thought with a chill.

But it wasn't going to come to *that*. Was it?

"So," said the Cat eventually, half turning to the general, "are you going to tell me what this is all about? What crazy plot have you cooked up in your overactive imagination, Halia? What am I supposed to have done, hm? Stolen weapons? Colluded with the enemy?"

"You are accused of purposely trying to prolong this war," Kingsley said abruptly. "Am I making it up?

The silence was total as the Cat looked at the General.

"Oh, that," he said eventually. "No, you're quite correct, I did do that. My apologies, please proceed."

There was a shocked gasp from the assembled crowd and it mirrored the shock and confusion that instantly flooded Arthur's head. Purposely extended the war? How? Why? Surely it wasn't-

"How did you find out?" the Cat asked.

"Not everything in war is easy to judge," the general said. "Not all battles end in an immediate victory or defeat. And even when they do, not every victory moves you closer to winning the war. Just as not every defeat moves you closer to losing it. Sometimes the value of your actions can only be determined weeks or months later, when you analyse what has happened as a result of them. So, as you know, we have analysts from Toria, the strategy isle, doing just that. They regularly give us reports on the previous few months of our activity and what effect we had on the war. From these, we make future plans."

"Yes, you're right, I do know all this," the Cat nodded. "I'm waiting to get to the part I don't know."

"Well, here is what you don't know, feline," said Kingsley. "What you don't know is, just before the attack on Titanium, our analysts gave me some extra information they had noticed. For the last several months, there have been certain actions the Resistance has taken - things we decided to do or not do - that have actually resulted in making the war last longer. Now, a certain amount of these actions is to be expected, of course. None of us is perfect and war is complicated. However, what the analysts noticed was a disturbing pattern."

Arthur sat forward in expectation, as did everyone on the ship - all in an eerie and complete silence.

"Every single decision that we took that ended up lengthening the war was made by..." Kingsley pointed a finger at the Cat, "...you."

Again, a rumbling murmur swept through the crowd as disbelief ran its fingers through everyone's puzzled, confused brains.

"Yep," the Cat nodded, "again... sorry about that."

At this admission, the ripples of confusion broke out into an explosion of outright anger and cries of rage broke out from sections of the gathered pack. Arthur was afraid they were about to change from a crowd to a mob. He glanced at Teresa and saw even her face was a pool of conflicted emotions. He had to admit, he didn't quite know what to think. They were used to the Cat being somewhat unconventional but this was a whole different level. If true, this wasn't just unconventional, it was outright malicious.

Kingsley continued.

"Every life that has been lost in the weeks and months of this war that we did not have to fight is on *your* head! Including the life of your long-time friend and our leader, Bamboo!"

The Cat bowed his head, slightly, and said nothing.

The general stood over the Cat. She was not enjoying this, Arthur could tell. She clashed with the Cat because they had different methods and personalities. It was nothing personal. It seemed clear to Arthur that she *wanted* the Cat to lead them, to be the symbol everyone needed, to lead them to victory. The overriding feeling Arthur got from the general wasn't one of relishing victory. It was of crushing disappointment.

"According to rumour," she went on, "rumour that you have never seen fit to dispel, you are apparently the King of Ends. The actual Ender, Pillar of Arilon! What worth, then, are the lives of mere mortals such as we? You don't care about us, isn't that right, *your highness*?" Kingsley stepped forward and spoke in a lower, harsher voice. "I don't know which is worse - you being deluded into thinking you're the King of Ends or you joining sides with our enemy to kill us!"

"The battle of Lumina Valley," said the Cat, suddenly and calmly.

Kingsley blinked. "I'm sorry, what?"

"Did your report include my actions at the battle of Lumina Valley?"

"Yes, if I recall…" Kingsley thought for a moment, "…yes, it did. You ordered our troops back from the edge of the valley on the third day. If we had pushed ahead, the analysts calculated that we would have ended the siege a week earlier than we eventually did. I'm afraid you chose the wrong evidence with which to defend yourself."

"When we pulled back, we encouraged the enemy to come out to us. It took a lot longer to break the siege, this is true. But how many more Resistance lives did we lose for the rest of that week?"

Kingsley's pause informed all present that she knew the answer. Eventually, she said it.

"Not a single one."

"You see? I wasn't consorting with the enemy to kill our own people. Some of my actions *saved* lives."

"What about the Graft offensive that you were in charge of? And the raids on Sedita that you convinced us not to carry out? Both of those decisions lengthened the war and ended up losing many Resistance lives."

The Cat bowed his head again.

"Yes. They did. And I am truly sorry."

"Perhaps you were not consorting with the enemy, then. Some of your choices saved lives and some lost them. That is irrelevant. What is clear, is that you made lots and lots of decisions that altogether had the effect of lengthening the war. In fact, the analysts are convinced that if not for those decisions, we might have actually won this war two or three months ago. So, to avoid execution for treason right here and now, you need to explain to us one thing. Why?"

"The Agency Engine," the Cat replied.

The rumbling discontent that had been rolling across the gathered crowds instantly died away. Mention of that machine always had that effect.

"The Agency Engine?" Kingsley was confused. "Explain yourself."

"We've been so focussed fighting this war, running here and there trying to defeat this royal advance over here or protect that Resistance piece of land over there, we forgot the reason we're here in the first place."

"We are here," said Kingsley, "because the Queen is a danger."

"And the Queen is a danger because…?"

Kingsley was surprised to find she was the one answering questions, now.

"Because for years, she has been trying to squash the will of the people of Arilon - resulting in the uprising coming in the wake of your attack on her castle."

"*My* castle, but I'll ignore that. Why were we attacking her castle?"

"To…" Kingsley stumbled, uncomfortable with the line of questioning. "To stop her from activating the first part of the Agency Engine in the human village. In Waterwhistle."

"Exactly. Don't let all these battles and ships and impressive fights against towering Chaos Armour warriors distract you. The main threat the Queen poses always was and always will be the Agency Engine." The Cat's voice had become more urgent now, imploring not just Kingsley but the whole crowd. "Something so powerful that we don't even know exactly what it's going to do. So devastating that the first, tiny piece of it that we stopped would have given the Queen complete control of everyone in Arilon. Yes! Complete control over everyone in Arilon as simply the *first step!*"

"Of course we don't forget that," Kingsley shot back. "But how does lengthening the war help you find the Agency Engine?"

"One word… Zane Rackham. Wait, sorry, two words… Zane Rackham."

The name meant nothing to most people present. But to a few in the know, it was almost as big a shock as the initial accusation had been.

"You found Rackham?" Teresa called out before she could stop herself.

"Indeed I did, Smithy," the Cat responded. "You see, Halia, while fighting - and yes, trying to win - the war, I was also trying to find the Engine. And the best person to help with that was the man who had helped design it and been driven mad for his troubles. I have many contacts, many eyes and ears across Arilon..."

Somewhere near the back of the crowd, Arthur could just see the Professor, Ajo and Lake doing their best to look innocent. The Professor was suddenly taking great interest in the floor.

"Ooh, look, a pebble," he mumbled.

"They found him and I put him to work," the Cat went on. "But you see, as our late, lamented friend Bamboo told myself and the non-cats many months ago, the Agency Engine is not in one single place. Do you remember his words from that day, Arthur?"

Arthur jumped a little as they realised he had a part to play. He gathered his wits and dipped into his memories, eventually replying.

"How do you smash something that has a piece in every building, every place, every man, woman and child in Arilon..." he recited.

"I wasn't looking for the entire Engine," the Cat continued. "By all accounts, that's all around us. No, I was looking for the machine core. And with Rackham's invaluable help, we realised how to track it. You see, as I said, the Agency

Engine is already plugged into each and every one of us. And do you know what it's doing, even now?"

Kingsley shook her head.

"It's feeding off us."

An uncomfortable silence washed over the crowd. Arthur found himself slowly rubbing his forearm, imagining invisible tentacles plugged into them, feeding on him. Judging by some of the expressions around him, he wasn't the only one having such visions.

"It's feeding off our fear," the Cat continued. "The fear of every single person in Arilon. Literally right now, this very second, it's sucking the energy from that fear and feeding it back to the machine core."

"So you're saying the machine is using our fear to power itself up?" Kingsley said.

The Cat nodded. "That's exactly what I'm saying. And once it has reached full power - which Rackham believes will be any time now - it will activate. And then, my dears, I'm afraid we will find out exactly what it was built for."

"But… you have still not explained why you were lengthening the war."

"Because the machine core is very well hidden. I needed time to locate it. I needed to follow the fear like a line of ants heading back to the ant hill. The war is the thing that's helping the Engine charge up so quickly, generating fear as only a war can. But the very thing that's helping the machine is also lighting up the way to its hidden heart for those who know how to look. If the war ends before the machine is fully charged, Arilon's fear levels will drop and it will be impossible to track."

"But if we end the war before the machine is fully charged, then the Queen will not be able to use it anyway," Kingsley argued.

"I wish it were that simple," said the Cat. "But even without war, there are always things to fear in life and the Queen will use those fears to continue to fuel the machine. It will much slower than using the war but it will be completely undetectable. No, the war is our best chance. Our *only* chance."

The Cat was pressing his point home to Kingsley, now, with an energy that Arthur could literally feel pulsing through the crowd. "This war isn't some great idealistic crusade for the Queen - for her, it's nothing more than a chance to quick-charge her machine. And if we don't want to lose the ultimate battle, we need to see the war in the same way. It's monstrous to say it, I know, but if this war were to last another ten years, the lives lost wouldn't come anywhere close to the danger of that machine turning on. It's not that I don't care for the thousands of lives lost due to my actions - it's that I care for the billions of lives that will be lost if the Agency Engine is not found."

Arthur stared at all the people present, trying to see what they thought of the Cat's words.

"I don't really care if you believe me to be the King of Ends or not," said the Cat to Kingsley. "But the reason I didn't tell you any of this wasn't down to some arrogant self-delusion. If such horrific actions must be taken, then I decided I would take the responsibility alone. My burden. My crime, if you like. But not yours. But make no mistake - once the Agency Engine is activated, Arilon as we know it will cease to be. We need to win this war, this is true. But if we don't find the Engine first, everything we know and love will be ended."

Arthur's brain was spinning. This was the oldest moral dilemma in the book, of course. Was it okay to sacrifice some lives to save even more lives? But this wasn't just 'more' lives. It was *all* lives. On the one hand, the maths was clear. Of course it makes sense to sacrifice a smaller number in order to save a much larger number. But on the other hand, the sacrifice of even a single life was too horrific to think about.

Arthur looked from face to face to try and see what the assembled crowd thought of the Cat's words. The thing that really defined Arilon was the connection everyone had to each other. But what this trial came down to, he supposed, was how strong that connection really was. It's easy to fight for the person next to you. You can see them and hear them. They have a name and a face. You might even like them. But what about all those people you can't see? All those people you'll never meet? People you don't know but who are still meant to be 'your people'. Can you fight for them? Can you sacrifice yourself for them? That's what the Cat was really asking. Words like 'bravery' and 'sacrifice' were really tested when you applied them like that.

"So you purchase the future of Arilon with the coin of the lives of your fellow Arilonian?" Kingsley said. "Well, let us see if that currency is one which your fellow Arilonian is willing to pay."

Arthur watched as Kingsley turned to the watching crowd.

"You have heard the accusations and you have heard the defence. Now it is your turn to make your feelings known."

At a glance from her, one of the deckhands pushed forward a crate of small metal rope-hooks. Maiz and Isaac each rolled out a small barrel and stood behind them.

"Every person present is to come forward, take a hook and place it into one of these two barrels. The one in front of Maiz means you believe the Cat is innocent of the crime of treason. It means you think he was justified and correct to keep the war going long enough to track down the Agency Engine, the greater threat."

Maiz shifted slightly as she stood in front of the 'innocent' barrel. Her expression was very hard to read and Arthur couldn't tell if she agreed with the 'innocent' verdict or not.

"Drop your hook in Isaac's barrel if you believe the Cat to be guilty of treason. If you believe he was not justified to hunt for the Agency Engine at the cost of so many lives."

As if to demonstrate, Kingsley took one of the small brass hooks out of the box and dropped it into Isaac's barrel. Well, Arthur thought, that vote wasn't a surprise.

"The lieutenants have both already voted. They will count the hooks as they go in and inform me of the crew's final verdict. Begin."

Kingsley's command was like a starter's pistol and people immediately began to shuffle forward. The Cat was generally seen as a hero. An iconic leader, even among those who didn't believe he was the King of Ends. But it was clear to Arthur that the revelations of the last several minutes had split the crowd down the middle. And that was immediately evident as the hooks began to fall into both barrels with equal rapidity. Each tiny piece of metal dropped into its barrel with a condemning clink.

One for 'guilty'. One for 'innocent'. Another two for 'guilty'. Another for 'guilty'. One for 'innocent'.

Very quickly, Arthur lost track and couldn't tell which barrel was filling quicker. Before long, Arthur found himself being nudged forward by one of the crew to pick his hook. He followed Teresa to the front of the queue.

Standing in front of the box of hooks, Arthur could finally see into each barrel but they looked too close to call. He saw Teresa, without a moment's hesitation, pick up a hook and drop it in the 'innocent' barrel. Arthur knew he should do the same. The Cat was his friend, and he didn't agree with execution in general, much less these impromptu affairs of executing combatants while they were in a war. He'd read about soldiers being shot for desertion or cowardice and it never seemed fair to Arthur to try and judge people while the war was still going on around them.

Avoiding looking at the Cat altogether, Arthur picked up a hook.

Perhaps due to his Seer power, Arthur was definitely able to see the bigger picture and understand what was at stake. There were so many lives hanging in the balance if the Queen's machine ever began to work. But he also couldn't shake the feeling that any victory bought with the unwilling or unknowing sacrifice of others was not the kind of victory he wanted to celebrate. However, he didn't want the Cat to be executed. Was it acceptable to vote based on his personal feelings towards his friend? Or against the punishment being used? He knew he was supposed to vote purely on the facts of the alleged crime, but those other questions jostled stubbornly for space in Arthur's thoughts and refused to be ignored.

Although Arthur's mind was flailing all over the place, he found that his hand was moving in a single fluid motion straight towards the innocent barrel. In went the hook and the arguing voices in his head were instantly silenced.

Lieutenant Maiz watched Arthur intently as he dropped in his vote. As he returned to his seat next to Teresa, Arthur realised he was the last one.

"Please give us the verdict," Kingsley called. "A draw means an innocent verdict."

"Guilty, forty-two."

"Innocent, forty-one."

The gasp that went up was even more dramatic than the ones that had gone before. Clearly, even the people that voted 'guilty' were surprised. From the expressions on some of their faces, Arthur thought perhaps one or two of them had voted 'guilty' to show how angry they were at the Cat's actions but didn't necessarily want him to be actually convicted. Now it had happened, they were perhaps thinking they should have voted the way they actually felt and instead found another way to protest their displeasure.

"The verdict has been given," said Kingsley. "Know that this gives me no pleasure, Cat. And I shall take this horrible task upon myself."

"I applaud your sacrifice, Halia," said the Cat. "However, word of advice - when you pull the trigger, you might want to step back a bit..."

"*Wait!*"

The crowd turned to see a small boy walk slowly forward. Bamboo's spokesperson.

"I have not yet cast my vote," said the boy. "People are not used to asking my opinion but I do have something to add."

The young boy stepped up, the shiny metal hook in his hand, and Arthur felt a wave of guilt. He was right. People only really spoke to him in order to speak to Bamboo. Now there was no Bamboo, what reason did anyone have to talk to the boy? People needed to start treating him as an individual in his own right. And it appeared that this individual had something to say.

"What the Cat has not mentioned – no doubt, in order to protect Bamboo's memory – is that the two of them conversed on this matter before the Cat acted on it. Bamboo agreed with the Cat's assessment and gave his blessing to proceed."

There was a murmur of surprise around the deck but not outrage. Bamboo was a kind of spiritual leader but not someone that joined them on the front line. The assembled crowd didn't seem so bothered that he would have agreed with this plan.

"I, myself, was against it," the boy said. A crushing disappointment fell on Arthur in that moment. Bamboo had been the Cat's last hope.

"When Lord Graves crushed his body, Bamboo left this place and went somewhere... else. I do not know where," the boy continued. "I now face a future where I speak not for him, but for myself. It is a future I look forward to... but still, I am sad to no longer have my friend with me. And so, for one last time, I shall speak for Bamboo."

And with that, he dropped another hook into the 'innocent' barrel.

Forty-two for both! Arthur almost punched the air. A draw!

Halia sighed before stepping to one side and gesturing to the Cat.

"You are free to go."

There were several cheers of delight from the assembled crowd - more than fifty percent, Arthur noted wryly. But clearly not everyone was happy about what the Cat had done.

"You are an excellent tactician," Kingsley said to the Cat. "And a fearless warrior, despite your size. I know, as many of us do, that your participation greatly increases our chances of winning this war."

Then she stepped close to the Cat.

"But as your commanding officer, I am telling you now that our immediate task is to win this war. We do not have the luxury or resources to do anything else on top of that. We deal with the immediate threat - and then if by some miracle we can actually win this thing, we will then have to find an alternative method to locate the Agency Engine. I allowed the people to judge your actions today. But if you disobey me again, your judgement and sentence will be swift and irreversible. Am I making myself perfectly understood?"

"Perfectly," said the Cat. And with a sense of seriousness most did not get from him, he continued. "I know the grave nature of my actions. I do not take them lightly. They are the actions of someone who has a larger judgement awaiting them. You have a list of all the decisions I made. Do you have a list of all the names of all the people who died as a result of those decisions?"

"No, I don't," Kingsley said.

"Well, I do," the Cat lightly tapped a paw to his head. "Up here."

Kingsley and the Cat exchanged hard stares and eventually, the General called out to the crew.

"We will arrive at Boricia within the hour. Make yourselves ready to end this war. Upon our arrival, we will make final preparations to launch Operation Hammer."

CHAPTER FIVE
THE ONE WHO TRIUMPHED

- TERESA -

Teresa's fingers traced the marks in the ancient stone.

The dense forest around them was hot and stuffy, despite the late hour, but the thousand year-old wall in front of her was cool to the touch. Vines and moss crawled all over it - the chaos of nature was doing its best to pull down the order and structure that people had tried to impose.

Teresa was surprised that an island whose Idea was 'building' would have quite so much vegetation. According to the Cat, Boricia had all kinds of extreme natural landscapes - not just forests but mountains and deserts too. But overcoming those landscapes was the point. The Borician mindset was that you take small blocks and create something big from them. You conquer the natural landscape and impose impressive structures. A valley tries to beat you? Build a huge bridge. A mountain tries to block your way? Carve a tunnel through it. On Boricia, the ultimate aim was to build monuments that would ultimately outlast their creators. It was the very act of pushing nature back and replacing it with buildings and structures that the Boricians thrived off.

Besides all that, though, General Kingsley said that it was exactly those thick forests that had led to the Resistance having one of its fallback bases here. The plan was to regroup here, catch a collective breath after Titanium and plan the launch of Operation Hammer.

The Galloping Snake had landed at an old, disused port on the deserted eastern side of the island. As the group had slowly made the two-hour trek from the port to the base, the Cat - always a fan of a captive audience - had been explaining how the isle of building and construction fell so completely and willingly under the controlling hand of the Primacy empire, over a thousand years ago.

"Back in what people depressingly call the 'olden days', castles and forts with walls that stretched miles were scattered all over this island," the Cat had said during their hike. "The Primacy's ideas of control aligned nicely with Boricia's ideas of structure and orderly creation. So, under the Primacy, Boricia prospered. On the eastern side of the island, not far from where we docked, were the famous and beautiful Shimmering Lakes. Many of the island's richest families - and those most loyal to the Primacy - had large houses on the lakes' golden banks. When the empire eventually fell, though, those families were the first to flee.

"The forces fighting back against the Primacy - led by Queen Elyen and her Painted Ones - were travelling across Arilon and freeing islands one bloody battlefield at a time. And those islands who had happily collaborated with the Primacy saw the most vigorous fighting. Not waiting for such retribution, the rich families packed up whatever gold and possessions they could carry and fled before the fury of the Painted Ones.

"Nowadays, life on most of Boricia has returned to normal," the Cat said, his tale coming to an end, "but the eastern coast remains mostly empty and barren. Like an ugly scar left by a wound that nobody wanted to heal."

Back in Waterwhistle, such talks of long-ago battles would have reminded Teresa of boring, old history lessons at school. But here, in Arilon, she found them fascinating. It brought the place to life. Plus, it provided a welcome distraction from thoughts of the Queen.

But distractions and interludes by their nature always have to come to an end and eventually, they had arrived at this tumble-down ruin in the woods. It had obviously been some kind of building. What kind, Teresa found it hard to say. But whatever kind it had been, one thing was clear - it had been massive.

Raising a hand against her eyes to block out the shafts of sunlight coming through the trees, Teresa peered up into the empty building's upper reaches. Terraces battled with treetops but she could still imagine rich Primacy citizens coming here centuries ago. She supposed some of the Primacy soldiers, like the ones she had met on Oblivia, would have come here too. Maybe even some of those exact ones, such as the Commander, Celius. Before they'd ended up on Oblivia and… Teresa cursed. All thoughts always came back to the Queen.

Forcing the monarch out of her mind, Teresa looked back down at the wall in front of her and the carvings that ran across it. A series of images were engraved into the stone, bright green moss running along the lines like highlights. They seemed to show pictures of people fighting one another.

"Wait here while I go inside and check if the other ships from Titanium have arrived," General Kingsley told the tired, rag-tag group. "Maiz, Reuben, with me." And with that, the three of them passed through the giant gateway and disappeared into the innards of the ancient structure.

"What is this place?" Arthur wondered aloud as he looked at all the different stone sections, trying to piece them together.

"This, my historically challenged friend, is the Redstone Coliseum," said the Professor. "Or it was, once upon a time."

"Very good, Professor," said the Cat. "Your knowledge of ancient, useless things is almost as good as mine."

Teresa took a step back and saw the overall shape of the stone sections, her mind's eye filling in the missing bits that the centuries and the trees had pulled down. And finally, she could see it. A coliseum - amazing!

The engravings made much more sense, now. The figures were obviously gladiators. The pictures showed scenes from various battles, images of victory and defeat. Eventually, Teresa's eyes rested on one particular picture of a female fighter surrounded by piles of defeated figures lying on the ground to her left. To her right, other, smaller figures stood, looking up at the gladiator, arms raised in... adoration? The Cat strode over to Teresa.

"What are these, do you think?" Teresa asked him.

"Oh, how interesting! Nice find, Smithy," said the Cat. "That is Elza the Indomitable."

Teresa was immediately intrigued.

Ami rushed over. "Elza the Indomitable? Seriously? I love that story! My mother used to read it to me when I was little. She was supposed to have been a gladiator on Boricia. Was that here, then, Cat? At this actual place?"

"No, it wasn't at this actual place," said Seb, "because the story of Elza the Indomitable is just that - a story. It didn't actually happen."

"What is the story?" Arthur asked.

"During the reign of the Primacy," the Cat said, gleeful to be able to impart yet more ancient knowledge to a rapt audience, "some people followed the new rules and ways of living that the Primacy emperors brought in. People that followed the new ways were known as Moderns. They did away with the old ideas of Balance and were all about seeing life as something to quantify and control. Something you could mold to your will. Those that stayed true to the old ways of Balance were known as Originals. They saw life not as something you could or should control, only learn to live within.

"Boricia was mainly Modern in its views and really persecuted its Originals who they saw as barbaric. The Moderns had better lives, nicer houses, better jobs. Originals, on the other hand, were forced to live in the poorest parts of the cities and towns. If you were an Original, it didn't take much for you to get arrested for some imagined crime. And when you did, you may have found yourself imprisoned in one of the battle pits, like this one. Fighting for your life, all for the entertainment of crowds of Moderns. And if you had any children, they would be shipped off to the local orphanage, seeing as you weren't expected to survive long here."

"Let me guess," Arthur said, "Elza was no fan of the Primacy and ended up here."

"She was a formidable warrior," Ami took up the tale. "Every day she would defeat her allotted opponent and return to her cell, alive. She lasted longer than any other fighter. In fact, she was so successful, she actually became really popular with the crowds, even though they were Moderns."

"Yes, too popular, by half," the Cat continued. "The district governor grew increasingly displeased with her growing fame. The last thing he wanted was some barbarian Original becoming a celebrity. He decided to bring her run to an end. So, one day, after she had won her daily fight as usual, he brought forward a second opponent immediately. It went against the normal way of doing things but he hoped to use the crowds to pressure Elza into accepting the extra battle - a battle he hoped she would be too tired to win. Much to the crowd's pleasure, she agreed. However, she had a condition. In the event she won, the governor had to release a child from the local orphanage, free its parents and set them all free together."

"Oh, I like her," Teresa smiled. "Called his bluff."

"And the crowds he'd used against her now proved to be a tool she used against him," Ami said. "He couldn't refuse her offer with everyone watching. He had to honour it."

"So, with that all sorted out, Elza fought and defeated her second opponent," said the Cat, "and the governor, as Ami said, was forced to keep his word. But he was so angry-"

"Let me guess," Teresa could already see where this story was going. "He came up with another fighter. And baited her with the freedom of another child."

"Exactly," said the Ami. "And of course, she accepted."

"And she won again," Seb said, rolling his eyes.

"And again, and again," said the Cat. "The legend goes that she emptied the orphanage and most of the governor's cells by the time she... you know..."

"Yeah," said Teresa, staring back at the engraving of the freed children all around Elza the Indomitable. "There's only one way that was going to end."

"But the point isn't that she died in the end. Everyone does that. The point is what she did for others while she had the chance," said the Cat. "Because of her selflessness, she ended up becoming something of a folk hero - not just for Originals but, incredibly for Moderns as well. During the wars when the Primacy fell and Boricia was liberated, you'd often find her picture painted on flags or the sides of buildings."

"It's a nice story," said Seb, "shame it's a fairy tale." Ami shot him a hostile stare. He ignored her and turned to Teresa. "It's a nice moral but you don't find genuine acts of selflessness like that. It's not how the world works. In reality, she probably said 'no thank you' to that first extra opponent and headed back down to the cells for dinner."

Teresa didn't reply, she just turned back to the thousand year old carving of Elza the Indomitable. Despite Seb's skeptical view, the idea of fighting tooth and claw to protect others from harm was one that totally appealed to her. She knew it was something she got from her mother. She held tight onto that thought - because that felt like the best way to keep from turning into a being as evil and selfish as the Queen.

"He's such a romantic, isn't he?" Arthur whispered. Teresa smiled as the pair began to stroll a little.

"Oh, he's alright," she said, glancing back at the young Quartermaster - who was, in turn, ignoring the daggers that Ami was giving him. "At the end of the day, whatever upbringing he had ended up with him becoming a pirate. I think that means he's likely to have a bit of a cynical view of the world."

Arthur nodded in agreement as they walked. "I suppose some people are there for the world, and others think the world is there for them."

Teresa fully agreed with that, but she had to wonder which category she fell into. She always tried to be in the first one, but she knew she had certain character traits - her fierceness, her ruthlessness - that threatened to dump her right into the second. Right alongside the Queen.

At the thought of the monarch, a terrible thought suddenly entered Teresa's head. "Arthur, the Queen! I shouldn't be here! Whatever I see, the Queen will remember. I'll lead her here like I lead her to Titanium!"

Before Arthur could reply, the Cat suddenly popped up on a tree stump in front of the pair.

"Hey, you two," said the Cat, "you shouldn't wander too far. There are bears in these woods. Well, not bears, more like squirrels. But big squirrels. With claws. And they love honey. Okay, they're basically bears…"

"I'm the Queen," Teresa said, suddenly, surprising herself and Arthur too, judging by his expression.

"I know, and I'm the King," said the Cat. "So what's the probl-"

"I'm. The. Queen," Teresa said, slowly this time, her gaze fixed on the Cat's green eyes.

The smile froze on the feline's small, rounded face. He looked at Arthur and saw the frozen stare in her brother's eyes. He looked back at Teresa, his smile gone, now.

This was the moment she feared. Just like before, when she was a Needleman and people started looking at her differently. It was happening again but this time, it would be a million times worse. Last time, they did stand by her. But this time, surely she would lose friends.

"Well, blow me down," said the Cat. "Well done. Something I didn't know."

"We just found out," said Arthur, "back on Titanium."

"I don't want my memories to become hers and lead her here," said Teresa. "I have to leave. I can't know the details of Operation Hammer." All she could think of was the Cat's family. She didn't know anything about them or what they looked like but she assumed the Cat had some pretty vivid and harrowing images surrounding whatever it was the Queen had done to them. And surely he was even now linking those images to Teresa. Surely he wouldn't-

"You're not going anywhere," said the Cat. "Number one, you are the most important person in Arilon right now, because you hold the key to defeating the Queen. Somehow.

67

And number two… you're my friend, Smithy. And I stand by my friends, no matter what."

Teresa felt like crying but for the first time in a long time, it was tears of happiness that were fighting to come out. It took a few moments before she trusted herself to speak again.

"Arthur and I already said we're going to change things," she said. "Stop me from becoming… her."

The Cat bobbed his head. "Well, changing the future isn't all that easy but it can certainly be done. And if there's anyone that could do it, it would certainly be the two of you. Ably assisted by myself, of course." The Cat winked and Teresa felt her spirits raise, just an inch. "Trust me," said the Cat, his face suddenly serious. "I will move the very skies to make sure that future doesn't happen."

A sudden rustling sound emanated from the depths of the coliseum and Kingsley emerged.

"Okay, they're here. Come on, everyone inside. Let's get this show on the road."

Everyone got to their feet and started towards the General. Teresa turned to the Cat, fear etched on her face.

"We won't be here that long," the Cat reassured her. "Plus, we don't know that every single memory you have is going straight to her. If that was the case, she would have been here to meet us. But… you're right. It would definitely be prudent to keep you away from the briefing. You trust your brother?"

"Of course."

"Then let him be your Seer. He will look and you will hold his hand. And we'll find our way out of this forest."

"Please," groaned Teresa, partly joking, partly with a sense of foreboding, "no more forests."

With the help of people like these, Teresa thought, surely she had a chance. Just one last, slim chance to free herself of this dark destiny. She would be glad to have Arthur guiding her - there was no-one she trusted more. For a second though, she saw the image from her dream of Arthur dragging her through the woods. The tiniest drop of the annoyance she'd felt in that dream suddenly seeped out into her mind. That, and the anger toward her mother for protecting Arthur and leaving her out in the cold. She saw her disassemble Arthur and destroy the statue of her mother.

But it passed instantly. It passed because she made a choice. She would not be that person.

She would destroy the Queen and the only involvement Arthur would have would be by her side, where she knew he would always be. She would break the loop.

Out of all the uncountable versions of Teresa that had lost that battle, she would be the one who triumphed.

CHAPTER SIX
OPERATION HAMMER

- KINGSLEY -

Despite appearances, Halia Kingsley didn't always know what she was doing.

Over the course of her career as head of Arilon's Peacekeepers and more recently as General of the Arilon Peoples' Army, she was often plagued with guilt or fear. They were natural feelings for any sensible person with her responsibilities. One thing she almost never suffered from, however, was indecision.

Hesitate and be lost, the ancient books said. She knew it was better to make a decision and it be wrong than to make no decision at all. Make a choice. Stick to it. If it turns out to be the wrong choice, change it if you can. If it's not possible, then learn from your mistake and make better choices next time.

But there was one conundrum she had been uncharacteristically dancing around for weeks without ever truly deciding on - and the time had finally come for her to make a decision.

Should she use the human children to fight this war?

"Shall I bring everyone in, General?" asked Maiz.

Kingsley looked around them. The coliseum's dungeons. When the gladiators were not fighting, this is where they were chained up. One floor up, above their heads, was the remains of a banqueting hall but Kingsley had opted to come down here instead. They stood now in a wide, low-ceilinged, stone corridor with cells on either side. All the metal gates had long since vanished but the dingy alcoves of the cells themselves remained. It would put everyone in the proper frame of mind, Kingsley thought. Lose this final battle and be forever imprisoned in whatever version of Arilon the Queen had planned for them.

The General nodded. "Yes, let's get underway."

The lieutenant left to go and gather the various captains and section heads. This was the briefing they had all been waiting for. They all knew of the mission's existence, but until now, could only guess at what it actually entailed. This was partially for reasons of secrecy but also because the General had not decided whether her soul would survive bringing in two twelve year-olds to fight in a savage war. And the plan looked very different with Arthur and Teresa than it did without them.

The common thought was that if you abandoned your morals and won, then the victory was not deserved. But right then and there, in the midst of all that war and fighting and death, with the grim spectre of the Queen's victory hanging over them, maybe it was worth winning and letting the philosophers figure it out afterwards.

And so, as her captains slowly filled the room, the decision was finally made. And may the Pillars of Arilon have mercy on her soul.

Kingsley watched as the captains that had survived the fall of Titanium assembled. After the briefing, the captains and commanders present would spread word of the attack to as many Resistance ships as they could in the short time they had. Everyone they needed right now was here. Well, nearly everyone.

Kingsley turned to the Cat as he and Arthur approached. "Where is Teresa?"

"I know you don't like me," said the Cat, "but do you trust me?"

"Absolutely not."

"Okay, fair enough," he shrugged. "Worth a try."

"Teresa can't know any of the details of this plan," Arthur said to the General under his breath. "There are good reasons. Really good reasons. She can help as long as I tell her what to do at the last minute. But that's all I can tell you."

"It's the Queen isn't it?" Halia said, equally quietly. "There's some kind of connection between them. That's how Teresa survived facing up to her."

There was a look of horror across Arthur's face but Kingsley raised a hand to put the young boy at ease.

"Don't worry. I won't pry and I won't judge. There are things happening with you that I don't fully understand. Things that are more in the purview of this one," she nodded toward the Cat. "But I've seen you both put yourselves on the line more than once. Your loyalty is not in question."

As far as Halia was concerned, it was what it was. She was just a soldier when it came down to it. Not because she didn't have the brains to be anything else - you didn't lead an entire army if that were the case. No, it's because she had chosen her path. Her place in the Great Tapestry. It was to serve Arilon by leading its troops.

"Fine, let's get on with it, then."

Everyone got comfortable - leaning against a wall, resting on an outcropping of stone or sitting on a tree stump from some stubborn bit of forest that had managed to force its way inside over the centuries.

Kingsley got started.

"The Queen is winning," she said, simply. "That is the truth and we might as well get it out of the way. Not only is

72

she winning, she is just this far," she held her thumb and forefinger an inch apart, "from victory. She was close *before* she destroyed Titanium. She's virtually there, now. The reports I've been getting from our forces all over Arilon for the last few weeks have been stark and clear. All the work the Queen's cutter ships had been doing for years is bearing fruit now. Duseeya, the self-reliance isle, is so lacking in self-reliance that the citizens there - despite being mostly against the Queen - are not aiding the Resistance forces that have come to help them. Now, they sit back and wait for someone else to fix everything for them.

"Medassa, the island of lies, is thriving. People all over Arilon are believing every barefaced lie the royals decide to spread. Royal forces will massacre an entire village to prevent an uprising but are able to turn around and say the Resistance did it because we're bandits and thugs. People lap it up - the power of the lies are overriding peoples' own common sense. And due to Savis being overwhelmed, Arilon is shockingly lacking in kindness." Ami shuffled uncomfortably in place, as though the woes of her home island were somehow her own personal fault.

"But of course, the main idea settling all over Arilon like a dark cloud... is fear. We've always known that to win this war, we need to topple the Queen's throne on Phobos. We take her headquarters, the Kymerion, and we win the war."

"So to bag victory, all we have to do is storm the most heavily guarded building in all of Arilon," said Thrace, "which is sittin' in the centre of the capital city on Phobos, an island with more Yarnbulls per square metre than anywhere else." He smiled, folding his arms. "For a minute there, I was gettin' worried, thinking this was goin' to be difficult."

Admirably, Kingsley held her tongue, pushed aside the fact she'd been interrupted and pressed on. "Before we can even think about taking the Queen's seat of power, though, we need to actually set foot on the ground. Which means a head-on assault on the shores of Phobos. Staring straight down the throat of the dragon."

A murmur rippled around the chamber. A head-on assault had been the rumour for some time, so Kingsley knew it came as no surprise. But to actually hear her say it must have brought the horrifying reality crashing home to everyone present. It wasn't just an idea. It was happening.

"Many will die in the assault, that's the sad reality," Kingsley said as matter-of-fact as she could. "But it is possible to get through the Phobos defences. We have enough ships to actually give them a good battle. But the number of ships isn't the problem. The problem with attacking Phobos has always been Pavidus."

A shiver rippled through the assembled people. Many of them knew about the Pavidus problem, of course, but she could see the surprise on Arthur's face.

"As you know, the Queen surprised everyone by raising a base on Pavidus. And not just any base. A ship factory. In the early part of the war, it housed several galleons ready to launch at a moment's notice if anyone dared attack Phobos. They would be trapped in between the Phobos defences and the Pavidan fleet. However, as the war proceeded, the fleets were needed elsewhere and they slowly left the island of dead monsters. But they were replaced by something else. The Warships.

"The Warships are the new type of vessel we have been seeing over the last several months. Bigger, faster, more heavily armed. A few were just used in the attack on Titanium. And it's on Pavidus that they are built and housed. If we are to launch any kind of attack on Phobos, the Warships of Pavidus must first be destroyed."

"There are only two lines to Pavidus, ain't there?" asked Gabriel, one of the lieutenants. "One to Phobos and one to Valia."

"Yes," confirmed Kingsley, "The Three Siblings as those islands are known. The Line between Phobos and Pavidus is obviously inaccessible to us as we would have to get onto Phobos to use it. And the Line between Valia and Pavidus is also impossible to use due to the massive royal garrison on Valia protecting it. There have been various attempts by the Valians to liberate the Line but the royal forces there are too strong."

Kingsley saw Iakob touch the scar on his face - a gift from the last big battle for control of that Travel Line.

"Pavidus is extremely defensible and with the Warships docked there, it's the perfect way to deter any attack on Phobos," she said. "There's only one way we can realistically put those ships out of commission in time for the main attack..."

She looked over at Arthur who had clearly been expecting this. He didn't need to be a Seer to tell which way this conversation had been heading.

"Arthur and Teresa will accompany a team aboard a small ship," Kingsley said the words that bound her to her long-postponed decision. "They will head towards Valia but before they reach, they will disconnect from the Line and fly directly to Pavidus."

An anxious buzz immediately whipped around the room. Many people present had heard tales of this unnatural occurrence but only a handful had ever seen it. Kingsley could tell there was some scepticism around trusting the entire war effort - not to mention all their lives - to the magical fairy tales of flying ships.

Captain Bela, fresh from three months fighting on the isle of Vindictum, voiced her doubts. "So, the human kids just fly us on over there and we just start bombing the Warships? That sounds too good to be true."

"That's because it is, Captain Bela," said Kingsley. "An assault from above is out of the question. Our intelligence informs us there are twelve fully functional Warships on the island at all times. Too many for a single ship to destroy before being shot down."

"Wait a minute," said Arthur, somewhat confused. "A dozen massive ships? Attached to what? There's barely room for even one ship up there. All they have is two Travel Lines hitting the ground about ten yards apart. There aren't any docks there."

"They have *built* docks," said Kingsley. "That spot you mention now houses the launching section of the factory. They moor the Warships there and a pulley system attaches any one of them to the Phobos or Valian line as needed in less than a minute." The General shook her head. "They have enough firepower inside that building to wipe out our entire fleet in minutes. And it can launch extremely quickly. For Operation Hammer to be a success, we can't allow even a single Warship to leave that facility."

"So the people accompanying Arthur and Teresa on the boat," Seb said, "they'll be a sabotage unit."

"Exactly," the general nodded. "They will be taken down to the surface and dropped off. Teresa and Arthur will find a spot to hide with the ship while the sabotage team heads to the facility. They will have two hours to plant explosives on either the vessels or around the factory before the ship returns to extract them from Pavidus. The explosives will be timed to go off just as the attack on Phobos begins."

The room was awash with excited buzz. Many of the assembled captains looked uncertainly at Arthur.

"Arthur," said Kingsley, "you know I have struggled with the idea of utilising you and your sister in this war. We always planned on attacking Phobos, once we had come up with a way to nullify the Pavidan threat. Unfortunately, Titanium has forced us into a corner. This option is now the only one we have time to carry out. So. Will you and your sister help us?"

Arthur coughed and stood up. All eyes turned on him but, impressively, he didn't let it faze him as he spoke.

"General Kingsley," he said, then smiled, "we thought you'd never ask."

CHAPTER SEVEN
SERVED ITS PURPOSE

- FLORIAN -

To say that the Kymerion was the seat of the Queen's power in Arilon was not one hundred percent correct. The Queen's true power lay in control through fear. And that fear could be found inside the hearts and heads of every person in Arilon. It was generated from her actions - such as her sacrilegious mission of pruning Travel Lines. It could be felt when travelling through the NothingSpace and wondering if you would suddenly come across the *Twilight Palace* looming ahead of you in the dark.

Nevertheless, the Kymerion was certainly the most visible aspect of the Queen's domination. Sitting directly in the centre of Gast, Phobos' capital city, the imposing building was a clear statement of the Queen's rule. Raised in the first year of the monarch's rule, the tall, thin tower was built from a black diamond-like material unique to Phobos. The substance had been mined in pits so dangerous that every single person who had worked in them had died. Not a single pair of eyes emerged from those mines to see the structure they had helped build. Their families, however, were gifted with seeing it. Every day they looked out of a window or up into the sky, they saw a dark, fearsome reminder of their own helplessness.

Fate had determined that it was the duty of this island's people to provide all of Arilon with its fear - and to do so meant they themselves had to be constantly frightened.

This is what it was like to live on Phobos.

The Queen herself wasn't often in residence at the Kymerion - she preferred to be on the move, never stopping, always going from one place to another, making her presence felt and her hands busy. But on this dark, rainy afternoon, any citizen of Gast that happened to look up, would be rewarded with another injection of fear as the shadowy underbelly of a massive galleon came sliding down a Travel Line. The intimidating spectre emerged from the thick cloud cover like a monstrous whale sinking toward the bottom of the ocean, scaring all the little fish below.

They would see its fearsome bulk slowly come to a stop on the roof of the Kymerion - and they would know that the dragon had returned to its lair.

"Please, sirs, we must come to a consensus," Florian tried to break through the endless babble. "The Queen will be with us soon and she will not thank us for conflicting advice."

The other three men of the Queen's War Council were not great admirers of Florian. They had guided the royal strategy, shaping the war for the last eighteen months - only for the Queen to bring in this newcomer right at the end. A "know-nothing school teacher" as Avani had called him more than once. It was an uncharitable description. Florian had been a respected lecturer on Doctreena, the most prestigious seat of learning in Arilon. Furthermore, his advice had helped close out the war in the royal fleet's favour. By rights, they should have been glad for his presence, Florian thought. Like many men, though, the other three seemed more bothered about their own careers than in the service they were supposed to be providing.

"Our advice does not conflict with each other," Avani growled at Florian. "It only conflicts with *you*."

"As I have said many times, your knowledge works well during the midst of total war," Florian explained, trying to remain as respectful as always. "However, my insight covers the forces that are at play as a war is coming to its end. People behave differently as they become more desperate, their behaviour becomes more unpredictable. Well, unpredictable to most, but not to me. And trust me when I say that, despite what you think, the insurgents are *not* retreating!"

"But look at these movements," Makai said, pointing at a set of sheets covered with grids of numbers. "Over the last day, known insurgent vessels have been spotted running all over the place. Her Majesty's attack on Titanium has cut off the head of this snake, and the body is thrashing around in its death throes."

"Yes, indeed," Avani chimed in. "None of them know what to do now Kingsley has been removed."

"Removed?" said Florian, exasperated. "Why do you think she's been-"

"They are scattering," Avani continued, oblivious. "Panicked. Running to their rat holes. We won't see them again, not in any great number."

"But that's just it," pleaded Florian, "I don't think they are scattering. I think they're moving in a very specific way. Look at this." He pulled across a large map. Dozens of red circles had been marked on it, each one with an arrow indicating its direction of movement between the islands.

"Several large troop carriers are moving in different directions," Florian continued. "Take this one… it's heading towards Graft."

"Not moving," said Makai, jabbing the paper with a withered old finger. "Running. They're *running* toward Graft.

Obviously hoping to go to ground. Too stupid to realise vessels that large are easily tracked."

"But think about it, what else is on Graft?" said Florian, pointing at the map.

Tarli saw what he was getting at. "Lots of insurgent soldiers."

"So?" said Makai.

"And what about here?" Florian pointed at another set of papers. "There are a few big ships heading for Savis and Rustica. Both places with large amounts of Resistance troops. They're not running…"

"They're picking them up!" Tarli said, finally getting it.

Even Makai was beginning to see the pattern now. "But, what are they picking them up for? Surely so they can escape the inevitable retribution from our Queen...?"

"If we're lucky," said Florian. "But I don't plan war strategy based on luck. I plan it based on worst case scenarios. And the worst case scenario for us is that they are planning one last big attack. Just as I predicted the other day."

"An attack? Not here on Phobos, surely?" said Makai.

"Where else?" Florian argued. "After Titanium, they have one last throw of the dice left. An all out attack on our power base."

"But that would be foolish!" Makai waved the suggestion away. "They'd be caught between our canons down below on Phobos and the Warships from Pavidus above them. They'd be torn to shreds! They would never be so stupid, Florian."

"Exactly," said Florian. "They wouldn't. Not unless…" he brought a map of Pavidus back on top of the pile of papers, "…unless they're expecting Pavidus not to be a problem."

"You mean attack the facility on Pavidus?" Tarli sounded sceptical.

"But we have the Travel Lines guarded at both ends," argued Avani. "They can't even *reach* the facility, much less attack it!"

"Well, we have to assume they can," said Florian.

"And how, exactly?" Makai scoffed. "I suppose you're going to start up again on this flying ship nonsense?"

"The Battle of Eris Island," Florian argued, vehemently and not for the first time. "That flying pirate ship turned the tide of that battle."

"Poppycock! It's insurgent propaganda," said Makai, his face getting red. "Dull-witted fools who don't know *what* they saw!"

"And before that?" Florian argued. "When those outlaws escaped Lady Eris' execution and flew a ship that made a new Travel Line to Valia? People could see it in the sky! There were riots on Phobos for days afterwards."

"Mass hysteria!" Makai shouted.

"But the Travel Line is out there right now! The cartographers have verified it! How can you ignore the evidence of your own eyes, you old fool?" Florian finally lost his patience. "We have to warn her majesty that Pavidus is about to come under attack!"

"We will do no such thing!" Makai shouted. "Go before the Queen of Arilon and tell her fairy tales about her Warships coming under attack by pixies and unicorns? She'll have our heads!"

"You have gone too far, this time, Florian," said Avani. "I think it's finally time the Queen separates you from this group."

"My dear Avani," said the Queen as she entered the room, "you are absolutely right. I shall do so with immediate effect."

Florian didn't even see her move. The next thing he knew, bloodstained swords were flying back into her hands and the rest of the War Council lay in scarlet pools on the chamber floor. He blinked and the swords were gone. Barely a second had passed.

Had that just happened?

The Queen stood to the side of the doorway and gently raised a hand, gesturing for Florian to come and walk with her. Hesitantly, the sole remnant of the Queen's War Council approached his monarch and together, they left the room - and the grisly scene - behind them.

Even though the outside coating and the inner skeleton of the Kymerion was made of the Phoban black diamond, the walls, floors and ceilings were all stone and wood. The corridor down which the Queen was now leading Florian was characteristically dark, despite regular windows showing the grey, depressing city of Gant outside. It was a far cry from the bright and hallowed halls of Doctreena, that was for sure. Florian tried to gather himself after the unceremonious disbandment of the War Council he had just witnessed.

"You are thinking about my dismissal of the War Council," the Queen said, matter-of-factly as they walked. "Do not concern yourself. Once a thing has served its purpose, you do not keep it," said the Queen, seemingly reading Florian's thoughts. "To keep something you no longer need would be cruel. And I am not cruel."

"No... no, of course not," Florian said quickly.

"So," the Queen said slowly as they walked. Her gaze was ahead of them, though Florian had the distinct impression she was not really seeing the corridor, but something else. Something unknowable. "Pavidus. Their next target is the Isle of Dead Monsters. This is what you believe?"

The chilling new meaning of the ancient title did not escape Florian. Dead monsters indeed.

"I believe so, your Grace," he said. "They will attempt some kind of attack on the Warships which will, in turn, allow them to launch an all-out assault on Phobos."

"What kind of attack do you think will work against our Warships? The facility prevents bombing from above."

The Queen's voice always put Florian on edge while at the same time making him feel completely at ease. Somehow, there was always the unsettling impression of bells ringing faintly in the distance. She was possessed of the most calming exterior - until it exploded and destroyed you without warning.

"There have been advancements in small-scale explosives over the past several months," he said in answer to his queen's question. "Gunpowder compressed within a small package with different length fuses for timed detonation. More reliable than ever, apparently. I think they will sneak a team in and hide explosives throughout the facility."

The Queen fell into silence as they strode the deserted halls, their footsteps echoing down the long, empty corridors. The lower floors of the Kymerion were filled with administrative staff, running the Queen's dominion. But these upper storeys were almost completely deserted. Apparently, the Queen disliked company.

The silence of his monarch continued as the pair came upon a giant set of doors, intricately designed with decorations of gold and ancient wood. The Queen's throne room. Florian was excited. Few people had ever been inside. The Queen gave the slightest nod as they approached and the giant doors opened as if pushed by an invisible hand. The display of such unnatural, primal Arilon power filled Florian with dread and excitement all at once.

Florian's initial reaction to the room was one of disappointment. It was virtually empty with almost no decoration at all. However, his disappointment swiftly gave way to a realisation that the room actually fit the Queen's demeanour perfectly. There were no fancy ornaments of gold or silver. No vainglorious portraits. No marble floor or pillars of ivory. Instead, the large room was grey and barren. The floors, walls and columns were all dark, dull stone. No possessions filled the room, no trinkets or trophies, no statues or artwork.

Well, there was one piece of artwork - if it was indeed art.

A painting of a giant tree adorned the far wall, stretching from floor to ceiling. The branches of the tree looked as if they were reaching out in an attempt to embrace the world and everything in it. Florian couldn't tell if it felt motherly or threatening.

As his eyes adjusted to the relative gloom, though, Florian noticed it wasn't a painting of a tree at all. It was actually hundreds upon hundreds of smaller pictures. A collection of images - drawings, paintings, sketches, even words… Some of them were on pieces of paper or cloth. Some were painted onto the wall itself, or carved into it. A thousand images, some huge, some almost too tiny to see. Instinctively, Florian knew it was the Queen herself who had produced the display, as disturbing as it was beautiful. And he also knew it was a glimpse into the inner workings of her mind.

In the centre of the room stood the throne itself. A simple stone, high-backed chair. Florian could not actually imagine the Queen ever sitting on it. Thrones were there to show power to others. The Queen didn't need to show off her power. She simply used it. All of Arilon was her throne.

With a start, Florian realised they were not alone in the room. Someone was waiting for them.

"General Graves," the Queen greeted her right-hand man. A replacement for her final Noir Lady. Lady Eris had failed at the Battle of Waterwhistle and nobody had seen her since. It wasn't hard to guess what had happened to her.

"Your Grace," the knight went down to one knee, his head bowed. Despite his face being concealed behind the polished, black metal of his faceless helmet, his deep, rumbling voice signalled his powerful presence.

"Rise," she said. He did so, his height only just shy of the Queen's. It was incredible, Florian thought. He was convinced Graves was taller than the Queen and yet she always seemed taller than him when they met. In fact, she was always taller than anyone. She had a way of twisting your perception of the world around you, Florian thought. Not just out there with the masses, but up close and personal too.

"So, you escaped."

"I did, your Grace, though I am shamed to have been captured in the first place. Making my escape was not easy but I was there to meet your second wave of ships when they arrived at the insurgents' base. Unfortunately, the insurgents themselves had since departed."

"I am pleased you were able to return to us," said the Queen. "But your report told me something much more interesting which I would like to hear from you in person."

"Yes, it is true," said Graves, knowing what the Queen was referring to. "Bamboo is dead. I killed him."

Florian's eyebrows raised in shock, though he knew better than to make a sound. Bamboo dead! This was a great victory for the royal forces and the Queen. It would have a hugely damaging impact on the insurgents' plans. Florian almost wanted to go back and apologise to Avani and the others. Almost.

"I see," said the Queen. An expression momentarily crossed her face and it seemed to Florian like she was trying to remember something. Some stubborn memory that would not come. She refocused her gaze on her Lord Knight. "Remove your helmet."

Florian had never seen Graves without his helmet but upon the Queen's command, he removed it immediately and without hesitation. The knight's dark eyes and hair and square face were certainly handsome, Florian thought. But immovable, like stone. He was from Ofisora, the isle of duty. He probably kept his helmet constantly on because it was a symbol of that duty. To his Queen and to Arilon. He lived and breathed to serve. Removing his helmet was probably like taking a rest - and, like his queen, General Graves did not rest.

Florian was taken aback as he realised the Queen was staring into Graves' eyes, intently. She was looking for something, he realised. But, looking for what?

Several uncomfortable seconds passed as Graves, to his credit, did not move or allow any sign of uncertainty or discomfort to cross his face. During his short service, Florian himself had once received a brief, sharp glance from the Queen - and with that glance, he had felt her staring into his mind, scrutinising his thoughts. It had felt like she was sifting through his soul with a hot knife, scraping the elements of his 'self' back and forth as she hunted for something. But for Florian, it had lasted a fraction of a second. If she was doing that same thing to Graves right now, Florian thought, with such a long and searching stare, it must have been an intense and painful experience indeed.

Eventually, the Queen turned away. Only then did Florian notice the most miniscule hint of relief flicker briefly across the general's stone face.

Whatever she had been looking for, she seemed satisfied.

"The insurgents are mounting a full-scale attack on this island, sometime within the next twenty-four hours," said the Queen, her back to them both as she walked slowly around the throne, her eyes running up and down the empty chair. "Prepare your forces, Lord Graves."

"Yes, your Grace," the knight bowed and replaced his helmet. Once more, the formidable General.

Graves turned his blank helmet toward Florian as he walked past and gave the man the slightest of nods, which Florian returned, slightly flustered. Within moments, he was once again alone with the Queen.

The monarch was on the other side of the throne room looking at the collage of the great tree. Florian was deciding whether to go over and join her when she spoke.

"Do you know why the insurgents are fighting us, Florian?"

Florian didn't know what he was expecting the Queen to say, but it wasn't that. Why was she asking him this? Did she want him to say something specific? Perhaps he should say 'because they are foolish'. Maybe that would make her happy.

But then, Florian realised, the Queen didn't encourage sycophants. She didn't like people who just told her what she wanted to hear, nor did she have people who were not good at their jobs. There was a pile of bodies in a room down the hall that was testament to that. No, what she wanted was Florian's actual opinion.

"They believe they are fighting to protect freedom," he said. "To them, you represent control. Restriction. They want to be free to act as they please rather than being told what to do or think."

"And...?"

"And they are right. You *do* want to take away their freedom," he said, curtly.

"So, I am the villain, after all," the Queen said. Her tone was flat and it was impossible to tell if she was being sarcastic or genuine.

"I disagree," said Florian. "Removing freedom is absolutely the right thing to do. Freedom is an evil we must completely do away with."

"Now *you* sound like the villain," the Queen said with the merest hint of amusement.

"Not at all. Freedom leads to choice. Choice leads to disagreement. Disagreement leads to chaos. To conflict. To death."

"And if I were to take away your freedom? Or that of your family?"

"If there's one thing I've learned from a lifetime of studying wars," said Florian, "it's that safety is more important than freedom."

The Queen smiled, now. Florian breathed a little easier to see it. He had decided to speak his true feelings but he hadn't been completely sure the Queen would have wanted to hear it. Now, though, he was inwardly ecstatic to see they were indeed on the same page.

"This war we are fighting serves a purpose," the Queen said, "but not the one you think. If it enables me to achieve the real victory, then I will not care one whit whose flag sits atop the Kymerion."

Florian's shock at this statement was obviously completely visible on his face because the Queen smiled in amusement. "Once a thing has served its purpose… remember?"

The ex-professor nodded quickly. His job wasn't to question the Queen - his job was to win the war. Everything else was above his station.

"I am not so different from our friend, Lord Graves," the Queen continued. "I have a duty to do and I intend to see it through. And nothing will stand in my way. Well…" the monarch turned to a painting on the wall behind her. "…almost nothing."

Florian's gaze switched from his queen to the painting that had taken her attention.

The lines that created the image were rough and incomplete. It looked to Florian as though it had been painted at great speed. He noticed a scattered pile of tiny brushes strewn haphazardly on the floor at the foot of the picture, each brush's colour now caked into its bristles. The image portrayed within the picture itself immediately made Florian feel sad.

Two girls sat by a vast, black lake. Though they sat next to each other, it wasn't clear if they were friends or enemies. Only the backs of their heads were visible and long, blonde hair fell down behind each of them. They stared out into the vast body of dark water while above, coming down from the dark sky were several tendrils covered in razor-sharp barbs. Florian thought that the black shapes looked like the tips of the RainHand legs.

"This image came to me in the dead of night," the Queen said. "I painted it immediately."

"What… what is it?"

"…the end of the future…" The Queen said, quietly. She turned to Florian. "That is the one obstacle that may yet derail everything we have fought for. In order to achieve victory, I must change the unchangeable."

"The future...?" Florian said, astounded. "You know the future?"

"Only one particular event, alas," she replied. "But it is one that is set to take place very soon. My own death."

Florian was once again rendered speechless by the Queen's candour. "That cannot be allowed to happen!" he exclaimed. "If you know the details of this vile future, then you certainly must change it!"

"If only it were so simple," said the Queen. "If you do not know the future, then you can act as you wish. Everything you do shapes the future. But if, like me, you have the power to pull back the curtain and take a brief glimpse at what is to come... then things become more complicated. You cannot change a future that you know."

Florian nodded in understanding. "Yes, I see... The future is fixed. Whether it's known or unknown, you rush toward it. Everything you do shapes it. If you don't know the future, all things are possible in your mind. But if you ever find out for sure what the future holds..."

"All possible futures collapse into one certain future," the Queen finished. "Precisely."

"And this is your problem," Florian nodded, understanding. "How can you change a future that you have set in stone by learning of it?"

The Queen stared at her advisor, clearly waiting for him to give an answer to the question. This was why she had summoned him, Florian realised. She was apparently due to die soon - she was approaching the final stages of her war. Florian's speciality.

"Okay… so the situation is that not knowing the future allows you to shape it… but knowing the future locks you into it," he nodded, stroking his chin, thoughtfully. "There appears to be only one answer… do not believe the future you have seen."

"Excuse me?"

Florian took a tentative step towards the Queen as he continued. "Knowing the future stops you changing it, so tell yourself this event you know isn't the future at all. It's a potential future. Or it's a mistake. Or a lie. If you simply do not believe it, the future will once more become unknown. Then you can shape it with your actions, as normal."

"Denial," the Queen said. "Lie to yourself until you believe the lie and it becomes your truth."

"You can get around anything if you simply alter what you believe or decide which facts to accept as true. People do it all the time. If you don't like the fact you're given, just pick an alternative one."

The Queen looked back at the painting. This time, however, Florian thought her expression was not so much sad acceptance as cold determination.

"There is one thing the Threads did not lie about," she said, eventually. The monarch turned back to look at Florian. "You. They promised you would have an important part to play. And so it has proved. Thank you, Florian Al-Sturzan."

Florian was overjoyed. He had helped the Queen!

"Please, I am only ever happy to serve my queen," Florian bowed. "I look forward to being of such use to you again in the future, if you ever need it?"

The Queen stepped closer to him and smiled once more. It was a sad smile.

"Once a thing has served its purpose..." she said, quietly. "I am not cruel."

Horror filled Florian as he looked down to see the Queen was once again holding her swords.

CHAPTER EIGHT
THE UNGATHERING

- TERESA -

Teresa did not mind admitting, being alone right now was not her idea of fun.

She sat on a stone seat at one end of a long table. The Cat had told her this was a banquet hall - the room was long and thin, mirroring the table, and had a high ceiling. The timbers and finer features of the hall might have long since rotted away but Teresa could still imagine the grand occasions and laughter that would have filled the place in its heyday (okay, it was fun and laughter of people who enjoyed watching others fight to the death, but putting that to one side...). It all made the fact she was here alone all the more stark and depressing.

She waited impatiently for everyone to finish with the briefing downstairs. Generally, Teresa didn't have a problem being alone. In fact, she quite liked her own company. As much as she enjoyed being around people, it was nice to get a break from them sometimes and just listen to the babble of a lazy brook or watch clouds sail by in a bright, blue sky. But right now, the problem wasn't so much being on her own - it was more being kept away from everyone else. Being on the outside while everyone else discussed what to do reminded her too much of when she was a Needleman. She'd been alone on the island while simultaneously being alone on the *Galloping Snake* as they headed to come and rescue her. (Having two sets of memories for the same period of time really was quite confusing sometimes). In some ways, being alone while on the ship had been the worse situation of the two - she was surrounded by people she was supposed to be close with, and yet they had avoided her. Distrusted her. Feared her. Abandoned her.

And now here it was, happening again. Not exactly in the same way - only Arthur and the Cat knew about her being the Queen and they were both standing by her. But the upshot was still the same. Everyone else was in one place - she was alone in another.

She resisted the urge to swing her bow and smash something. She was so tired of this! Tired of being the thing to fear. She wanted to be in the briefing. She had good ideas. She was *great* at having good ideas!

Back in Waterwhistle, whenever the teacher left the room, Teresa had often taken it upon herself to organise the class. The teacher was always surprised to return to a calm, orderly and under-control classroom. Teresa knew how to get people to sit still and get along. On occasion, the teacher would try to enlist Teresa's help so they could look after the class together - but that never worked out quite as well. The teacher's methods would always clash with Teresa's. She preferred to just be allowed to get on with it herself. She knew what to do.

Thinking of home reminded her how much she missed her father and Sam. Calming herself down, she sat on the edge of the stone table and took out the photo of her family. She still had no idea who the mysterious man was that had given the picture to her and started this whole adventure off. But when she looked at the image, that riddle faded into insignificance. Just seeing her father's face brought calm back to her mind. Seeing Albert and little baby Sam just filled her with a sense of belonging. This was her place. And her mother... how she missed her mother.

Teresa had still been so young when her mother had died of influenza. On the one hand, her memories were fuzzy but at the same time, her mother lived in sharp focus in Teresa's mind. She sometimes felt like she recalled her mother holding her as a baby, even though that was impossible. But she held onto the image anyway. It had always made her feel safe and loved.

But over the last few months, that feeling was slipping away from her. She could try and blame the Needlemen and the Queen but all they had done was highlight something Teresa had always feared in the back of her mind. There was a darkness in her and her mother had known it. That was why she'd sent Arthur away - to keep him safe from his sister. The suspicion was slowly growing that her mother hadn't loved her as much as she'd always believed.

Frustrated, Teresa shoved the photograph back into her trouser pocket. The picture had failed to calm her down for long and her thoughts returned to the briefing in the dungeons below.

They really ought to have let her join in, she reckoned. If she'd been allowed in the briefing, she could have seen if there were any flaws or problems with the plan and corrected them. Teresa smiled to herself - what made her such a great military expert? But then she reminded herself about surviving on the Needleman island for a year and a half. Rescuing all those Sleepers. So yes, she *did* have a thing or two to contribute.

How long did it take to plan a war-ending battle, anyway?

As if on cue, there was the sudden and welcome sound of dozens of boots ascending the worn, stone stairs. Moments later, people started to stream down the corridor, past the banquet hall's entrance. Soon, Arthur and the Cat emerged, peeling off from the throng and headed into the room to join Teresa.

"Well?" Teresa said, impatiently running up to them. "What happened?"

"I think you might have forgotten the point of you not being there, Smithy…" the Cat teased.

Teresa knocked her head. "Oh yeah, of course…"

"Suffice it to say, there's a plan and you pair will be playing your part."

"Knock knock," said Stick, pretending to rap on the non-existent door.

"You know, you can just say 'knock knock' without actually doing the actions," Ami smiled at her friend.

Stick shrugged. "That seems a bit silly. Like, what you gonna do with your hands while you're sayin' 'knock knock'? You might as well pretend-knock while you goin' to all that trouble."

"I'm going to miss your philosophical insights while we're on this mission, Stick," Teresa grinned.

"We're goin' ta miss you guys too," said Stick. "We're headin' off to Graft to help bring people from our old resistance cell back to Phobos for the second wave."

"Assuming there is a second wave, and everyone doesn't die in the initial assault," said the Cat. He looked around at the horrified expressions around him. "I'm sorry, I mean, we'll be waiting for you on the surface of Phobos with a pop-up ice cream stall."

"Even if we didn't have that task to carry out, we wouldn't be around for the actual big drop," said Ami.

"Kingsley wants all non-seasoned fighters well away during the main assault."

"And she's right too," said the Cat. "You've all been involved in some hairy situations but... well, there are some things I'd be much happier if you never have to witness."

"At least you'll be out of harm's way," Arthur said to Ami.

"Yes, but you'll be in it," she said, before quickly turning away.

Teresa didn't miss the catch in the Savisian girl's throat and she knew what it meant.

"Well, we won't really," said Arthur, oblivious. "I mean we'll be in the neighbourhood but we're going to be little more than glorified bus drivers!"

"Nothing 'glorified' about it," said the Cat. "You'll be *actual* bus drivers. And well away from any fighting. There's more than just Kingsley who'll have my pretty little hide if anything happens to you two."

Well, don't ask me what we're doing, Teresa wanted to say. *I don't have a clue until someone sees fit to tell me with five minute's notice.*

Ami shrugged. "I'm just worried for my friends," she said, forcing a brave smile and nudging Teresa's shoulder with her own. Teresa fought back the guilt she felt whenever Ami was nice to her. Whenever she looked at the Savisian, all she could imagine was the Queen laying waste to her island and slaughtering her friends and family. Banishing the image as much as possible, she surprised Ami with a sudden hug and spoke quietly into her ear.

"Don't worry," she whispered. "I'll keep him safe."

"What is happening in here?" a deep Russian-sounding voice boomed all of a sudden. "Is party going on? My invite is lost in post, yes?"

"Iakob!" Teresa cried. "Iosef! Grom! You're right, this is a party. I hope you brought food."

"Do not mention food to Iakob," said Iosef. "He is still being obsessed with our mother's Flossberry Bread Cake. Ever since mine siege on Graft, he is always talking about it. Is getting very boring."

"I speak with mother," Iakob said. "She is bringing Flossberry Bread Cake to Operation Hammer. When we get to surface, she says she will give to me. Is my incentive for not getting killed!"

Despite the morbid nature of the joke, everyone laughed. That's what war gave you, Teresa supposed. What do they call it - gallows humour?

"Here they are! I told you they were hiding from us," said the Professor as he entered the room. Ajo and Lake trailed behind him.

"Nope," said Lake.

"Oh no?" the Professor said as he walked into the room, staring at everyone. "If they're not hiding from us, who are they hiding from?"

"You," said Lake.

"You know, Professor," said Ajo, "sometimes when people are not in the same place as you, it does not mean they are hiding from you. Sometimes, it simply means they are just not in the same place as you."

"You're just saying that because you're on their side, now," the Professor sniffed, looking away.

"What do you mean?" Arthur said.

"The Professor and Lake are going to try and find our ship," said Ajo, "but I am staying to join in the Operation Hammer assault, this is true."

99

"This is excellent news!" Iakob said, clapping Ajo on the back. "The more Valians the better!"

"Just do not expect any of Flossberry Bread Cake," grumbled Iosef. "Is all destined only for Iakob's belly."

Everyone laughed - even Grom seemed to have an air of amusement to his huge, stern face. Teresa laughed most of all. This is what she had missed. It was all she wanted. She had been alone moments ago but now she was surrounded by so many of the people she had befriended since arriving in Arilon. Friends, allies, comrades. Family. These were the things that separated her from the Queen. This is what she, Teresa, was fighting for.

The shining moment was all too brief, though. There was a lot of work to be done and very quickly, duty began to pull people away. First, Ami and Stick left as they had a long way to go in a short time. Stick gave Arthur his 'everything will be ok' metal badge. "For luck," he said. "Really, I s'pose it's from Ami, since she paid for it." Ami turned away so Arthur couldn't see her blush.

Lake and the Professor went with the pair as they were getting a lift with them back to Graft. The hard-working isle was the last place they'd seen the *Rogue's Run*, so that was where they were going to start looking.

Soon after that, Grom, Iakob and Iosef headed out and they took Ajo with them. The Valians wanted to get in some last minute sword practice before their ship left for Phobos. Hugs from the mountainous Eastern Knights and even one from Grom were their leaving presents. Ajo offered a polite hand since they didn't know him so well but Teresa grabbed him in for a hug as well and told him to stop being so silly.

"Well, well," said the Cat when it was just the three of them. "Bet you didn't realise all this was going to happen when you met Kingsley at Nottingham Castle for tea and cake!"

Teresa nodded. "It feels like absolutely years since then. Not just because of everything that's happened but also I now have an extra eighteen months of memories in my head. I feel like it'll be a totally different person that eventually returns home to that castle. Assuming I ever actually-"

"I'm going to stop you there," said Arthur, before Teresa could finish her downbeat thought, "because I just remembered something really important about that meeting in the castle."

Teresa raised her eyebrows in surprise. "What is it?"

"I never finished your cake!"

Teresa and the Cat burst out laughing but Arthur wasn't amused. "What? It's cake! Uneaten cake! It's an actual tragedy, why are you laughing?"

"Perhaps Iakob will give you some of his Flossberry Bread Cake later," chuckled Teresa, wiping a laughter tear from her cheek.

"Yes, well, I wouldn't pin too many hopes on that," said the Cat, shaking his head.

Teresa admitted that both Arthur and the Cat had been annoying her at times, lately. But she'd been going through a lot and it was moments like these that reminded her they were her closest friends.

"Well," the Cat said eventually, "keep yourselves safe. And stay away from those crazy cavemen up on that island."

"You too, Cat," said Teresa. "And... I really do appreciate... you know... you not hating me for being... well, for being *her*."

"Well, there's a simple reason for that, Smithy," the feline smiled. "You're not her. See you on Phobos."

And with that, he was gone.

"Well, that's everyone," said Arthur. "Just us humans left, now."

"Yeah," said Teresa, mock-punching Arthur's arm. "The dream team. Let's face it, we're the only ones who really matter."

The pair laughed, but it was a nervous laugh. They had a big job in front of them and they didn't know which of the people that had just left they would ever see again. But at least, for right now, it was the two of them. The Cat was right, it had been non-stop since Nottingham Castle but now felt like a good moment to just pause and be thankful they had each oth-

"Ah, there you both are," said Maiz as she came in through the doorway. "You drew the short straw - I'm heading the team for our mission."

"Ah, don't worry about it. You'll enjoy our boat," said Teresa. "It's the party boat."

"I'm sure," said Maiz. "Just as long as the party boat doesn't leave without me. Again."

Teresa was just about to babble an apology for that day when the lieutenant actually smirked. *Wow*, Teresa thought. *Stonefaced Maiz actually has a sense of humour!*

"I actually came to borrow Arthur, if I may," said the lieutenant. "We need to make final plans for our mission. Teresa, if you'll excuse us?"

For a second, Teresa was a little confused as to why only Arthur was being invited but it suddenly came back to her.

"Oh yeah, sure, take him off my hands," she waved them away. "All I hear is cake, cake, cake from this one. Go, go."

Maiz nodded and left, Arthur trailing behind her. He gave his sister a quick, apologetic wave as he left. "Won't be long," he said.

Teresa just waved him away, forcing a smile and a fake laugh. And then she was by herself, once again.

She looked around the empty room and sighed.

CHAPTER NINE

THE DISQUIET BEFORE THE STORM

- GRAVES -

The island of Phobos was designed to induce the maximum amount of fear from its inhabitants. It generally achieved this through its wide array of fear-inspiring monuments and landmarks, both man-made and natural.

The Kymerion was obviously one of the man-made variety. Buildings, statues, monuments, giant paintings. Generally huge in size so as to make people feel small and insignificant when they craned their head back to look up at them.

But the natural monuments were just as effective. Some were just as obvious and unsubtle as the Kymerion - places like the Plummeting Cliffs or the immense Mount Tormant. However, the power of some locations was more understated. Insidious, even.

The Shores of Disquiet was one such place.

General Graves had never liked it here. There was nowhere like it on his home isle, Ofisora. They had beaches and shorelines, certainly. But none quite as unsettling as this.

Located several dozen miles sunward of the Queen's seat of power, the Shores of Disquiet was the part of the coastline where the city of Gast met the dark, turbulent waters of the Night Ocean. Flat and featureless as an unengraved tombstone, the beach stretched for several miles. It was also extremely deep - the distance from the bluff down to the water was vast. A person standing midway down the beach would be surrounded by nothing but dark, flat, wet sand for what felt like miles in all directions. It would make them feel abandoned and alone, as though everything in the world was so far away and they themselves had been completely abandoned by everything alive.

However, the most disturbing aspect of the Shores of Disquiet was the silence of the water. Tall, powerful waves would constantly rush in towards the land at breakneck speed and crash onto the shore. And yet, neither the rolling waves nor the crashing surf made any real noise. The dark, freezing waters of the great expanse attacked and pounded the rocks and sand in almost total silence. It was like watching a crazed creature bashing at the bars of its cage, its mouth wide and roaring... but without a single whisper of sound either from its roar or its fists.

For Lord Graves, the summary of this place was simple - it slowly drove you mad.

Standing on the shore now, Graves was beginning to wonder if he was in danger of such a fate.

"The cannons are situated in the locations you specified, Lord Graves." The words were spoken by Graves' trusted second, Captain Rigs, as she held her helmet in the crook of her arm. "The gunners are now laying out the tracks for the ammunition re-supply carts."

"Excellent." The knight nodded his faceless mask as he observed the endless activity going on around him in preparation for the insurgents' invasion. "And the super-cannons?"

"They are ready and waiting," Captain Rigs motioned to the row of monstrously huge cannons located at the top of the beach, near the bluff. The five beasts sat silent right now but the noise to come when they began to roar would be beyond deafening. They represented the pinnacle of weapons design and formed the backbone of the royals' defence of the beach. They had a range far superior to any ship-bound guns, including those of the attacking insurgents.

"The tests were successful and the range was confirmed," said Captain Rigs, proudly. "We will be able to hit the insurgents while their own guns are still out of range. They will be obliterated twice over before they get anywhere near the beach."

Graves nodded, satisfied. Preparations were coming along well.

The Shores of Disquiet was the only feasible location from which an invading force could attack Gast. The Travel Lines that passed over the city were extremely high - a lot higher than in many other places on the island. This made it all but impossible for attackers to come in from overhead as there was then no way they could easily get their forces down onto the ground before being blown out of the skies by the city defences.

The best options for coming down to the surface were all outside the city boundaries - and those boundaries were formidable. In the sunward direction was the Night Ocean. To darkward was the near-impenetrable Dagger Forest, home of the infamously bad-tempered, ridiculously numerous and endlessly violent tribe of talking grizzly bears, the Kopesch Family. The southern approach was protected by the unscalable Plummeting Cliffs. There were no Travel Lines near to this natural sheer drop and anyone foolish enough to attempt an invasion here would be very easily and quickly destroyed from above. Finally, to the north of Gast, beyond the fifty-foot city-protection wall were miles and miles of Yarnbull fields. It contained many hundreds of the fearsome creatures in various states of growth. Some were no more than seeds, some were part way emerged from the ground. Maybe just a head but often the entire upper torso, complete with inescapable grasping arms, was free from the soil. On top of that, there were always vast numbers of fully harvested Yarnbulls roaming around that would give any attacking hostiles a very bad day.

And so Graves had set up his defences in the only place the resistance had any hopes of landing. He knew that's where they would be coming from and Kingsley would know he would be waiting. Graves shook his head when he considered the impending loss of life. A needless massacre. But a massacre, it would be.

Was that what was concerning Graves? Something *was* bothering him, but he couldn't quite tell what it was. Perhaps it was just this infernal, silent ocean, he thought. But, no, there was something else-

"Lord Graves?"

Graves was suddenly aware that Captain Rigs had asked him a question. "I'm sorry, Captain, what did you say?"

"I asked if you still wanted me to deploy the new Yarnbulls here on the beach, my lord."

"Is this the defective batch?"

"Yes, sir," the captain nodded. "The farmers say they were forced to harvest the batch before they were ready, so apparently, the creatures' self-control instinct is... under-developed."

"Understood," said Graves. "Do not use them on the beach. Keep them back for use in the event the insurgents manage to take the beach and march on the city. We will deploy them along the route to Gast. Push them into the heart of the enemy forces and let them run riot. Their lack of self-control will work in our favour."

"An excellent idea, my Lord," said Rigs. "I will see to it."

Yes, using those poor, enslaved creatures is quite the honourable move for a man of duty.

Immediately upon having this thought, Graves looked away from his captain. It was random, out of place notions like that which he'd been having for the last few hours. Perhaps it was this place, he thought. This silent beach slowly burrowing into his sanity, like a splinter in his mind.

What was the Queen looking for?

Yes, this is something he had wondered. When she had summoned him to her throne room, she had looked long and hard into his eyes. What had she been looking for? Had she found it?

Graves was beginning to doubt his own sanity. He was increasingly feeling like a passenger in his own mind.

"...so, we will therefore not have our full complement available on the beach," Captain Rigs said, finishing a sentence that Graves realised he had not heard her begin.

"Captain, I'm going to need you to repeat that," he said, curtly.

Captain Rigs tried - and failed - to hide her bemusement and confusion over Graves' current distracted disposition.

"My apologies," she stammered. "I said only half the Chaos Armour units will be available. The Raptors are on their way down from the city but the engineers say the two-man Devastators will struggle on this sand, due to their size."

Graves was incredulous. "We have the ultimate in advanced weaponry capable of destroying entire battalions of soldiers... but it can't handle *sand?!*"

Rigs shuffled uncomfortably. "Apparently, most sand is okay - but this beach has the wrong kind of sand..."

As a warrior, Graves thought, if there was one thing he hated, it was technology that didn't do its job. Graves took a deep breath and exhaled his frustrations away.

"Very well, keep them back to defend the city. We do not want to lose valuable firepower to avoidable mechanical faults. Is there anything else to report?"

"No, my Lord. All else is in readiness."

"Good. According to our intelligence, the attack is due to begin anytime in the next few hours. We must be ready."

"We will defend our Queen, my Lord. I will lay my life down if need be, as will we all."

"We pledged our duty to the Queen and to our world of Arilon," Graves said, before saying the words of his island motto. "Duty before all."

"Duty before all," Rigs responded. She was also from Ofisora - a fact that, paired with her skill as a warrior, made it an easy decision for Graves to make her his second-in-command. She was a fierce leader and could certainly handle a sword. But above all, she knew that duty was the defining trait in a civilised person - the thing that drove all actions and choices.

We don't do what we please, Graves knew, nor do we pass judgement on the tasks we are called to do. We simply do what our duty demands.

For someone who has viewed their entire life through duty, you really don't understand it at all, do you? We can only hope the Threads will provide someone who can teach you before it's too late.

Another random thought! Graves was growing more and more convinced that he was losing control of his mind. He didn't know if it was because of this unnatural shore or some other reason. Whatever the case, he had a job to do and needed to ensure it was completed before whatever this infirmity was

109

took hold. After all, to him, his island motto was not just words.

It was his very life.

"You are dismissed," Graves said to Rigs. She nodded and took her leave.

CHAPTER TEN

RETURN TO PAVIDUS

- TERESA -

The *Beggar's Bones* glided silently and swiftly along the Travel Line towards Valia. It was the line Arthur had created all those months ago during their escape from Phobos. Teresa could still remember the giddy excitement of realising they had all survived Arthur's harebrained escape plan. Now, what seemed like an eternity had passed and they had connected from another line in Arilon's vast network to this one that Arthur had created. Maiz had already warned that they couldn't get too close to the bravery isle on this trip or they'd be spotted by the crownies who controlled the Travel Line endpoint down on the surface.

Valia was constantly under attack from royal forces, as it had been throughout the war. Not only was it the home of some of the Queen's staunchest enemies, but it still only had three Travel Lines. Over the years, the Queen had cut almost all of Valia's lines to disconnect the idea of bravery from the rest of Arilon. She had left the line to Pavidus and one other line, both of which were constantly guarded by royal forces. The third line was the one Arthur had defiantly created and which was sometimes the only way in or out of Valia.

The royals knew they could control the Valian threat if they could control the endpoints of all three lines on the island. They had a firm hold of the Pavidus line, around which they had managed to raise a large and permanent base. The other two, they had less success with. Ownership of those lines changed hands constantly with the ebb and flow of the fighting. The endpoints of both lines were the scenes of almost constant battle and Maiz definitely wanted to avoid them.

"Ten minutes to go," Maiz announced. "Last chance to make sure your kit's ready, folks."

That last instruction was aimed less towards Teresa and Arthur and more to her fellow soldiers. Teresa wondered how they felt being on this mission instead of the big push down towards Phobos. Everyone else had left Boricia for some other location - a closely guarded secret - to rendezvous with the rest of the attacking fleet. Would these guys have preferred to be there, alongside their friends and comrades?

Teresa hadn't been told much but she could guess most of it - and everyone knew the Queen had probably guessed it, too. The first wave would be the big one. Lots of casualties in a very short space of time. High chance of failure. But assuming a miracle happened and they actually managed to get a foothold on Phobos, that's when the second wave would come in. What Stick and Ami were doing on Graft, so were a hundred different agents doing on a hundred different islands. Gathering forces to come back to Phobos to help with the push inland, towards the city of Gast. Towards the Kymerion.

Maiz would rather be fighting alongside her general, Teresa guessed. The others, she didn't know so well but she imagined they had similar feelings. But without this mission, that larger one was doomed to failure anyway. The best way to keep their friends alive, they knew, was to make sure they were successful in their task here.

"Everyone looks so serious," Seb whispered to Teresa as he sat down next to her. "It's like they've never infiltrated a massively defended royal base before."

"Have you fought with any of these guys before now?" Teresa asked him, nodding toward the rest of the squad. Seb pointed out each of them in turn.

"Reuben was in my unit during the Sedita campaign. Weeks of mud, cannons and his terrible singing is enough for anyone to want the war to end. He'd make a good pirate, though. Mykal is a sharpshooter like nothing I've ever seen. After this is all over, I will stop at nothing to recruit him for the *Snake's* crew. Isaac is the one that knows all about these fancy explosives we're using. Yet another member of my crew, he just doesn't know it yet. And Gabriel, I don't know so well, but I have played cards with him several times. I lost every time. He's a wizard at taking peoples' money with those cards."

"Let me guess. Another future crewmate."

Seb nodded. "What can I say? This war has been great for piracy recruitment."

Teresa had hoped that Iakob, Iosef or maybe Grom might have been put on this mission. But she knew their raw power would be more suited to the big push than all the sneaking around that would be needed on Pavidus. These guys looked solid, though. She had a good feeling about the mission.

Valia was getting larger in the sky above them, now. What had originally been nothing more than one silver dot among many was now slowly growing in size. Teresa could just about make out a mountain range and perhaps a sea. She wondered if it was the famed Eastern Sea where Iakob and Iosef came from.

Pavidus, on the other hand, was much smaller and so was still obscured by the darkness. They'd have to get a lot closer before they could see it properly. By Teresa's reckoning, it would soon be time to change course and begin heading toward the Isle of Dead Monsters.

113

"I don't know about you," said Arthur joining the pair on the bench, "but I cannot *wait* to get back to Pavidus. It was such fun last time."

Teresa laughed. "You're right. Getting almost ripped limb from limb by violent hordes of Fearless is like a trip to Goose Fair."

"Oh, yes, the island that's so terrible, even the big, bad Valians don't go there?" Seb said, rearranging his rucksack on his lap. "Yeah, it sounds like a total party. You never know, maybe the Fearless aren't as bad as everyone says. Maybe they're just misunderstood and all they want is a hug."

"The only thing that kept them at bay last time was the fact I was a Needleman - something even they were afraid of," said Teresa.

"Got any of that left?" Seb cocked an eyebrow. "No? Not even a hat?"

Laughing, Teresa went to hit the pirate.

"Fair enough," he shrugged, ducking the mock blow. "Looks like we'll have to rely on Maiz's warm sense of humour to calm them down."

"We can't all be as funny as you, quartermaster," Maiz joined in the conversation as she checked the clasps on her rucksack. "The rest of us have actual work to do."

"She's right," said Seb shrugging at Teresa. "I *am* funny."

Maiz was wearing dark clothes instead of her usual suit of armour. It was weird seeing her like that, Teresa thought. At the end of the day, though, this was a stealth mission. If they found themselves in need of armour, the mission would already have failed. Having said all that, the lieutenant still had her twin combat batons. Teresa watched as she slid them into her boots, making sure they were both secure and accessible.

114

Satisfied she could get to her weapons quickly and easily, Maiz stood up and turned to the human children.

"Are you two ready? We're nearly ready to... detach." The pause in her sentence betrayed nervousness felt by the usually stoic soldier. Everyone had heard of the twins' flying ships but being aboard one was going to be another matter.

"We're ready, just give us the nod," said Arthur.

"I am," said Maiz. "This is me giving you the nod. The nod is given."

"Oh, right, sorry," Arthur saluted, getting to his feet. Teresa stood as well and he cast a sideways grin at her. "Come on then, Tee. Let's wow these folks."

With everything else happening, even with this very mission, Teresa was glad to be doing this with Arthur. Making ships fly free of the Travel Lines was the most magical and exhilarating experience they had discovered during their time in Arilon. It was the freedom of slipping free of the normal rules and constraints of how you were meant to get from one idea to another. You just let go of convention and soared off into the darkness of the unknown - free to make your own path. Your own rules.

The pair of them stood at the ship's wheel, each with one hand on it. Teresa looked at the faces of the team. They were a team of mighty warriors but right now, they had the air of frightened children.

"I feel for them," said Arthur, obviously seeing the same thing. "It must be like telling the first ever parachute wearer to jump out of an aeroplane."

"Well let's hope we show them a soft landing," Teresa turned to her brother. "Ready?"

Arthur nodded and they both closed their eyes. The last time they'd tried this, Teresa had been a Needleman so the whole thing had been very difficult for them both. But this time, Teresa could immediately feel how easy it was. Together, they reached out to the endless Threads around them and pulled them close, wrapping them tightly around the small tugboat. They enveloped themselves in a complex criss-cross of the natural Arilon life energy. It felt to Teresa like Arilon was giving them a hug.

After several seconds, Teresa instinctively felt when she and Arthur had a secure hold of the ship. She felt a mental confirmation from her brother, letting her know he was similarly satisfied they had full control. With that, Teresa pulled the anchor-ring plunger, disconnecting the boat from the Travel Line. There was an audible gasp from the others as they were momentarily overcome by the instinctive Arilonian fear of falling away from the Travel Lines and being swallowed by the Black.

Except they didn't fall.

"Amazing…" Maiz whispered. Teresa opened her eyes, as did Arthur a moment later. The ship was flying away from the line, swooping upwards. They altered course away from Valia and towards the Isle of Dead Monsters. They were moving faster, too, now they were no longer restrained by the friction of the anchor-ring on the Travel Line.

The *Beggar's Bones* was on its way.

"We'll be there in five minutes," said Arthur to Maiz. The lieutenant took a deep breath and composed herself as she turned to the rest of the crew.

"Okay people," she said, "stand by the gangplank."

"Make sure you have your fuse cutters," said Isaac, the explosives expert. "And make sure each block of explosive is securely in its wrapper. We don't want any premature explosions in anyone's backpacks."

"Indeed," bellowed the deep-voiced Reuben. "Blowing yourself up is painful, embarrassing and tends to give the enemy a really good clue where to find what's left of you."

Maiz' five-man squad stood by the gangplank, even though they wouldn't actually be using it to disembark. The plan was to swoop down low and let them jump out. ('Getting kicked out of a moving cart - sounds like the perfect end to a night on the town' Seb had joked.)

The island had grown quickly in the last couple of minutes and it was soon sprawling below them. The buildings and houses looked old-fashioned, even for Arilon standards - but from a distance, they looked perfectly normal. As you got closer, though, you could suddenly see the missing windows, the open doors, the crumbling bricks. The roads and streets were entirely deserted, just as Arthur had said they were the last time - before the Fearless had suddenly emerged from wherever it was they hid themselves.

Teresa, moving in smooth concert with Arthur, aimed downwards, towards the ground. Broken and derelict roofs swept up to meet them as the tugboat dived for the cover of a sea of old, run down buildings. The small boat swooped below the skyline, hopefully keeping out of sight of prying royal eyes.

The ship-building facility was clearly visible in the distance now, a huge, black dome rising above the skyline of ruined, deserted buildings. The imposing structure was covered in a shiny, black material that reflected the Arilon sun back out in harsh, blinding rays. Teresa marvelled at how quickly the royals must have erected it since her and Arthur's last visit.

The *Beggar's Bones* nimbly sped through the crumbling stone and foliage canyons, making its way towards the facility.

"Where are the Fearless?" Arthur wondered as the landscape flew by. Teresa looked around as they passed temples and courtyards and streets. Arthur was right. There wasn't a single person to be seen. Even if they tended to stay hidden until disturbed, surely they should have seen some by now?

"Hiding in their holes, waiting to jump out and scare us," said Reuben. Teresa wasn't sure.

"Maybe not," said Mykal. "Look!"

Pavidus had fallen into slow ruin over the decades but the young soldier had spotted something new. Large, spidery black marks dotted the landscape. Now Teresa looked again, she noticed them everywhere. Burn marks. Craters. Signs of mass bonfires. An ice-cold chill descended over the crew as they realised what had happened.

"Well, I think we've discovered how the royals solved the problem of being constantly besieged by Fearless," said Seb, darkly.

"They wiped them all out..." Arthur whispered under his breath. "Not even the Fearless deserved that..."

"Really is the isle of dead monsters now," Reuben said, shaking his head.

Teresa clenched her fists with rage. Mass murder. Another calling card of the evil monarch - or at least those under her command, which came to the same thing. How could she do that to her own subjects? People she was meant to protect? It was moments like these that Teresa couldn't at all envisage becoming the Queen.

Very soon, Maiz gave Teresa and Arthur the signal to come to a halt. The pair stopped the boat in the middle of a road junction and lowered the boat so it was almost touching the ground. They were as close to the giant, ebony dome as they dared get.

"Okay, people, time to walk," said Maiz. She turned to Teresa and Arthur. "Keep out of sight. Be back here in exactly ninety minutes. If we're not already here, waiting for you, leave immediately. Do *not* come looking for us, do you understand?"

"But, what if you're in trouble?" Teresa said, "I don't like the sound of those instructions."

"This is a military operation, so they aren't instructions," said Maiz. "They're orders. And orders are followed, not questioned."

"Yes, ma'am," Arthur saluted. Teresa glared at him and he shrugged. "What? She scares me."

Teresa sighed. "Okay, fine. Ditch you if you're late. Got it."

Maiz looked dangerously close to an actual smile. She saluted back and then dropped off the side of the boat onto the road below. The other five quickly followed her lead. As soon as they were on the ground, Teresa and Arthur took the boat back into the air and went to find a good hiding spot.

It didn't take long to discover somewhere suitable. A series of house stacks - decrepit dwellings piled one ontop of another - were arranged in a circle. They looked like a bunch of old drunks leaning against each other for support. The *Beggar's Bones* dropped down into the centre of the circle, nestling out of sight among the houses - which they now knew would all be devoid of any Fearless.

"Well..." Teresa said into the sudden silence. "Got a book?"

Arthur took a seat next to his sister. "Well, maybe we can use the time to figure out how we're going to... you know..."

"Stop me from turning into an evil rage monster?" Teresa said, flatly.

"Exactly," said Arthur. "So let's look at this logically. What do we know?"

"We know that at some point in the near future, I'm going to kill the Queen," said Teresa. "That's what she told me. And that's what causes me to *become* her, eventually."

"The question…" Arthur said, rolling the thoughts around his head, "…is how exactly do you manage to destroy her? I mean, where does that power come from?"

Teresa shrugged. "I'm not sure," she lied. There was no way she could make herself say the words.

I strip you of all your power until you cease to exist.

"When we were on Oblivia," Arthur said, "Lon-Jinus told me that together, we had virtually limitless power. Maybe we join forces and tap into that?"

Teresa closed her eyes and turned away. "Maybe."

"But then why does that somehow result in you becoming the Queen? Unless…" Arthur trailed off. "Oh, I see."

"What?"

"Well, maybe it's not killing the Queen that drives you down the road into becoming her. Maybe it's what she does right before you kill her."

"What do you mean?"

"Well, if you go off and become the Queen, it might be because I'm not around. So perhaps, what happens is that we face the Queen together but she… she kills me."

Teresa closed her eyes but Arthur continued.

"That makes you so angry and your anger super-charges your powers… and you destroy her in revenge."

Teresa didn't trust herself to speak. The picture Arthur was describing was traumatic enough but, unfortunately, it didn't scratch the surface of the true horror of the situation. How could she tell him that he was wrong? That it was *her*, not the Queen, who-

The Queen, who...

...was standing right there on the deck.

"Hello, Teresa," she said.

"You!" Teresa yelled, leaping to her feet. She swiped her hand towards the Queen and a wooden crate launched from its resting place and flew into the monarch's body... passing right through and smashing harmlessly on the deck beyond her.

"Teresa?" Arthur leaped to his feet in alarm. "What is it? What's going on?"

Arthur couldn't see her! The Queen must have been sending some kind of projection into her mind. Teresa felt the ice in her veins, as if she were facing down dog-men back in the night forest. She couldn't allow herself to be scared, not even in the face of such danger and evil.

"How are things, dear?" the Queen asked as if they were catching up over a cup of tea. "How does it feel to know you are destined to rule this entire world? You are welcome, by the way."

"I would never rule like you! Not through fear!"

"I'm sure I said exactly the same thing when I was in your position," said the Queen. "I can't really remember being in your position, so one can only assume."

Arthur jumped in front of Teresa, glowering at the empty space in front of her, trying to protect her from a threat he couldn't see. "You get away from her! You can't have her - she'll never become you!"

121

"And here he is," the Queen said, mocking and disdainful. "Returned from the dead. The one memory I could never rid myself of." The monarch tried to keep her usual air of menacing calm but it was immediately clear to Teresa that the sight of Arthur genuinely disturbed her.

With what seemed like an effort, she turned her gaze back to Teresa. "Still running to your rescue? Your white knight? Still holding you back? Keeping your rightful power from you? Stopping you from helping everyone you want to help? From being all you want to be?"

"You're so twisted, so far beyond love and compassion that you don't even recognise it anymore!" Teresa accused her future self. "You can't tell the difference between love and imprisonment."

"There *is* no difference between love and imprisonment," she replied, coldly. "This, I have learned. My horizons have been widened. As will yours. From the very moment you take your brother's life-force as your own."

Teresa cast a horrified, guilty glance at Arthur.

"Is she still talking?" Arthur hissed at his sister. "What's she saying?"

Even amidst the terrifying situation, part of Teresa breathed a sigh of relief. Her terrible secret was still safe.

"This future you're pinning your hopes on," Teresa said, "I wouldn't get too excited about it. We're going to put an end to it."

"Yes, all of this I would have said when I was you," said the Queen. "When I was facing this supposed dark, evil future version of myself. All you are doing is repeating history. You are following your brother through the forest and he will lead you to a future you do not want."

"But you want it, though, don't you? So why complain?"

122

"Well, considering what you are soon supposed to do to me," said the Queen, "perhaps I'm not as thrilled with that outcome as you might think."

Teresa froze. What was the Queen suggesting?

" I do not want to fight with you, Teresa. Perhaps if we join together, we can create a new future. One that is better for us both. You need to leave your brother's influence behind - but I am not heartless. He does not have to die. You don't have to kill him. We can escape this loop and save Arilon. Together."

For a moment, Teresa was taken back to the Needlemen house. When the two versions of her were stuck in that loop, trying to get up the stairs and out of the room. Only when they stopped fighting each other and worked as one person could they succeed.

She glanced slowly at Arthur. Could it be? Could there be another way? Could his life be saved?

"People are self-destructive, Teresa, you know that. They need to be saved. Remember Waterwhistle? You tried to tell the villagers about Lady Eris. You were taken away before you could convince them and what happened? The village fell. Only your return saved them."

"Yes..." Teresa breathed, finally. "Saved them from you! You're the threat!"

The Queen shook her head, slowly. "Your perspective is still so small. But that is okay. I cannot simply tell you what is best. You must see it for yourself. And so, I will do the very best thing for you that I can. The thing that will convince you to come to me of your own free will."

"Oh yes?" Teresa said. "And what's that?"

"Nothing. I will leave you alone. Go. Complete your mission. I knew you were coming but I have not alerted my

123

forces. Do as you will. The future has already been written. Now, we just have to make it." The Queen opened her palms to her young self. "I will see you again soon. You can give me your answer then."

"You can have my answer *now!*" Teresa screamed, throwing a dozen crates at the deadly apparition. The wooden boxes smashed into the spot where the Queen stood sending rope and metal rigging equipment crashing all over the deck. But even as they landed, there was no-one there.

The Queen was gone.

Teresa was rooted to the spot for a moment, stunned and shocked. Then, as the fact of the Queen's presence hit her, she dropped to her knees, suddenly feeling emotionally and physically drained.

"Teresa, are you okay?" Arthur knelt down beside his sister, his arms around her shoulders.

"She lied," Teresa said, breathing heavily.

"About what?"

Teresa remembered he hadn't heard anything the Queen had said. "She knows where we are," she explained. "She claimed she wasn't going to come after us, that she was going to just let us carry on our mission."

"Willingly let us destroy the one thing that would end the resistance attack in its tracks?" Arthur was as incredulous as his sister. "No way."

"My thoughts exactly. How long have Maiz and the others had?"

"Not long. Maybe half the time."

"It'll have to do," Teresa grunted as she pushed herself to her feet. "Let's get this ship in the air. The *Twilight Palace* is coming."

CHAPTER ELEVEN
EXPLOSIVES ARE NOT TOYS

- SEB -

Seb held his breath as he hid in the shadows.

Two crownies were standing just the other side of some cargo crates. They'd been there for the last couple of minutes, chatting quietly between themselves. Seb shook his head in frustration. There were two types of royal soldier. One type was the silent, faceless, barely-even-alive creatures that the Queen had brought with her when she'd arrived in Arilon. The ones here in front of Seb were the other type - regular Arilonians who had signed up to defend the crown. *Wish these were the silent ones*, Seb thought. *At least they wouldn't be slacking off and getting in my way like these losers.*

The pirate quartermaster held his rucksack close to his chest like a baby's comfort blanket while willing the soldiers to move on. After another eternal thirty seconds, the soldiers finally obeyed his mental pleas and wandered off, rifles in hand, still chatting. Seb let out a long, slow breath of relief and annoyance.

"Cripes, fellas," he whispered to himself as he got back to business, "Some of us actually have work to do."

The soldiers would not be short of places to continue their chat - the hangar was a massive, cavernous expanse. It felt even bigger on the inside than it did on the outside, the way huge buildings often do. It housed no fewer than twelve of the gigantic Warships, as promised by the mission's intelligence. The vessels were arranged in a huge circle, all facing inward. In the centre of the giant, circular room were the two Travel Lines

Arthur had described - about ten yards apart and both heading out of a circular opening in the centre of the ceiling. One headed to Valia and the other, to Phobos. Both of them grew out of the ground in the way Travel Lines did - placed there by the Thinker and the Beginner at the start of Creation.

Seb had to admit, this entire place was a very impressive structure. Shame the only way they'd been able to build it was to wipe out the island's native inhabitants. Cruel, genocidal, mass-murder. The Isle of Dead Monsters had new monsters in residence now, Seb thought, and they were most certainly not dead.

No longer at risk of being overheard, the pirate opened his backpack and took out his final explosive. Like the previous five he'd already planted, the small package of brown paper was brushed with grease and was, appropriately enough, dome-shaped. The grease made it slightly slippery but since the grease was there to protect it from sparks or anything that might set it off prematurely, Seb didn't mind so much. Rather sticky fingers than surprise sunburn.

Anyway, you're a thieving pirate, he imagined Teresa saying as if she were here beside him. *Sticky fingers is part of your job description.*

The package apparently contained super-compressed gunpowder which, Seb had been told, would make an even bigger explosion than some cannons. This, Seb was excited to see - but preferably from a safe distance. He carefully peeled the paper off the dome's flat underside, revealing the sticky base, and pushed it against the stone column in front of him.

A single piece of string hung out of the top of the dome - it was over a foot long and had blue marks every few centimetres along it. The markings indicated the differing lengths of time it would take for the fuse to burn all the way

126

down to the gunpowder. He checked his pocket watch - the family heirloom he had taken from the man on the cliff. He remembered telling Teresa the story and for the first time, he actually felt guilty about how he'd acquired it. That annoyed him. It really was a very nice watch.

Gauging the time that he'd planted the other explosives, Seb snipped the string to the twenty minutes mark. That should have them all going off at the same time, he thought. His and the rest of the team's. And hopefully, as the big boom was going up, they'd all be sipping cocktails on the *Beggar's Bones* and enjoying the fireworks from a safe distance.

He allowed his thoughts to briefly travel to his partners in crime. With any luck, Maiz, Isaac and the others were getting on as well as he had. When they'd arrived at the facility, after their brief jog across the eerily deserted city, they had quickly assessed their task. Isaac, being the explosives expert, identified the structural points they would need to blow to bring the whole place down - it would be quicker than trying to blow up the ships themselves. Seb had been assigned to the group setting bombs on the main building support columns, while Maiz and Gabriel had gone to the upper floor to take care of the roof struts. Soon, the whole facility would be falling in on itself, burying the Warships in the process. They would definitely not be in a position to gate crash the big party down on Phobos.

For what felt like the hundredth time, Seb reflected on the fact he never expected to be playing war hero. Sebastian J Falkes was a Pirate of the NothingSpace. A Brigand of the Black. He sailed for gold, not foolish, heroic ideals. In his short career, he'd gone from a pirating nobody to Quartermaster of one of the most notorious ships in the NothingSpace. That was some going. And it proved that the young man wasn't as useless as his violent father used to delight in telling him he was. Seb glanced again at the watch, feeling that unfamiliar pang of guilt. He had to admit it - a lot had changed during this stupid war. Including, it seemed, he himself.

"Hands up."

Seb froze. Sounded like a royal officer, standing right behind him. Okay. That was fine. He'd been caught red-handed lots of times. All he needed to do was the same thing he did that time in the Duke's jewellery walk-in closet. Time to engage the silver tongue.

He turned around to face the officer, but his plan immediately fell apart when he saw that the man was not alone.

The secret, covert team was no longer secret or covert. Royal soldiers had every single one of Seb's comrades handcuffed with either a pistol to the head or a sword to the throat. In the circumstances, Seb reluctantly did as he was told and raised his hands.

"Looks like you're the last one," the officer said. This one was an actual person, like the two chatterboxes earlier. He wore the armour but had removed his helmet, all the better to gloat at his captors. "I don't know what you're doing here, but you can't have been foolish enough to believe you could escape detection forever?"

Apparently, they were exactly that foolish. As a soldier roughly yanked his arms behind his back and cuffed his wrists together, the pirate glanced at Maiz but her face was stone, as usual. A hard glance from her warned him to say nothing. Confirm nothing.

"We're not Resistance," said Seb. "We're travellers. We just got a bit lost."

"I never said you were Resistance," said the officer, his tone triumphant. "But thank you for confirming it."

Maiz closed her eyes and shook her head in despair. *Hmm*, Seb thought, *the old silver tongue seems to have gone a bit rusty.*

"Your paltry, laughable band cannot hope to win this war," the officer crowed. "The Queen's power is implacable. Now you will all wait here for her majesty to arrive and-"

"Immovable," said Seb.

The officer blinked, shocked at being interrupted. "Excuse me?"

"You said implacable but I don't think you mean implacable. Implacable means 'unable to be appeased or placated'. As in - the baby was crying endlessly, it was implacable. I'm sure you probably meant to say the Queen's power is *immovable*."

The officer was caught off guard. "I'm sure I know how to-"

"Or maybe 'invincible'? 'Unconquerable'?"

"I think I-"

"Wait, how about 'inevitable'!" Seb grinned, happy with his word choice, but then, "...wait no, that's not exactly the same thing..."

"Oh, for the love of Creation will you *please* shut up!" Maiz had had enough.

"I'm just trying to help him not sound like an idiot," Seb argued.

The officer glanced at his soldiers as if to say meekly 'but... I don't sound like an idiot do I?'.

"Do you not recognise when it's time to stop talking and take things seriously?" Maiz shouted.

"Okay, scum" the officer yelled, "that's enou-"

"Not sounding like an idiot is something I take *very* seriously!"

129

"Really? Do you think maybe you should apply it to yourself sometime?"

"Both of you, you will apply with my command!"

"You see? He's doing it again..!" said Seb before turning back to the officer. "*Comply* not *apply!* Did you even go to school? What's wrong with you?"

"Well, I'm in agreement with the crownie," yelled Maiz at the young pirate. "You need to be quiet immediately!"

"But if I'm quiet, how will I distract these royal goons from the fact I've just picked the lock on my handcuffs?" Seb said, holding up his now empty handcuffs.

Everyone froze for a second.

"What?" Seb said, quizzically to Maiz. "Did you not realise that's what I was doing?"

Immediately, Maiz shoulder-barged the soldier holding her and the others all launched into action at the same time. Seb launched a kick straight into the stomach of the officer, doubling the hapless man over in pain.

"That's for not paying attention in school!" Seb berated his would-be captor.

"Nice kick!" Reuben grinned as he smashed his soldier into the wall.

"Not really," Seb shrugged, flicking his hair out of his face. "I missed the parts I was actually aiming for."

"Great, nice chat," said Maiz. "Now how about getting the key from our royal friend?"

Seb rifled through the officer's pockets until he found a ring of keys, then picked through them, finding the right one as he stood up. He was about to move toward the lieutenant with the key to her freedom when the sound of more soldiers' boots filled the air. The team may have gotten rid of their immediate captors but, even now, more were running to investigate the commotion. There was no way they'd be able to dodge everybody. Their escape was over before it had even begun.

Worse, their mission was a failure.

That was the moment an immense explosion filled the air - followed by the sight of the *Beggar's Bones* diving down into the base through the roof launch gate. The small boat let off another cannon shot, blasting soldiers and equipment in all directions. It nimbly dodged between the sails of the giant Warships and made its way over to Seb and the others.

Being inside a flying ship was one thing, Seb marvelled, but seeing it from the outside...

"Seb!" Maiz barked with the tone of an annoyed teacher. "Key!"

Shaken from his gawping, Seb ran over to Maiz and quickly uncuffed her and the rest of the team. Meanwhile, royal soldiers all around them ran for cover as the *Bones'* single cannon continued to take potshots, sowing confusion and trying its best to keep at bay any kind of co-ordinated counter-attack. The boat came to a stop above the team and three rope ladders unfurled over the edge, tumbling down toward the ground.

"Let's go! Up, up!" Maiz shouted as one or two soldiers began to regain their wits and started to return rifle fire.

Isaac and Gabriel clambered up one ladder, Reuben and Mykal up another. Maiz and Seb leaped onto the final one and the *Beggar's Bones* immediately lifted up and began soaring forwards.

The six saboteurs did their best to climb while the boat swung from side to side, evading gunshots while trying to let off more of their own. Climbing up a rope ladder was always hard enough, Seb thought, without being flung about like a half-empty bottle of rum.

"The columns!" Maiz yelled as she neared the top of the ladder. "Blast one of the columns!"

Seb realised she wasn't talking to him but to whoever was manning the gun above them. Whoever it was - Arthur or Teresa - took heed of Maiz's commands and turned the weapon on the nearest column. The blast hit the building support dead on, setting off the explosive that had been clinging to it. That's when things *really* got loud.

Each explosive set off the one next to it in an ever-expanding chain reaction. One by one, the bombs around the edge of the gigantic circular building spewed red-hot destruction into the hangar. A wall of flames and exploding stone began chasing the *Beggar's Bones* around the edge of the room as the small boat raced ahead of the burning death.

Seb clung to the ladder as the fire reached out for him, roaring with a deafening anger that echoed all around the giant dome.

"Maiz, I'm going to kill you!" he yelled over the pandemonium. "This is *not* a safe distance!"

Seb knew why Maiz had issued the order, of course. At least one of the Warships was surely bringing its cannons into position right now, to swat this annoying fly. They had to set off the explosives immediately or they may not have been going off at all.

Maiz was clearly okay with sacrificing herself for the cause. Seb, despite running around with resistance fighters, didn't feel he was quite there yet.

The pirate finally reached the top of the ladder, allowing him to see onto the deck of the *Beggar's Bones*. Teresa was standing at the wheel, swooping the boat left and right, nimbly avoiding flames, stone and gunfire. Arthur was loading and aiming the cannon with impressive speed, doing maximum damage to the facility and keeping the crownies' heads down as much as possible. Any falling debris from the explosions that came too close, he or his sister waved a hand and the rock shattered or flew out of their way. These two children were unstoppable, Seb marvelled. Even dangling half over the edge of the boat as he was, there was a part of the quartermaster's mind that couldn't help but be impressed by these two. Impressed and a little scared.

Finally the young pirate tumbled clumsily over the top of the gunwale and down onto the boat's deck. "Get us out of here!"

"I'm so glad you're here to give us these blatantly obvious ideas," Teresa shouted as she began to spin the wheel in a new direction and reached for the speed lever. "Now shut up and hang on."

"I don't think you meant *blatantly*, I think the word you were looking for is *patentl-*"

Seb fell over as Teresa flung the boat towards the hole in the ceiling.

The *Beggar's Bones* raced along on invisible Threads, fighting to stay ahead of the angry firestorm that chased it out of the rapidly collapsing dome. Engulfing everything inside the hangar, there was nowhere else for the fury to go but out through the launch gate after them. However, as Seb looked back at the rising conflagration, a dark shape formed within the flames and warned him that the fire wasn't the only thing they needed to outrun.

"Um…" he shouted, pointing and trying to get someone's attention. "Warship. Warship, warship, warship!"

Maiz and the others turned to see the intimidating bulk, bristling with weapons, spring from the flames like some evil sea creature leaping out of the waves.

Very quickly and with unbelievable speed, it began gaining on them.

"It must have already been attached to the Line!" Maiz yelled. "We can't let it get away!"

"What exactly do you plan to-"

"Already on it," cried Teresa, swinging them round and bringing their tiny boat close to the mammoth vessel. Seb immediately saw what she was trying to do - being so close meant two things. One, they were too close for the Warship's guns to be able to swivel and take aim at them. And two...

"For Arilon!" Maiz cried as she leapt overboard, batons in hand, and dropped several metres onto the deck of the Warship. Upon landing, she immediately began tearing into the royal soldiers.

"She's kind of scary, right?" Seb said to Arthur who had appeared next to him. Before the human could reply, a blast emanated from one of the Warship's smaller guns, dispelling the idea that they were too close to be fired upon. The single shot was devastating. It completely demolished the centre of the deck, breaking the spine of the small boat. The main mast immediately began to list to one side - and the entire vessel began to sway in the opposite direction.

"Boat's coming apart!" Teresa shouted as she ran past Seb and Arthur. "Time to get a new one!"

She leapt down, sword in hand, to the enemy deck, landing next to Maiz. Isaac and the others quickly followed. Seb glanced at Arthur.

"That one is crazy, you know," he said, drawing his cutlass.

"Yeah…" Arthur grabbed his own shortsword and shook his head, steeling himself. "Apparently, we're related." And the pair jumped over the side, leaving the *Beggar's Bones,* flaming and falling apart, to stream down towards the desolate surface of Pavidus, its final mission accomplished.

CHAPTER TWELVE

ENEMIES ABOARD

- TERESA -

Teresa was not sure if she found this terrifying or exciting. Being in the middle of battle, using her power, fighting alongside Arthur, standing shoulder to shoulder with Arilon freedom fighters, taking on the might of the Queen's forces, always just a moment away from death, a mistake away from defeat, a risk away from victory. She was pretty sure that when she'd been yearning to return to Arilon, this was exactly what she'd been hoping for.

"Tee, behind you!" Arthur cried.

"I feel them," said Teresa, facing the other way. She swiped away the soldiers in front of her and without turning around, the ones behind her as well. Arthur used the Threads to fling a cannon toward her and she caught it, swung it around to increase its momentum before shoving it at a group emerging from a door to the lower decks.

The deck of the *Gauntlet* was alive with chaos. Teresa was pretty sure nobody had ever before had the audacity to bring fighting like this to the doorstep of the mighty Warship.

Like pocket lightning, Maiz was right in the centre of the fighting, swinging her customised batons in lethal arcs, taking out soldiers, knights and ship's crew alike. Without her armour weighing her down, Teresa was astounded to see the soldier moved even faster than usual. Seb was in his element, of course. Shipboard battle was his bread and butter. He usually had better odds than this, Teresa guessed, but he wasn't letting a little thing like being ridiculously outnumbered spoil his fun.

This kind of brawl also appeared to be right up Reuben and Mykal's street and they seemed to be enjoying themselves immensely. Teresa knew Isaac and Gabriel were more tactical warriors but they were clearly no slouches at close-quarters combat either. Between them, they employed sword, lance and pistol with a vigour and efficiency that Teresa was sure would have made General Kingsley very proud.

It was a shame, of course, that they were all on a losing streak. This ship probably had hundreds of people aboard. It had already been attached to the Travel Line, so it had presumably been at least partially crewed and ready to go. No matter how bravely the Resistance fighters battled away, it was only a matter of time before the tide overwhelmed them.

When Maiz had leaped onto the deck of the *Gauntlet*, everyone had instinctively known the situation. This wasn't about fighting their way to survival. This was about stopping the last remaining Pavidus Warship from outflanking the Resistance forces that at this very moment, would be beginning their attack on Phobos. This was a mission Teresa took very seriously. She would not allow a single Resistance life to be lost because she had failed to do her part.

Rather than let that happen, she would rip this ship apart with her bare hands.

Maiz suddenly appeared next to Teresa, her batons swinging intermittently as she spoke.

"This ship's going to be within range of our forces any moment. If you have any ideas how to stop it before we get there, now's the time," she said, bashing a soldier in the face before kicking him into a nearby group of his own comrades.

"Well, we won't be able to make the ship fly far so there's only one thing I can think of," said Teresa, "and you're not going to like it."

"If you're thinking of pulling us off this Travel Line and throwing us into the Black, you're right, I don't like it," grunted Maiz, "but it's what I was expecting you to say. Do it."

Arthur and Seb, swords flashing, were forced backwards towards Teresa and Maiz and the four of them formed a circle, back to back, holding off the incoming swarms as best they could. Isaac, Gabriel and Reuben weaved themselves in and out of the enemy forces as they moved back and forth across the deck causing mayhem. Mykal had managed to get himself situated somewhere in the rigging and was taking shot after rapid, accurate shot with two pistols - every one a hit, not a single bullet was wasted.

"If I just heard what I think I heard," shouted Seb over the din, "I'd like to register my opposition to the plan. Why can't we just fly out of here?"

"It takes a lot of concentration," Arthur shouted back. "If you could ask all these people to kindly stop trying to kill us for a minute, then maybe we'd be in business."

"If we're extremely lucky, we might be able to fly for a few seconds," Teresa shouted. "We'll get nowhere in that time. All we can do is shove ourselves away from-"

The entire deck shook with a massive explosion and everyone was thrown to the ground.

"What was *that?*" Seb groaned, holding his head.

"I think Gabriel just hit one of those weapons crates over there," Maiz grunted as she picked herself up. Many of the soldiers nearby were still stunned.

"Ha!" Teresa grinned, swiping a dazed crewman away from her as she got back to her feet. "How do you like that, crownies? Not so big now are-"

The words died in her throat as her gaze was caught by the sight of Phobos appearing out of the darkness. What she saw was pure horror.

The words 'Operation Hammer' didn't even begin to describe the destruction happening before her eyes. Resistance ships of all sizes were charging the island on a series of adjacent Travel Lines, trying to force their way down towards a beach hundreds of feet below. However, powerful cannonfire on the ground was mercilessly shredding the attacking ships, sending torn, broken hulls and tiny, lifeless bodies spinning out into the Black. Below a certain height, all that remained of most ships were their anchor rings, sliding aimlessly down the Travel Lines, short lengths of anchor chains trailing behind them.

A few ships had managed to get past the initial barrage, closer to the surface. However, many of them were fully on fire - hull, mast and sail. Some Resistance fighters opted to jump from burning ships in the hope they would hit the sea before enemy gunfire could pick them off. A few of them did make it all the way down to the water but most of those were not surviving the impact from such a height.

Of the few exhausted remnants that made it through the cannon barrage, the burning ships, the drop into the ocean and the swim to the shore, swarms of royal soldiers waited for them on the sand, swords drawn.

From start to finish, it was merciless, hellish, futile and cruel.

"What a waste..." Teresa's voice struggled to crawl up her throat. "What a terrible, terrible waste..."

This was war, she realised. All the battles fought across great distances over weeks, months or even years... they just came down to this. People falling on each others' swords for what everyone hoped was a worthy cause.

139

In the distance, striking out high against the Phobos skyline was the tall, black shiny building Teresa had seen once before. The object of the day's exertions; the Kymerion. And moored next to it was *The Twilight Palace*. The Queen had been telling the truth… she really wasn't coming for them! But why would-

The deck shook again as another crate of gunpowder was blown up. Again, everyone was sent flying. But Teresa managed to keep a hold of the side of the ship, as did Arthur next to her, and in doing so, she suddenly spotted something important far below on the beach.

"Arthur, Maiz, look!" Teresa grabbed Maiz to her feet and pointed at the battle below. There was a row of five gigantic canons along the ridge that was providing the majority of the devastating blanket of suppressing fire keeping the Resistance from getting to the ground. "If we can take out those cannons…"

"We'd give them a chance." Maiz nodded. "You said you might get a few seconds of flight."

Arthur glanced at Maiz. "For this, we'll only need a few seconds."

A thin smile briefly flitted across the lieutenant's mouth. "We'll get them for you."

"Well," Seb shrugged as he re-grasped his cutlass, "this would seem to be one of those self-sacrificing moments I've heard about. Ah well, maybe Elza might have decided it was worth sacrificing herself for others after all." He flashed one last grin at Teresa before he and Maiz leapt at the oncoming soldiers, joining the others in buying the time Arthur and Teresa needed to win this fight.

"Come on!" Teresa shouted and Arthur followed her on their journey to the ship's wheel.

The pair ran through the storm together, pulling and pushing the Threads to forge a path through the endless storm of soldiers. The trip was definitely made easier by Maiz and the others drawing more of the fighting onto themselves and after seconds that felt like hours, Teresa laid hands on the ship's wheel.

"Do it," said Arthur as he pulled the anchor ring plunger. The Warship left the Travel Line.

There was no time to properly prepare a smooth transition and the abnormal lurch of the ship drew cries of fear and shock from several crew members - although not the inhuman, faceless soldiers who continued to fight regardless. Ignoring the battle around her, Teresa felt Arthur's mind latch onto hers and together they shaped the Threads into a road - almost like a slide down an icy hill and the ship was the sledge. They laid the road as they rode it, continually placing the next section, allowing the ship to immediately skid onto it. Concentrating as much as the melee would allow, the pair aimed the invisible highway towards the row of monster cannons on the beach hundreds of feet below.

Teresa and Arthur's minds were connected in this moment. She could feel his thoughts and she knew he could feel hers. Together, they felt the panic on the ground as, one by one, people began to notice the ship heading in their direction. They could also feel the spark of hope ignite in the air- and sea-borne Resistance forces as they saw something finally going in their favour.

Teresa felt Arthur flinging away any soldiers that came too close, his attention momentarily diverted away from flying the ship. Any fleeting thoughts she'd had of them being able to properly control the ship after all were dashed. Rather than the usual controlled flight, they were basically hurling the

141

massive vessel at the canons like a massive rock. And they had just one chance to get their aim right.

Teresa could feel Arthur's fear, determination and even a few streaks of uncharacteristic anger all mixed up into an armour that he wrapped around the pair of them while he continued to strike out at the enemy. It was very impressive and Teresa felt warm and safe knowing her brother, very literally had her back.

The ground raced closer and closer as Teresa felt everything going on around her. She felt Maiz' indomitable bravery but also the intense emotions the lieutenant had buried deep down. Suddenly, springing out of the lieutenant's mind was the image of her life back home. Maiz and her wife Sara had a ranch back home where they looked after their beloved horses. It was a place the combative lieutenant had planned to spend all her days on. This sudden insight into the secret history of the no-nonsense warrior grabbed Teresa's breath, stopping it in her chest.

And in that moment, she felt it all.

Isaac wanted to become an author. Mykal and his wife ran a travelling puppet theatre. The bombastic Reuben actually designed buildings. Gabriel had fought to be the first person from his island to be accepted onto a course at a prestigious university on Doctreena. He had finally been admitted but felt it was his duty to come and fight for Arilon instead. All the hidden things that no-one ever saw. They weren't just warriors or soldiers, Teresa realised, they were real people. She already knew that in her head, of course, but now it hit her right in her heart. Like everyone else in this war, their real selves had been buried beneath a shell of battles and swords and explosions.

And suddenly, it wasn't just her team Teresa felt, but also the living crew of the *Gauntlet* - the ones who weren't the

Queen's mindless automatons. And the royal fighters on the ground. Yes, she was about to save lives but hundreds were about to lose their lives, too. And they deserved to live, even the royalist ones. And she deserved not to be the one forced to kill them.

Not to mention Arthur, her other half who, even now, strained every fibre to protect her. Why should he be turned into a mass killer?

Teresa's anger suddenly flared from zero to volcano. It erupted so quickly, so frighteningly fast, it took her completely by surprise - but as soon as she was aware of it, she embraced it. The ground was right there, just a couple of metres below them now. The masthead of the ship was literally about to touch the central cannon and within the next second, the rest of the ship and all aboard would follow.

No.

As easily as turning her head, Teresa reached into Arthur's mind - linked as it already was to hers - and grabbed his power with both hands. Mixing it with her own, she stretched and span the Threads into a fine gossamer film, enveloping every person she could sense - Arthur, Maiz, Seb, the rest of her team, the rest of the *Gauntlet's* living crew, and all the people manning the cannons. Every single one of them. Once it was spread thinly around everyone, with a nudge of her mind, she hardened it.

The ship hit the ground.

The most monstrous explosion imaginable raced outwards, the heat instantly fusing the sand into glass. Then it raced up into the air as the entire Warship with its endless store of gunpowder met the row of cannons. The two elements impacted into a cataclysmic eruption of fire and destruction. It was white and hot and deafening but Teresa stood in the centre of it and all around her, hundreds of confused-looking people hung suspended in mid-air, all of them staring with wonder at the inside of the explosion.

It felt like a million years and no time at all. Teresa could feel every fibre of Arilon, every Thread, every island. Just for that endless instant, she was Arilon and Arilon was her.

And then the moment passed and indescribable pain flashed through Teresa's head. The strain of what she was doing was pulling her head apart and the link between her and Arthur's power was already beginning to break down. She needed to tidy up quickly.

With a wave of both hands, the all-engulfing flames dissipated into wisps of fire and then scraps of smoke and then nothing. Everyone dropped to the ground.

Teresa cried out in pain as the sensation of Arilon rushed out of her head like air out of a balloon. Even with all that shared power, what she had just done was nearly impossible. As the essence of Arilon left her, Teresa was convinced she sensed a feeling of surprise coming from *within* the Threads.

And then it was all gone.

She opened her eyes and all around her lay the scorched wreckage of the *Gauntlet* and the twisted metal remnants of the five giant cannons. The faceless, empty royal soldiers and knights were all gone, burned away to nothing. But all the actual, living royal soldiers were still alive. Immediately, despite outnumbering the resistance warriors, they ran. They ran from the power, Teresa realised. They were terrified. She felt a pang of anger at them - that power had just saved their lives. How ungrateful they were! But the pang passed as she saw Seb, Maiz and the others standing there, dazed but alive. The anger and exhaustion was instantly washed away by a wave of joy. But before she could even say anything, that joy was itself washed away as her eyes fell on Arthur. And all she was left with was a sudden shower of realisation and guilt.

She rushed over to her brother as he stumbled to his feet.

"Arthur-" she reached out to him but he was staggering and holding his head in pain. He swept out a hand, knocking hers away.

"You… you did it again…" he stammered, his head clearly splitting as much as Teresa's had been. Probably worse, Teresa guessed, since the whole thing had taken him by surprise.

"I'm… I'm sorry Arthur! I really am," Teresa pleaded, "I didn't want you to die. I didn't want anyone to die. I just had to-"

"You're going to kill me," he said.

The words struck her in the chest. All the swords Arthur had just protected her from couldn't have hurt as much as the words he now flung at her.

"What… What are you-"

"I saw it," he said, still breathing heavily. "In your mind, when we were linked. That's how you destroy the Queen. You take my power - all of it, until there's nothing left of me. And you do it by choice."

Teresa was bombarded by emotions. Guilt and shame at breaking her promise and hurting Arthur, shame at Arthur's discovery of her secret, but confidence too. Confidence that they could handle all that power swirling around them. They didn't need to be afraid of it or approach it timidly like Arthur or the Cat kept preaching. And finally there was anger. Anger that she had just saved Arthur's life and he was complaining. Anger that the royal soldiers and crew had run from her in fear instead of falling at her feet in thanks.

"So…" Seb's voice suddenly broke the silence as he patted himself down, "…I'm not dead because…?"

"You're not dead because this young woman," said Maiz, putting her hand on Teresa's shoulder, "possesses bravery, power and skill the likes of which none of us have ever seen. Look!"

The soldier pointed at the dark sky and everyone could see the Resistance ships descending through the lessened royal bombardment in far greater numbers. More of the ships were making it to the surface and more troops were making it farther up the beach. With more troops on the ground, the royal line of defence was quickly beginning to crumble.

"If I'm not mistaken," Maiz said, "we are watching the first phase of Operation Hammer literally being won before our eyes!"

Seb let out a whoop of victory as did Reuben, Isaac, Mykal and Gabriel. Even Maiz allowed herself a laugh as Reuben twirled her around on the sand in a dance of victory. In the distance, their compatriots chased the royals off the beach and Resistance ships and boats began to land on the fabled Shores of Disquiet.

But Teresa watched her brother turn away from her and collapse heavily onto a broken piece of ship hull. Down the way, the almost-silent waves crashed onto the beach and she felt the desolation and loneliness fall onto her like a fine, salty spray of ocean water.

CHAPTER THIRTEEN
THE NEXT MISSION

- THE CAT -

Well, thought the Cat, *isn't this awkward.*

"Would... um... would either of you like a biscuit?"

Teresa and Arthur walked just behind the Cat and Kingsley as they headed towards the command tent of the hastily erected beach-head camp. All around them was the frantic activity of Resistance soldiers establishing their first foothold on the isle of Phobos. They were sharpening swords, checking rifles, fixing armour, getting a quick bite to eat, tending wounds and holding brief, impromptu memorials to their recently fallen comrades. All this life and activity and noise was in stark contrast to the silence coming from the two humans trailing sullenly in the Cat's wake.

He'd noticed something was wrong from the moment he'd laid eyes on the pair, of course. They had walked into the camp along with the rest of their team to cheers and a thunderous heroes' welcome. They had been overjoyed to discover that their friends had all survived but they were uncharacteristically cold toward each other. When the Cat had asked about it, he'd gotten a firm 'everything is fine' from each of them. This was despite the fact each of them now had a face like the wet end of a fish.

The silent reply to his question informed him that, apparently, nobody wanted a biscuit.

He moved on.

"Can I just tell you both that what you did today saved hundreds upon hundreds of lives?" said the Cat. Still, the human children said nothing. They just walked on behind him, glancing at the scenes around them. At all the people who would have been dead if not for their actions. Once, the Cat glimpsed Teresa catch Arthur's eye but then they both quickly looked away again. He sighed, inwardly.

"We were basically beginning to think this was the end. Even I wasn't going to escape from this one," the Cat continued as he paced along. "Those cannons were really tearing us up. And then you two beautiful, brilliant humans threw a ship at them. One heck of a way to deal with the problem."

Still no response. Yep. *So* awkward.

"We eventually managed to secure the beach and push all the royal forces inland," said Kingsley. "But we don't have any time to waste. Within the hour, we're going to start the push towards Gast. Towards the Kymerion."

The General stopped and turned to the children. "We have had a rocky relationship, I know. From the moment I tried to capture you both in the museum on your world, we have not exactly hit it off. I perhaps took the wrong approach and for that I apologise. I am still not proud of my decision to use children - regardless of their power - in war. But I have to say right now that whether it was right or wrong, I thank you for your service to Arilon. It was, quite possibly the most important moment in our history."

The Cat watched as this last comment seemed to unlock something in the pair. They glanced at each other but this time, they didn't look away. Arthur might have even given a tiny half-smile. Teresa turned to Kingsley.

"It's all we wanted to do all along," she said. "To come here and help. I'm glad we were able to do that, finally."

A fine thing, thought the Cat, when he couldn't get through to his friends but General Kingsley could.

"Hopefully, you can take it from here, now we've done the hard part," Arthur grinned, cheekily.

The General - to the surprise of everyone - came dangerously close to cracking a smile. "I think we just might." The not-quite-smile soon disappeared, though. "Even now, the royal forces will be reinforcing the route to Gast, not to mention the city gates. Breaking through all that will require yet more sacrifice."

The group stopped as they approached a team of engineers trying to assemble the one-man, raptor-class Chaos Armour on the beach. They seemed to be having trouble lighting the furnace needed to power the walking weapon.

"We have the beach," Kingsley continued, "which means we can begin shipping in reinforcements from other islands. Unfortunately, the Queen has dozens of ports on Phobos that will allow her to do the same thing - but in much greater numbers. We need to get to Gast within the next day or so - if we don't, we will be completely overrun by the Queen's reinforcements." The general sighed an exhausted sigh. "One way or another, this will all be over by sundown tomorrow."

"We certainly have a lot to do," said the Cat. "I heard that the crownies have a cache of cream cakes that they plan on destroying. We have to get to them before they can carry out such a dastardly war crime."

Kingsley ignored the Cat and went on. "I know it's pointless to try and send you back to your world. I can't spare the people anyway. But maybe you can at least get to a safe distance, away from the rest of the fighting. And that," she warned, "I will not hear a word against!"

"Don't worry," said the Cat, "I'll make sure they get far away from here."

"You do realise," said Kingsley to the Cat, "that any sentence of yours that starts 'don't worry' is exactly when I worry the most."

"As well it should be," said the Cat.

The General shook her head and looked back at the children. "My thanks again."

"Good luck, General," said Teresa.

"See you in Gast," said Arthur.

The General shook their hands and left to go and give the Chaos Armour-wranglers a hand.

The Cat started talking. "Now, look, you two, this argument can't be allowed to-"

"Arthur, I'm sorry," Teresa said, suddenly.

"-well, you have to-"

"It's okay, Tee, I know how fast everything was moving."

"-erm, and-"

"I know I shouldn't have done it. It's exactly the kind of thing that's likely to lead us down the one road we don't want to go…"

"-so, I need you to-"

"It's okay, we'll figure it all out, together. And, well, it *was* pretty awesome what you did."

Teresa gave Arthur a hug. The Cat nodded. "Well… okay, good. I'm glad we had this talk."

Arthur turned to the Cat. "We're glad you survived the attack, Cat."

"It looked *horrible*," said Teresa. Then a worried expression suddenly came over her. "Should I be seeing all this? The Queen's memories…"

"Don't worry," said the Cat. "None of this is a secret anymore. The enemy knows exactly what we're doing. We just have to do it better than them, that's all. We need to make sure it wasn't all for nothing."

"By taking the Kymerion," said Teresa.

"Well that, but also by you guys tracking down the Agency Engine," said the Cat. "Remember, that's the real end-game here. The General made me give my word not to go chasing it - but I didn't give *your* word," he smirked. "You need to go to Zane Rackham. He's been working for me, looking for the Engine. You need to take his calculations, find where the Engine is hidden and destroy it. And you need to do it before sunset tomorrow."

"So where is he?" Arthur asked.

The Cat beckoned Arthur to come close and he whispered in the boy's ear. As Arthur stood up, the Cat glanced at Teresa.

"Sorry, Smithy. You know how it is. You'll find out when you get there."

"Anything a bit more specific than just the island and the name of a snack?" asked Arthur. "Maybe an actual address..?"

"To be honest, I don't know where Rackham is. He moves around a lot. I'm fairly sure he's still in that city. I mean, he's definitely on the island. Probably."

"So… how will we find him, then?" Arthur asked.

"One of you is a Seer, and the other is really, really stubborn. And you're both very intelligent. You'll find him. And hopefully, you'll get the info you need and be out of there before the Queen catches up with you."

151

"Don't worry," said Arthur. "We'll do it. We won't let Arilon down."

"That's the ticket," said the Cat, turning to Teresa. "You up for a bit of world-saving, Smithy?"

There was a brief flash of an expression that crossed Teresa's face that betrayed something other than Arthur's enthusiasm. "Of course," she said eventually. "When am I not?"

The Cat stood a little closer to the pair. "I have faith in you two. Especially you, Teresa. You'll find a way to not become her. You know why? Because you're not her. It's quite simple."

It was clear Teresa didn't fully understand what the Cat meant - or at least, she didn't agree with it. But she forced a stony smile anyway.

"Okay, then," he said. "Let's hope we meet again, some sunny day."

"Bye, Cat," said Arthur. "Good luck."

"Yeah, try to avoid losing anymore lives," said Teresa.

The Cat could tell they were both worried, despite his long history of surviving improbable odds.

"You can… ahem… cash in your hug tokens if you want."

The humans smiled and happily cashed in their tokens, getting a hug each from the fearsome King of Ends.

"Now, get out of here," said the Cat. "We will meet again, soon. We'll share a blastberry juice on the roof of the Kymerion."

"And this time, no standing on catapult trapdoors," said Arthur. "I rescued everyone once, I'm not doing it again!"

The three friends laughed before saying a final farewell. The Cat watched the humans walk off toward the beach to get a ship. Not bad for a couple of non-cats.

"Cat!" called Kingsley, the Chaos Armour now fully working. "Let's get to the command tent."

The Cat sighed. Okay. Time to end this war.

CHAPTER FOURTEEN
ARTHUR'S MISSION

- ARTHUR -

Arthur was feeling a lot happier now. Sure, they were still in the middle of a warzone but at least he and Teresa had made up. All siblings fell out. That was fine. Making up's the important part.

Of course, it wasn't as if they'd argued over who'd eaten the last slice of bread or ridden the other's bicycle without asking. This had been pretty big. In a lot of ways, it was difficult to even describe what was so bad about it. Anything Arthur had, as far as he was concerned, was Teresa's. If she wanted any of it, she didn't even have to ask. If he had a mountain of sweets, piles of money... if they were on a deserted island and he had the last cake. All hers, without even blinking.

But this power, their connection to the Threads. It was different. It wasn't the power itself, Arthur didn't care about that. No, there was something else about it. Like it was directly stitched into his very being. The deepest part of himself. When Teresa grabbed it, it was like she was grabbing his soul and crushing it. It hurt in a way he couldn't even describe. Not like a physical pain. It felt like... betrayal. And, instinctively, Arthur knew Teresa's connection to the Threads felt exactly the same. She knew what it would feel like if he were to do the same thing to her, which is why it confounded Arthur why she would willingly do it to him. Twice.

But - Arthur shook the feeling away.

It was fine.

They were talking again now and that meant they would be able to sort it all out.

The waves from the Night Ocean were busily crashing down onto the shore, the giant waves barely making a sound. The Travel Lines came sweeping down out of the dark skies - some of them ended on the beach while others disappeared into the freezing waters. Some of the Resistance boats and ships sat on the water, bobbing back and forth, following the movements of the sea as though they were being conducted in an orchestra. Other vessels were still connected to the lines, floating partway up in the air. The pair strode quickly along the waterfront, looking for something abandoned that they could make use of.

"I hope the Cat will be okay," said Arthur. "That next phase sounds like it's going to be intense."

"Don't worry, he'll survive. He always does, he's the Cat! Come on," Teresa said, as they walked quickly through the slightly organised chaos. "We need to find a boat and get out of here."

"We'll have to be careful once we get up there," said Arthur. "There'll be all kinds of people heading this way. Resistance and royal. We'll have to keep out of the way of any skirmishes."

"Oh, for sure," Teresa agreed, her eyes scanning the water. "Although hopefully there'll be less traffic once we get closer to Terminus."

"Wait… Terminus?" Arthur stopped dead in his tracks, fixing his sister with a confused stare. "We're not going to Terminus, we're going to find Rackham!"

Now it was Teresa's turn to stop. She turned to face her brother who was now a couple of steps behind her. "What are

155

you talking about?" she said. "You just said we were going to figure out how to stop me becoming the Queen."

"Yes, but I meant at the same time as following our mission."

"We can't do it at the same time as that mission, there's no time!" Teresa stepped closer to her brother, her voice hard but low, shielding her words from a young private carrying a bundle of swords as he stomped past them up the beach, his feet splashing through the shallow water. "Sometime soon, I'm going to turn into her and I'm going to kill you to do it! We can't allow this to happen, which part of that are you not getting?"

"There are millions of lives at stake if we don't locate the Agency Engine - which part of that are *you* not getting?" Arthur found himself shooting back. "We just gave our word that we'd help! We can't go running off to Terminus. We have to carry out our mission!"

"It's not *our* mission!" said Teresa, getting angry. "It's the Cat's mission!"

Arthur couldn't believe they'd misunderstood each other so badly. He ran his fingers through his hair in frustration. He had to calm down and think this conversation through.

Teresa was his priority, no doubt. They had to stop her becoming the Queen. But at the same time the *entirety* of Arilon was going to end if they didn't find the Agency Engine. And not only that, they knew the Queen would then take her show to the Human World - their home. They couldn't ignore that.

They had to figure out a way to help Teresa while carrying out the Cat's mission.

"Okay," he said, finally. "Let's say we're doing this, why Terminus?"

"We already had this conversation, Arthur," Teresa sighed in frustration. "To see the Blind Dressmaker, just like we talked about before. She's the only one who'll be able to see the stories around all this. She'll be able to see exactly how and why that moment happens and tell us how to avoid it. To be honest, I already know it's probably got something to do with the fact that our mother preferred you over me."

Arthur's mind blew.

"What? How…" he struggled for words, "…how did you even come to that conclusion?"

"It's obvious!" Teresa argued, her voice bitter. "She knew I was dangerous, that I had this potential to be cruel and ruthless. And she sent you away to protect you from me."

"No way! There's no way she saw that in you because it's just not *in* you!"

"Oh no? Did we not just argue about me ripping your power out of you not once, but twice now? And that's despite the fact I *knew* that's how I am supposed to kill you and become *her*! And did I not almost abandon you when we were escaping from the Needlemen island while you were hanging off the bottom of the ship? I think there's plenty of evidence to prove I definitely have it in me!"

"You… you're twisting all those situations! All those things, they sound bad when you say them in a simple way like that but … they don't mean you're cruel! They just mean you were under stress in some really difficult situations…"

"And I made the wrong choice every time, Arthur!" Teresa kicked an empty, broken helmet across the sand in anger and frustration. "Our mother knew it, she knew what I was capable of, from the moment we were born. But there must be a way for the Dressmaker to look into the story that surrounds that moment. She can tell me about myself, about what I end up doing. She'll be able to help us figure out a way around it. She'll be able to save us both!"

Arthur struggled to even put his thoughts into words. There were so many things just rolling around inside his head and crashing into each other. Had Teresa thought this all along? That her mother had considered her to be some kind of monster? That really isn't the impression Arthur got from the way Sam and Hector spoke about her.

"You are *so* wrong," he said in the end. "There's no way she thought that about you! If anything, she wanted you near to her which is why she sent *me* away."

"Of course she wanted me near - to keep an eye on me! She wasn't going to inflict me on some poor, unsuspecting strangers desperate for a nice baby! You, on the other hand, even as a baby, I bet you were perfect."

Something in Teresa's voice made that sound like an accusation. Even a little bit cruel. But no, Arthur dismissed the thought even as it formed. From everything he'd heard about their mother, she was a caring, protective woman and Teresa was a complete copy of her.

Of course he wanted to find the Dressmaker too. When they had been in the *Hector Smith* story, they'd seen the young Elsie Smith. At that time, Arthur had no idea he was looking at his own mother. He wanted more than anything to go back into that story - or any other one she was in - and see her again. And, yes, he wanted to ask her why she had sent him away. He was sure she loved him. He was convinced there was a good reason. Well, he hoped so… Okay, if he was honest, he really had no idea. Whatever had happened, his presence had been so thoroughly scrubbed that nobody even remembered him being born. Not the doctors and nurses, no-one. He had to admit, to cast him out so thoroughly did seem a bit cruel, after all. And if his mother was responsible for that, and if Teresa really was a copy of their mother...

"Listen, here's the choice," said Teresa finally, "either you're helping me, or you're helping the Cat. Which one is it?"

"Sometimes it's impossible to put one thing above another," said Arthur. "You know you mean the world to me. But the world itself's in danger, too. It's impossible to concentrate on only one of those without the other. We have to find a way to do them both!"

"Fine, you've made your decision." Teresa took a step backwards, her face like stone. It was like she didn't even care about Arthur anymore. "You go and be the Cat's errand boy. I'll help myself."

And with that, Teresa turned and walked away, quickly becoming obscured by a crowd of soldiers disembarking a boat and coming up the beach.

For a moment, Arthur couldn't believe she'd left him. His body held him fast to the spot, convinced it was some mistake and she'd come back any moment. She hadn't understood what he meant. She was seeing things in a really simple, black and white manner. Just like...

...just like the Queen.

His brain burst to life, suddenly, breaking the spell rooting him to the spot, and he forced his legs forward. He fought his way through the crowds of black and white armour to where Teresa had been standing moments before but the beach was just too thick with-

An explosion rocked the ground nearby sending a plume of sand and a couple of soldiers flying high into the air. Particles of sand rained down on everyone, forcing Arthur to cover his eyes.

"Move!" someone shouted. "They've started bombarding us already! Come on, get to your units!"

It had been difficult to spot Teresa before but it was impossible now. People were running back and forth with even more urgency and it seemed as though the amount of people on the beach had suddenly doubled. The next phase had started and Arthur had lost his sister.

"Hey! Don' just stand there! You wanna get blowed up?"

The voice was familiar and it came with a hand which grabbed Arthur's arm.

"Stick!" Arthur exclaimed as the young man pulled him out of the way of several soldiers wrangling horses across the sand. "What are you doing here?"

"We're back from Graft already, bringin' troops to join the fight," said Stick. "I mean, we can stands here and chats some more but… you know… explosions and stuff…"

"Yeah, good point."

"Come on," the tall bartender ushered Arthur back along the beach. "We was told to get offa the island once we'd dropped the soldiers off. No place for the likes of us, not with all this fightin'." He was clearly not happy about it but Stick always did as he was told. "Hey, wait, where's Teresa?"

"She's…" Through the chaos, Arthur saw a boat lifting off along one of the Travel Lines and he could feel Teresa was on it. "She's not coming."

"Uh, okay…" Stick said. Arthur could feel he wanted to ask for more details but another explosion rocked the beach. "Well, okay, come on then!"

The pair raced along the sand, dodging the personnel who were making their way up towards the forward positions.

Soon, they arrived at a small, white boat with one other occupant.

"Look who I found!" called Stick.

"Arthur!" Ami cried.

"Ami!" Arthur clambered over the side, "I'm glad to see you."

"You survived being glorified bus drivers, then," the girl from Savis beamed as she helped Arthur aboard. "We heard what you and Teresa did. Amazing!"

Arthur shrugged but didn't say anything. At the end of the day, amazing though it was, it was the very event that they'd fallen out over.

"Where is Teresa?" Ami said, looking past Arthur.

"She ain't comin'," said Stick as he pulled a small, red tin from his pocket and rattled it. "My badges," he replied to Arthur's puzzled look. "I fergot 'em when I took the soldiers to their unit. It's only cuz I went back for 'em that I even saw you!"

"Not coming?" said Ami, ignoring the badges. "What do you mean, not coming? Is she alright?"

Arthur didn't even know how to answer that question.

"She's fine," he said in the end. "She has a different mission to me."

Another muffled cannon shot could be heard from miles away and seconds later, the beach exploded once again.

"Time to go," Stick said, pushing the speed lever and swinging the boat around. Within seconds, the small tug was headed upwards and away from the Shores of Disquiet.

Arthur did his best to ignore Ami and Stick's frequent glances of concern at Teresa's absence. They were trying not to mention it but they might as well have put up posters. It was only to be expected, though. He and Teresa were always

161

together. Before now, the only time either of them had walked away from the other was when Arthur had asked to go back home after their escape from Labyrinth. The day he'd abandoned his sister.

But then, he remembered Teresa abandoning him as they escaped from the Needlemen island. He'd instantly forgiven her for that, putting it down to the stress of the moment - not to mention that version of her had never actually met him before. It was tempting to fixate on those two moments of abandonment - but Arthur realised that they were the *only* two. They'd spent pretty much the entire time in Arilon by each other's side.

Who knew - maybe a little time apart would do them both good. Maybe.

Arthur tried to see the other boat, the one that Teresa was on. But the darkness was already hiding her from view.

CHAPTER FIFTEEN
TERESA'S MISSION

- TERESA -

"Listen, here's the choice," said Teresa finally, "either you're helping me, or you're helping the Cat. Which one is it?"

"Sometimes it's impossible to put one thing above another," said Arthur. "You know you mean the world to me. But the world itself's in danger, too. It's impossible to concentrate on only one of those without the other. We have to find a way to do them both!"

Words, Teresa realised. Lots of fancy words. All to disguise the truth - Arthur cared more about following the Cat's orders than helping his own sister. It should have been a simple choice for him to make. But apparently, the dream team was something he had now woken up from.

Teresa felt the same way she'd felt after Labyrinth. When he'd abandoned her to go home. He'd promised he wouldn't do it again, yet here he was. Doing it again.

"Fine, you've made your decision." Teresa took a step backwards and she tried her best to force down the hot pain she was feeling over what Arthur was forcing her to do. "You go and be the Cat's errand boy. I'll help myself."

And with that, Teresa turned and walked away. After no more than three steps, the anger suddenly drained out of her. What was she doing? Arthur was right, they needed to talk about this. She turned back to look at Arthur again but a crowd of soldiers came rushing up the beach out of the water and blocked her view of him.

She was annoyed at him but at the same time, he was right. It wasn't a simple situation. They had to talk and maybe they could figure out a-

The ground suddenly erupted in a deafening explosion of sand and stone. The concussive force threw her off her feet and into a crowd of soldiers. The men and women didn't seem to notice the young girl lying on the ground in their midst - they were busy facing up to a potential royal attack - and Teresa had to throw up her arms to protect herself from their stampeding feet.

"Move!" someone somewhere shouted. "They've started bombarding us already! Come on, get to your units!"

Clambering to her feet, Teresa forced her way out of the crowd of armoured bodies before she got trampled. Coughing and wiping sand from her eyes, she regarded the beach around her. The frantic preparation of a few minutes ago had exploded into all out chaos and the amount of people seemed to have increased tenfold. She was completely turned around and had no idea where Arthur was anymore.

"I don't know if you noticed," a voice called out to her, "but someone's dropping cannonballs on us."

Teresa turned to the voice, coming from within a group of soldiers running out of the water. The figure of the young pirate came striding out of the chaos.

"Seb?" Teresa couldn't quite believe her eyes.

"I usually like spending time on beaches but just this once, I think we ought to get off this one," said the quartermaster.

Immediately upon seeing Seb, Teresa's mind was made up. Arthur had made his choice and he'd obviously already taken himself off on his little mission. She needed to stop being indecisive and stick to her guns. Arthur was going his way and Teresa was going hers. She was absolutely okay with that.

"That's my plan," said Teresa. "Can you get us a ship?"

"Of course. Where are we going?"

"You're helping me get off Phobos but where I'm going after that, I'm going on my own."

"Nope," Seb shook his head. "Every ship needs a quartermaster. Arilon law. I have to come or else I'll have to call the peacekeepers on you. Hey, just doing my duty as an Arilon citizen."

Teresa sighed. This one was incorrigible. "Fine. But I'm in charge, just so you know."

"Aye aye, Captain. So where are we heading?"

"Terminus."

"*That* dead end? What are we going there for?"

"I'm going there to save my life."

"Okay. And where's your brother?"

"Saving everyone else's."

Seb nodded. "Hold on then, Captain. I think I've spotted something that will do us nicely."

Seb tromped into the water, Teresa in his wake. The pair headed toward a small, posh-looking yacht. It looked fast and small - exactly what the doctor ordered.

Teresa could tell that Seb was confused - he had no idea what she was talking about or what she was doing. Yet he was still willing to go with her. Unlike her own brother.

Well, Arthur may have abandoned her, but even in her disappointment, she would not abandon him. She was going to find out from the Blind Dressmaker everything she needed to know about herself, her mother and how that all results in her becoming the Queen. Then, she'd be able to stop it and in doing so, save Arthur's life.

165

As the pair launched the boat and it swiftly left the beach behind, the distance between her and her brother suddenly grew and Teresa had the overwhelming feeling of losing a limb. She tried to pick him out among the many ant-like dots on the ground but even if she could have done such an impossible task, she soon ran out of time - the darkness was already hiding him from view.

CHAPTER SIXTEEN
THE WELL

- THE QUEEN -

The late morning sun was slowly swimming high through the sky above the sprawling city of Gast. The sunlight shone down harsh and hard, reflecting off the shiny, ebony surface of the Kymerion. The roof of Gast's tallest building tapered to a point and that point into a thin, metal spire, barely the width of a child's fist. It was on top of that spire that the Queen stood.

Balancing impossibly, the monarch stood so still she could easily have been mistaken for a statue. Her crimson red gown barely moved and even her obsidian black cloak hung straight down behind her. Her hair - a yellow so washed out it was practically bone-white - swayed ever so slightly. There was barely any wind, even this high up. The air on Phobos was always still and oppressive.

Up on her perch, the Queen's eyes gazed over her city. Her mind was in the here and now, working and evaluating. But it was also thinking of a long-ago day on a far-away island.

The years she'd spent after Arthur's death, slowly becoming the Queen, were mostly a blur to her now. But one day she did remember very clearly was the day she truly learned the importance of fear. It was the day she climbed out of the Well of Eyes. And she knew the lessons of that day would benefit her now.

The Queen's own eyes pointed sunward of the city towards the Night Ocean. Her excellent vision showed her what was happening miles in that direction, on the Shores of

Disquiet. She had watched as General Graves' defences had been obliterated by a falling Warship. No, it hadn't fallen.

It had been thrown.

As infuriated as she had been to see the insurgents profane the surface of her island with their presence, the Queen had been delighted to observe Teresa's use of her power. She wasn't sure, but it felt in the Threads as though some of Arthur's power had been forcibly conscripted too. The thought had made her smile.

However, now the feeling of pride and promise was gone. She watched tiny specs riding down the Travel Lines in endless droves, heading down to her beach. As all those insurgent vessels came and disgorged their insurrectionist payloads, the only thing the Queen now felt was anger. Those ungrateful wretches. After all she had done for Arilon. All she had sacrificed. And all they could do was either run scared or put up swords and fight her.

Graves had wasted no time and had started the bombardment of the invaders as soon as his own troops were clear. The insurgents would have to plan their next move while dodging cannonballs. But, the Queen knew, dodging cannonballs would not deter the likes of Halia Kingsley nor the damnable Cat. They would still plan and they would still march. Indeed, the first wave was drawing close to the city gates even now. Their Chaos Armour units would soon begin smashing down the ancient gates and then it would only be a matter of time before the true fighting began.

The darkness of the Well of Eyes was still clear in her memory. The tiny circle of light that was the sun shining into the top of the well had been the goal - but the fuel that had enabled her to reach that goal had not been the light from above. It had been the fear from below. Hand over hand, she

168

had pulled herself out of that hellish pit. And the only reason she had survived had been because fear had held her hand. Fear had been her friend on that day, pushing her to safety. Fear would help her again now.

The Queen's eyes - two dark pits, each dotted with a single, white diamond - now drifted downwards, into the city itself. Through the lines of Yarnbulls deployed in the fields near the gates. Past the endless units of soldiers positioned in the narrow lanes and streets. Eventually, her gaze came to rest on Valyard Hall. Like many halls, schools, cellars, office blocks and temples across Gast, Valyard Hall contained the true treasure of Phobos. The jewels that the insurgents wanted so desperately to get their hands on. It was time to visit that treasure.

The Queen had made her decision regarding Teresa. She had chosen her course of action - or inaction, so to speak - and she had no choice now but to allow it to play out and hope she had chosen wisely. For now, she had to concentrate on her other objective. The Agency Engine had to be fully fuelled before the Cat set foot inside the Kymerion.

After all this time, her fingertips were finally brushing the cold, hard surface of victory. She needed to flex her fingers just a little more and total victory would finally be in her grasp. To ensure that happened, she had to visit Valyard Hall and ensure the treasures within did not fall into her enemy's hands.

The Queen leaned slightly forward and stepped off the edge of the spire. Her body began to race towards the ground. Plummeting unnaturally swiftly, the monarch rode the Threads downwards but when her feet eventually touched the ground, it was with no more impact than a feather.

A short walk brought the Queen to her destination. Valyard Hall reached into the sky above her and its infamous engraved ironwood doors filled her vision. Positioned outside the ancient building were several dozen royal soldiers. The crimson and ebony armour stood out against the hall's bleached white steps. They parted as the Queen ascended the stairs, heading towards the giant doors.

The carvings on the door, centuries old, depicted the subjugation of Phobos by Elef the Destroyer. The legend had been told since the Age of Isolation - centuries before the first ships ever took to the skies. It was one of Phobos' oldest stories but it was told and re-told endlessly.

The most frightful stories always were.

As their Queen approached, the soldiers at the entrance slid back huge, metal bolts and pulled open the double doors.

The Queen's vision adjusted itself immediately as she stepped into the relative darkness of the stone hall. Inside, a few hundred citizens of Phobos were huddled. Scared and confused. The people were what gave Phobos its power. They were the island's treasure.

The mass of scared citizens shivered collectively as petrified eyes watched their ruler come inside the hall to join them. The Queen was not seen often, even on Phobos, so for her to be here, in front of them, was quite terrifying.

The Queen looked upon them all, petrified as they were, and was pleased. This was excellent.

But it could be better.

"My people," she spoke, finally. "Like all your fellow citizens, you have done as instructed and taken refuge. You have huddled in halls and schools and offices and down in cellars. In doing this, you hope to find some safety and protection from what is about to happen."

The Queen cast her dark eyes over the assembled citizens in front of her.

"I have come to tell you that your efforts will fail."

Some of the citizens gasped, others kept their tongue. All were shocked.

"Outside the city gates at this very moment, thousands of invading soldiers are gathering, waiting for their moment to strike at your town. And let me tell you, these people are not like you. They want to destroy your way of life."

The Queen could feel the tension and fear ratchet up an extra notch.

"They are from a thousand different islands," she continued. "They mix their ideas and cultures together in a profane attempt at Balance. An unholy diversity of ideas that all amount to one thing - they think they know better than you. They come believing that if you could only see them, see their freedom of thought, that you would instantly want to be like them. The real truth is, this invading army has only one objective." The Queen fixed her audience with a glare they could not look away from. "They want to destroy fear."

Two crimson soldiers brought in a man adorned in black leathers and threw him to the ground at the Queen's feet. She spoke to him but her eyes remained on her citizens.

"Am I lying?" the monarch asked him.

The soldier coughed back the beatings he had just received from the royal soldiers. Gingerly, he lifted his head and looked through bruised eyes at the scared citizens cowering in the dark. When he came sneaking into the town on his reconnaissance mission for the insurgents, he probably didn't expect to get caught and brought to a town hall meeting, the Queen thought.

"Well?" she repeated, her hard gaze looking down on him now. "I have just told my people that you represent a threat they cannot hope to combat. This is your chance to turn them against me. Proceed."

"We… we just want to help you," the soldier croaked, addressing the citizens. "We know you're Phobians and it's your Idea to be afraid. That's okay."

The people looked uncertainly at him. An old man at the front flicked his weathered gaze between the young soldier and the Queen.

"We don't want to stop all fear. We wouldn't do that, we know that's part of your identity," the soldier went on. "But the Queen is not good for you. You should be as afraid as you want to be, not as afraid as she forces you to be."

The old man took a step forward, bending his weathered face slightly down to the soldier.

"That's not how fear works, laddie," he said, simply.

Though her expression didn't show it, the Queen was amused to see the soldier's face fall. The truth of the situation was beginning to dawn on him, she thought. The old man continued.

"You don't choose how scared you are. If you could, it wouldn't be fear, would it? Fear is something used by someone with power over you, so they can control you. *They* choose how scared you are, not you. The Queen understands fear much better than any other ruler we've had. Better than the old Phobos governors. Better even than the Primacy. We love the Queen *because* she terrifies us."

The monarch stared into the eyes of the soldier and watched his reaction closely as she casually reached out and killed the old man with a single swipe of her sword. The sudden violence triggered cries of terror from all parts of the room. The sudden appearance and disappearance of the Queen's glinting steel and a life suddenly ended. This is what it was to live in fear.

"You see it now, do you not?" the Queen said to the quivering soldier. Like everyone else in the room, he couldn't believe what he had just seen. "This is the Balance declared by the Four Pillars. Balance dictates that the people unlucky enough to have been born on this isle must forever live in fear. They must, in fact, *want* to live in fear. This is the philosophy you fight to protect. And because of that, I can freely send you back to your people." She turned to the crowd. "If anyone here wishes to go with him to the invaders, you may do so. I will not stop you. Step forward now."

Not a single person moved. The Queen smiled.

"Well done, citizens. You have proven me wrong. Perhaps you will be able to resist the invaders after all." She turned back to the soldier and nodded to the still open door. "Go. Tell General Kingsley what you have seen in this room."

The young man scrambled to his feet, still expecting to be prevented from leaving. With a last glance at the citizens of Gast, he ran from the hall, past the soldiers and out into the street.

The Queen smiled. The people in here were more afraid than ever. And that was exactly as they wanted it. Soon, the insurgents would hear what had happened and understand. Their invasion was doomed to failure. They would still try, of course. They had no choice but to delude themselves into thinking the people could still be saved from fear. But Kingsley's people would in fact be afraid that their attempt to pry the Phobians' loyalty from the Queen was already doomed to failure.

Because the old man had been wrong. That is what she learned climbing from the well. Fear does control you - but only if you are weak. For those with the will, fear becomes a fuel they use to spur themselves on. And, if they wish it, those people can then become the very thing that others fear.

This was the nature of power and control.

All the extra fear she had just generated brought a smile to the Queen's lips as she left Valyard Hall. It would help power the Agency Engine just that little bit faster. And once the Engine was ready to activate, control would take over. A control the likes of which nobody had ever seen before.

And nobody would need to be - or indeed, be capable of being - afraid ever again.

"Commander," the Queen said as she re-emerged onto the great steps of the hall, "make sure you allow the fighting to be seen from the windows of the hall. I want the people to-"

The Queen stopped in her tracks. The Threads. A very distinct vibration flickered through them. Subtle yet unmistakable.

Arthur and Teresa had separated.

They had fought, the Queen sensed, and now they were going their separate ways. A dark cloud hung over them both. Her decision was vindicated. It was the right choice, after all. She didn't need attack their relationship any further - she had already done the required damage.

The moment was approaching. She could see the top of the well and the light was beginning to fall on her face.

"Send word to my ship," the Queen said to the Commander. "We leave for Terminus."

THREAD FOUR

SHADOWFALL ON TERMINUS

CHAPTER SEVENTEEN
THE STONE RABBIT

- TERESA -

Even as Teresa brought the yacht slowly to a stop, she could feel eyes watching her.

That was the strangest thing - Seb was with her, so any eyes should really have been watching the pair of them. But no, the eyes weren't watching *them*.

They were watching *her*.

"You know, this is even worse than the middle of nowhere," said Seb. Teresa pulled the speed-lever to the all-stop position and the yacht shuddered and then was completely still. The small vessel was surrounded by a sparse scattering of trees that was trying its best to be a forest. But the wide expanse of nothing that stretched for miles was visible through the skimpy collection of foliage.

She turned to the pirate with an air of irritation.

"What do you mean?" she sighed.

"The middle is too glamorous for this place," he said, staring out at the deserted expanse. "This is off to one side of nowhere. The backside of nowhere. This is the secluded part of nowhere that all the nowhere people try to escape from in order to *get* to the middle of nowhere."

Teresa rolled her eyes but, if she was being honest with herself, she knew she was pretending to be irritated when in fact, she was glad Seb was there. For some reason, though, she couldn't admit it out loud, to him.

"You didn't have to come," she said, picking up her bow and testing the string with an imaginary arrow. "In fact, now

177

you've dropped me off, feel free to head off back into the Black with your stolen pleasure boat."

"Seriously?" Seb said, staring at her. It made her stop for a moment, bow in hand. Had she gone too far? Had she actually managed to hurt his feeli-

"Go on, then, get yourself off my new ship," he grinned. "I'm going to find some unsuspecting traveller to rob and then I'm going to spend the rest of the war sunning myself on a beach on the island of Elysium, drinking blastberry rum."

It took Teresa a second to realise he was joking - and when she did, she was unable to prevent a smile spreading across her face as she shook her head. Seb shrugged as he strapped on his sword belt.

"Fine, maybe I'll hang around here for a bit longer before I go," he said. "Give you someone to chat to in case this dressmaker of yours turns out to be totally boring."

Teresa's smile was replaced by a scowl. "I don't need help, if that's the only reason you're staying. I can do this on my own."

"I just saw you throw a Warship at a bunch of super-cannons," said Seb as he drew his cutlass and began checking it. "And then somehow hold everyone aboard in the centre of the explosion while magically keeping us all from dying."

He held his sword up, closed one eye and looked down its length with the other. "And before that, you jumped headlong onto the deck of said Warship to face down dozens of enemy soldiers. And before *that*," he brought the sword back down and carefully ran his fingers along it's edge, feeling for damage, "you flew - *flew* - a junky little boat into an enemy base to rescue your teammates before flying out of said base and escaping a flaming, fiery death."

The pirate slid his cutlass back into its scabbard with a metallic clunk and finally turned to Teresa. "By my count, you've already saved my life three or four times this morning. So yeah. I'm all caught up with you not needing any help." His gaze softened a little bit, now. "It just seemed like a friend wouldn't go amiss."

Something hot began to well up behind Teresa's eyes. After a couple of seconds, she nodded.

"You're probably right. I suppose one of those would be quite nice at the moment."

"Good," Seb clapped his hands and headed over to the side of the boat. "Now you can stop pretending like you don't want me here."

"What..?" Teresa smiled as she watched the pirate climb over the side and drop to the ground. "I don't know what you mean."

The walk through the trees was as brief as expected and soon, the pair were trekking across the featureless plains of Terminus. The land rose and dipped slightly as it vanished into the horizon. There were some rocky valleys and passes here and there. A few bushes and trees dotted about the place. But mostly, it was just flat, rocky nothingness in all directions.

"You sure you know where you're going?" Seb said, squinting into the sun as he surveyed the horizon. "I don't fancy ending up as one of those skeletons you sometimes see in pictures of the desert."

Teresa remembered arriving here all those months ago with the Cat, Iakob, Iosef (and Arthur, she reluctantly admitted). Looking around at the desert, she'd thought back then that they'd be walking for days. They'd followed the Cat, blindly (a thought which irritated her right now) but,

179

fortunately, he'd known where he was going. They'd come upon a sudden dip in the path and a rock shaped like a bunny, all but invisible from a distance. Once you were at the bunny-rock, you were led down into an underpass that ran all the way to the little wooden cabin where the Dressmaker lived.

"I'm pretty sure we're heading in the right direction," she said.

"Are you?" Seb glanced at her as they walked. "Because usually, for you, the right direction is the same one Arthur's going in."

Teresa's half-decent mood was shoved off the rails, nearly forcing her to a stop walking altogether.

"Well," she said, not looking at her companion as she continued to stride along, "it's always good to try something new."

"Oh, I know," said Seb. "I once tried a new type of rum, flavoured with prunes."

"Is that what you are?" Teresa said, icily. "Prunes?"

"No, I'm rum," Seb bounced back. "*Flavoured* with prunes."

"Listen, I'm fine. We're both fine, me and Arthur," Teresa played nervously with the bow string. "We're still heading in the same direction, I think. Just… different paths."

Seb lightly touched Teresa's shoulder, bringing her, finally, to a stop and he stepped close. She looked up into his steely, brown eyes.

"It's Arthur and I," he said. "Not me and Arthur."

Annoyed, Teresa started to walk away. "Look if you're not going to take this seriously…"

"Repeat after me," he said, holding her gently in place. "Arthur and I."

"Seb…" she shook her head and tried to turn away.

180

"Arthur and I will be fine," he said.

Hearing the words held her still and silent.

"Go on," said Seb. "It's your own time you're wasting. Let's hear it."

"Arthur..." she began, faltered, regrouped and started again. "Arthur and I will be fine."

"Again."

She stared into Seb's eyes again, the words coming firmly and confidently. "Arthur and I will be fine."

Seb nodded and tapped her shoulder as he turned away. "Good. There's no excuse for lazy language."

Teresa resumed walking, a few strides behind the pirate and watched him as he walked. There was definitely something more to him than he liked to let on. His dismissive, sometimes arrogant air was what he used to keep people at arm's length, where he could manage them. All the anxiety and confusion she was feeling was even more tumultuous now, since her falling out with Arthur. Having people at arm's length certainly appealed to Teresa at the moment. But at the same time, being completely alone was probably not the best thing, either. Perhaps Seb had been right. He was just the kind of friend she needed right now.

"What is it with you and language, anyway? Maiz told me about the whole thing with the guard in the base," Teresa grinned at the thought of Seb arguing correct word usage with royal soldiers. "What are you, a secret English teacher?"

"What's English?" Seb asked, puzzled. Teresa was about to answer when he continued. "My mother was a school teacher. She used to read to me. She was always very insistent on language being used properly."

181

Teresa thought back to Seb's bashing of the story of Elza the Indomitable and wondered if that had actually been one of the stories his mother had read to him as a child.

"She sounds nice," Teresa said, trying not to think of her own mother and failing miserably. "And what about your father? Was he a teacher too?"

"We don't talk about him," was Seb's flat reply. It took Teresa aback - Seb looked more serious than he ever usually did. Serious, sad and maybe a tiny bit afraid.

Any further thoughts on the secret history of Sebastian J Falkes were immediately cut short, though, when a particular rock formation up ahead caught Teresa's eye.

"There it is!" Teresa pointed at the rocky scenery in front of them.

Seb looked around, puzzled. "There *what* is?"

"That rock!"

Seb glanced where Teresa was pointing. "Oh yes! The rock that looks exactly the same as all the other rocks!" Seb nodded, sarcastically. "Yep, there it is, alright."

"No, the big one," Teresa pointed to the rock formation slightly overhanging the path they were following. "The one that looks like a giant bunny."

"Yeesh..." Seb cringed as he looked at the free-standing boulder formation. It's bunny-ness was clearly not immediately apparent to him. "If your bunnies look like that, I am *never* going to the Human World."

"We're on the right track. It's this way!"

A wave of optimism suddenly swept over Teresa. She had found the right path after all! And they were close to the cabin, now. The answers she was after were tantalisingly close.

She strode past the giant bunny with a feeling of hope.

The feeling didn't last.

"This place is kind of deserted," Seb said, taking in the empty shop floor. Teresa emerged from the back room.

"All her books are gone," she said. "She can't have taken them all with her, surely? Do you think someone's been by and stolen them?"

"Look at this," Seb said, running his fingers over a shelf. His finger left a clean trail in the dust. "Anywhere else, I'd say this was several weeks' worth of dust - but on this abandoned desert of an island…" he bobbed his head to one side, estimating, "I'd guess maybe a week since she left..?"

Teresa's eyes drifted over the whole room, as if the Dressmaker was going to pop up from behind a shelf. There were several dresses hanging up in various states of completion. In the centre of the room was the spinning wheel where the Dressmaker did most of her work. Teresa remembered, as though it were yesterday, the feeling of spinning that wheel. The exhilaration of creation, of moulding something new to her own design. But the exhilaration had been swiftly followed by the horror of realising that her mind had gone from creating something beautiful to something ugly and creepy.

Had the Queen been nestling inside her, even then? Waiting for her chance to come to life? Teresa shook away the unpleasant thought.

A soft buzzing brought Teresa's attention down to the counter to her left. Next to the Dressmaker's till was a bowl of half-finished soup and a piece of stale bread. Only the flies were enjoying the meal now.

"Where is she…?" Teresa didn't know whether to feel angry, worried, cheated or sad.

A shadow suddenly cast itself across the floor, stretching all the way back to the still-open door. The unmistakable click of a gun followed.

"Hands up, you varmints."

CHAPTER EIGHTEEN
BY THE VICTORS

- ARTHUR -

Arthur enjoyed visiting islands he'd never been to. Unfortunately, wartime wasn't the best time to be doing it on account that everyone was spending all their time trying to kill each other.

Narrato was the isle of histories. According to what Ami and Stick had told him on their way here, it was the place that harboured Arilon's feelings of looking after the past. Learning about it, knowing it, passing it on to new generations so the stories of history are never lost. Not only did they generally hold the idea of looking after history, they actually recorded it as well. This wasn't just the isle of histories but of actual historians. In normal times, Narrato History Gatherers would travel throughout Arilon, speaking to people on various islands, learning about their past. What was life like on their island fifty years ago? A hundred? A thousand? What jobs did people do? What wars did they fight? What discoveries did they make? Then they would return to Narrato and record those histories and store them safely. They kept Arilon history alive and made sure that it never faded from living memory.

"The best bit is that they don't jus' write 'em all down, neither," Stick told Arthur as their boat rode a Travel Line down through the clouds and towards the island's surface. "That'd be too borin'. No, they got all kinds a' ways they keeps historical stories alive."

Arthur was just about to ask Stick what he meant when he saw the answer with his own eyes.

Spread across the side of a group of hills below was a gigantic image of a ship flying up a Travel Line with people at the bottom, staring up in amazement.

"It's carved into the chalk underneath the hills," said Ami, joining Arthur at the edge of the boat. "All Narrato's hills and fields sit on chalk deposits. There are pictures like this all over the island."

"I think we have the same thing back home in my country," said Arthur. "Some giant horses, I think? I've seen pictures of them in books. But this... this is even more amazing."

The picture was incredibly detailed and incredibly big. Although the people didn't have facial features, their positions and the way they were standing showed quite clearly how amazed and shocked they were at the sight of a ship flying up the Travel Line.

"They look like they've never seen a ship do that before," he said.

"They hadn't," said Ami. "If I'm not mistaken, that's an image of the First Flight. Back before people knew there were other islands besides their own. Zachary and Zsia figured out how to capture the energy of the Life Lines and use them to power a ship. And off they went into the Nothing Space, discovering new islands for the first time."

"I used to love hearin' that tale in nurs'ry," Stick nodded.

"So the Narratans record history as giant carvings in hillsides?" Arthur asked.

"And paintings inside the carvings, sometimes. Or statues in museums or out in fields. Or carved into their buildings and architecture," said Ami.

"Sounds like a lot of effort..! Don't they ever just, you know, write it down in a book?" Arthur shook his head.

"Of course they do," Ami laughed. "They have massive libraries and vaults here, crammed with books and scrolls. But they don't want to just lock this stuff away. To the Narratans, history isn't something you write down and stick on a shelf. To them, it's something that's around you all the time. You yourself are part of history, every day, so their surroundings reflect that."

"That's just so cool," Stick murmured in awe as he leaned against the side of the ship, staring down at the grand, sprawling artwork below. Everything in Arilon was so new to Arthur, he forgot that everyone who lived here hadn't actually seen it all either. Stick probably knew all about Narrato from school or whatever but this was obviously his first time here in person. Clearly, Arilon could be just as mind-blowing for Arilonians as it was for him.

"But like I said on our way over here," Ami said, "we're going to have to be careful. The commander on Graft told us that there are some islands that the royals are desperate to control. Narrato is one of them."

As the boat swam down closer to the island's surface, Arthur could spy royal forces on the ground, clashing with Resistance soldiers and local fighters. The little boat had travelled several miles since the First Flight hillside. Now, they flew over a series of smaller white shapes carved on a flat, wide open field with thick forest on either side. Royal forces were pouring from one forest, Resistance forces from the other. In between them were the white silhouettes of seven or eight disc shapes that were clearly meant to be islands. Outlines of a swarm of birds were swooping towards each island and landing on them. Every island had at least one bird shape that stood on it, wings spread in Imperial majesty.

"What are those birds?"

"They're hawks," said Stick. "Symbol of the Primacy."

"Oh, I see," said Arthur. "It's showing the spread of the Primacy across Arilon."

Ami nodded. "If you were to get closer, I'm sure there'd be some more detail saying the names of the islands and the dates when the Primacy colonised them. A timeline of the spread of imperial rule."

"So why are they fighting over it?" Arthur asked. But even as he asked, he saw the answer unfold below. As the Resistance was pushed back, the royals began scratching at the ground with large digging machines. "They're changing it!" Arthur leaned forward with surprise and no small amount of anger. "They're changing the picture."

"Not jus' the picture," said Stick, sadly. "The history."

The large, metallic figure of a royal Chaos Armour turned its massive upper body toward them as they flew overhead.

"Let's get out of here before they take too much interest in us," Ami said, rushing over to the ship's wheel. "We have to buy Fish Pops - that's what the Cat said, right?"

Arthur nodded. "I have no idea what a Fish Pop is, but he said we need to buy one. That's where we start looking for Rackham."

"Okay then," said Stick, "well that's fine. That means there's only one town on all a' Narrato we have to look. Cuz there's only one place in all a' Narrato that sells 'em."

Arthur turned to look at his companions as the battlefield disappeared into the misty distance behind them. "But, I still don't know - what even *is* a Fish Pop?"

"Oh, hold on to your hat, Arthur Ness," Ami smiled, knowingly. "You're in for a treat."

There was a wooden stall. Above the old man's head was a sign proclaiming the stall's name; *Fish Knees - Fantastic Fishy Snacks'*. Just below that was a smaller sign saying *'Home of the Arilon-wide Famous Fish Pops'*. And just below that was yet another, even smaller sign, saying *'Will be here every day, war or no war'*. Inside the stall was an old man, grinning from ear to ear. He was grinning because Arthur was standing there, holding the Fish Pop he'd just bought, looking at it and trying to decide exactly what he was supposed to do with it.

"This is a fish…" Arthur said, staring at the thing in his hand, "tied to a stick."

"It's a fish lollipop," Stick exclaimed. "What you *think* a Fishpop wuz gonna be?"

Arthur looked up at Ami, as if for help. She was too busy laughing at Arthur's expression.

With a final half-smile of thanks to the old 'Fish Knees' man, Arthur turned and surveyed the scenery around them. Perhaps the seriousness of their mission would distract from the smell of the fish.

"So, this is the town of Eren," said Arthur. "Not much left of it, is there?"

Ami's gaze drifted over the rubble and bricks around them. The Fish Pop had given them a much-needed moment of mirth. Much-needed because as soon as they'd seen this place, the suffering was as clear as day.

Ami had described Eren from pictures in books she'd read. It was a pretty seaside town with cute little buildings dating back hundreds of years. Houses and shops were mingled together around a large town square where they held the market every week and a parade celebrating their history at least once a year.

None of that was there anymore.

189

The trio stood in the middle of the town square but it was deserted and completely destroyed. Statues and monuments were just rubble and the ground itself was cracked and full of holes from cannonfire. Virtually every single building they could see had been all but gutted - roofless and windowless. A few people went by here and there but there were no smiles or friendly chatting. The townspeople shuffled around like ghosts.

Directly in front of 'Fish Knees' was a multi-piece sculpture showing a group of knights. Arthur could tell the armour looked just like Iakob and Iosef's, so it was clear they were meant to be Valian Towering Knights of the Eastern Sea. They weren't behaving like those knights, though, Arthur thought. They were attacking unarmed men and women and only a group of Primacy soldiers, carved to look super-heroic, were there to stop the apparently evil Valians.

"Let me guess," Arthur said, "This is one that's been altered."

"Yep. I've seen this sculpture before, in a book," said Ami. "Well, the original, anyway. It showed the Valians defending the people from the Primacy."

"This must have been what all the fightin' in this town wuz over," said Stick. "The crownies wanted to change it to this. Make the Valians look like the bad 'uns and Primacy like heroes. Make it seem like when the Primacy took over, they wuz jus' protectin' everyone from Valians an' such."

"But everyone knows that's not what happened," said Arthur. "Why are they even wasting all this effort changing pictures and statues?"

"Because people rely on their history," said Ami. "Our memories tell us who we are. The stories we tell ourselves about our past help us understand the here and now. They tell

190

us what our values are, who are friends or enemies are... everything. Change the memories or remove them, and we become something completely different."

Arthur nodded. "If we tell ourselves we're defending something precious, then our personal story is that our enemies are against that precious thing."

"Tells us we're the good guys - and our enemies is the bad guys," said Stick.

Arthur thought of all the men and women who had tried to land on that beach earlier today. Each and every one of them must have had such a story - be it personal or else one that everyone on their island shared. A story that drove them on, giving them the strength to fight - and die - for a cause they believed in.

"But here's the kicker - what if those stories change?" Ami said. "What if someone tells you that some of the people you're fighting alongside actually hate you? And that secretly, they want to destroy your home and people?"

"Sure would damage the Resistance if some a' the heavyweights like the Valians or the Forteans suddenly had to split cuz no-one trusted 'em."

"Divide and conquer," said Ami. "It's always been the Queen's style."

Arthur tried his best to ignore the sudden gut-punch that reminded him that all of this was down to some evil version of Teresa... and that these two who had helped him so much, and who liked Teresa so much, had no idea.

"But..." Arthur pulled his brain back on track, "...again, why would changing these statues make everyone forget what actually happened?"

"Because a' the Travel Lines," Stick said. "Whatever people feel here will 'ventually get transmitted out t' the rest a' Arilon."

"And the people here will see these altered pictures every day," Ami said. "Over and over. Every time they walk down the street. It doesn't matter what you knew in the beginning, if you're shown something often enough, you start to believe it."

Arthur understood. The very strength of the Narrato way of life – keeping history alive by having it around them every day – now becomes a weakness. That same method now burns false history into their minds instead.

"And to answer your next question…" Ami held up a hand as Arthur's mouth began to form the words, "…the reason the Narratans don't just change them back is because they simply don't believe in altering history. To them, it's sacrilege. They're fighting tooth and nail to protect the books and carvings and statues from being altered - but once they get altered, they won't change them back. To them, that would be an evil as great as the initial change."

"Changing history to what you want it to say," Arthur nodded. "Even if you know it to be true."

"That's just the point," said Ami, "once it changes, people start to believe the new version. They can't even be sure if the older version they remember even *is* the truth."

Arthur shook his head. 'History is written by the victors'. A phrase he'd heard many times before but in Arilon, it had a whole new significance.

What a mess. The things people allow to happen when they're afraid. And war certainly makes people afraid. Which is exactly what the Queen wants, Arthur reminded himself. She needed their fear to power the Agency Engine. Well, they'd better get on with finding it, then.

192

Arthur scanned the surroundings. Where would Zane Rackham be? Where would a genius driven mad by the super-destructive weapon he helped create actually set up shop? Where would he put a place that would allow him to concentrate on his job of tracking down the Agency Engine?

"If there was fighting here until recently, why would he even come here?" Arthur was talking to himself but he was talking out loud. Ami answered.

"Perhaps he came here before the fighting started?"

"Maybe…" Arthur whispered. "But the Cat believes he's still here somewhere. So he didn't leave even after the fighting began."

"So… maybe he *needed* to be here?" Ami guessed.

Arthur pointed his Fishpop at her, absently. "Exactly. Something here helps him track down the Engine."

"But there ain't hardly no buildin's still standin," said Stick. "Maybe he's underground? Like in a beer cellar."

"I know you worked in a pub," Ami said to Stick, smiling, "but there are other types of cellars than just beer cellars."

"That's true enough," said Stick. "There's wine cellars."

"Underground would normally be a good shout…" Arthur looked from building to building. "But a cellar, out here? When he knew there was likely to be fighting and he could just be buried by a collapsing building? I just can't see it…"

Arthur realised that was the problem. He was thinking too much and not seeing enough. He was meant to be a Seer, not a Thinker. He took a deep breath and quietened his brain down, squashing his analytical mind for now. He closed his eyes but opened his inner eye. Don't look at the surface, he told himself. Look beneath.

193

Suddenly, it was like he could actually see the Threads. Sort of like with Lon-Jinus' complicated viewing tool but with his own actual eyes. It was a strange feeling - like a cross between seeing and feeling, tasting and hearing. Arthur felt as though he was briefly linking with the *real* world around them. Getting past what they could normally see to what was *really* happening.

Different flavours of energy flowed in different directions. He could see Threads related to despair and hopelessness swirling around them and he could even taste the bitterness of desolation left after conflict had decimated the town. Bunches of these Threads - despair, desolation, hopelessness - were concentrated around people as they walked past, clinging to them like malicious spirits. Far away over the horizon, the hot, red feeling of ongoing conflict continued to swirl and storm. White and crimson tendrils of anger and violence and fear periodically flicking up over the horizon showing that there was fighting happening right now, several miles to the east.

Trying to filter out the misery and anger of the war, Arthur homed in on the natural Threads themselves. The fabric of the world around them that was untouched by the activities of people. A cool, light blue shimmered around and underneath everything and it intensified as it headed away in a particular direction.

"There," Arthur pointed, his eyes still closed.

Slightly puzzled, the other two followed his gesture. There was a narrow alleyway between two pubs and the building behind the alleyway was completely destroyed, revealing a different landscape entirely. All three of them could see right through the alleyway and glimpse out to what lay beyond.

"The sea..?" Ami said. She squinted harder. "Is that... is that a boat?"

Arthur opened his eyes and the coloured energy disappeared, bringing back his regular sight. There was indeed a tiny dot bobbing on the water.

"I think that's him. The Threads seem really concentrated out there." Arthur smiled, uncertainly. Had he just purposely accessed his abilities as a Seer for the first time?

"Well, okay then," said Stick, beginning to walk towards the alleyway. "The Agency Engin' ain't gettin' any less complete. Let's get hikin'."

The trek down to the waterfront took the trio less than an hour and they were mercifully free from any hostile encounters with royal patrols. (When Arthur suggested that a good way to chase away any royal soldiers would be to wave the Fishpop at them, Stick put Arthur out of his misery and happily ate it). Their good fortune held up further when they found dozens of small fishing boats lined up on the beach. They grabbed one - along with a couple of oars - and headed out onto the smooth, calm waters.

After a couple of false starts where the trio experimented with different pairings, they finally settled on Arthur and Ami doing the rowing as they seemed to have the best rhythm (which was just a polite way of saying Stick couldn't row to save his life). Stick sat at the stern of the boat, facing forward. His job was to direct the pair towards their destination and keep them on course.

"Nice rowing, Arthur!" Ami smiled. "Anyone would think you were always taking girls out on romantic boat trips!"

Arthur blushed - he had just been thinking that, under different circumstances, going out on a boat in the sunshine with Ami would be a great way to spend an afternoon.

"I... er... I used to go out rowing with my dad," Arthur bumbled.

"That sounds nice," Ami smiled back.

Great, thought Arthur. *Used to go rowing with my dad? Oh, that sounded really smooth.*

"I don' mean to sound like a moanin' mushroom," said Stick, "but didn't you say Mister Zane was loopier than a whole bag a' weasels?"

"Um... I'm pretty sure I *didn't* say that," replied Arthur. "But yes, I think he is kind of... unhinged. I think building the Agency Engine did something to his mind. Why?"

"Oh, I wuz jus' wondrin' why he's standin' there with jus' his pants on."

Arthur and Ami stopped rowing and twisted around to see they had arrived at the rusted, old fishing boat and Zane Rackham was indeed standing on the deck wearing just a pair of shorts. His beard was even thicker than before. Arthur thought the man's eyes didn't seem quite as distracted as before, but they were still definitely buzzing around, betraying a mind that was thinking very fast about a great many things.

Right now, he seemed to be tapping his fingers impatiently on the side of the boat. Arthur was about to say how good it was to see him again but the man started talking first.

"Been waiting ages for you, I have, ages!" he called. "We've got a lot to look at and read and think about and read and look at and think about. Come on, get into my boat. I have to take you somewhere."

Arthur was about to bring their little row-boat alongside the fishing vessel when he realised Rackham wasn't referring to that boat - but to another little row-boat that was moored just off his main one.

A little row-boat that sat upside down in the water, it's rounded hull poking up towards the sunny air.

Ami turned to Arthur, a concerned look on her face that mirrored his own rising uncertainty. They both looked at Stick who was just shaking his head, slowly.

"A whole bag a' weasels…" he said softly.

CHAPTER NINETEEN
THE COWBOY

- TERESA -

"Okay, come out where I can see you," said the figure at the door. "Real slow, like."

Teresa and Seb did as they were told, their hands raised high in the air. The figure stepped forward into the cabin so he was no longer silhouetted against the setting sun. A soft, jangling sound accompanied his footsteps on the hard floor and Teresa saw he had spurs attached to his boots. He wore a dark shirt and a leather waistcoat. A crimson scarf was tied around his neck and it was all topped off with a stetson hat.

He kept the gun trained on the pair but his voice was steady and calm. "Now, how about you tell me just who you are and why you're riflin' through this here house."

"My… my name's Teresa, and this," she motioned with her raised hands to her partner, "is Seb. We came to see the Blind Dressmaker."

"Did you now?" the cowboy said through narrow eyes. "Or perhaps you're just a couple a' rogues takin' advantage of an abandoned property to line your pockets."

"Please sir, mister cowboy sir," said Seb, "We really did come a long way to see the lady. We're pretty disappointed, truth be told. Speaking to the dressmaker was kind of a matter of life and death."

Teresa watched the cowboy as he scrutinised them closely. He looked them all over with a quiet and calm thoroughness which strangely enough, put Teresa at ease. She felt that this was someone who prided himself on being a sure and thorough judge of character.

After a few seconds, the cowboy lowered his pistol and released the hammer, slowly.

"Okay," he said, sliding his gun back into its holster, "I reckon you're on the level. Sorry to frighten you, I can see you're only young. My apologies." He tipped the peak of his hat. "The name's Joshua. I'm the Deputy over in Reliance."

"Reliance?" said Teresa, lowering her hands.

"The local town," said Joshua. "About a half-mile behind us."

"Nice to meet you, Joshua," Teresa said with a sigh of relief the situation was over. "It seems like you're as perplexed as we are over the dressmaker's disappearance."

"Perplexed ain't the word," said the deputy. "I'm downright worried. She ain't the type to go walkabout. What's this life and death thing you needed to see her for?"

Seb shrugged. "I need a new dress."

"I've got personal questions to ask her," said Teresa, ignoring Seb.

Joshua nodded. "Sorry, I don't mean to pry. It's just you're the only ones been here since she vanished. Thought maybe you might be linked or related somehow. Maybe give me some clue as to what happened to her."

Teresa nodded. Joshua seemed trustworthy enough but she decided it was best not to come completely clean with him just yet.

Joshua spoke again as he glanced briefly around the shop. "Well, there ain't nothin' out here. I've checked a hundred times. No clues, no nothin'. Plus, you really don't want to be out on these plains after sundown, not with the rock cats and rattlers and such. You might as well head on back to

Reliance with me. I'll make sure you get squared away with a place to stay and somethin' to eat."

"Sounds like a plan," said Seb to Teresa. "We can figure out our next move a lot better with a hot meal inside us."

Teresa looked around. Joshua was right - there was nothing to be found out here but they really did need to track the Dressmaker down. Whether she'd gone somewhere under her own steam or - heaven forbid - been kidnapped, the local town was probably a good place to start. On top of which, those plains really did look like the kind of place you wanted to avoid at night.

"Okay, fine," she said. "Let's go."

The sun was really beginning to dip low behind the horizon, now. *Really gets dark fast out here*, Teresa thought to herself. A horse was waiting for them outside and Joshua took the reins. Teresa waited to see if the cowboy talked to it but when he didn't, it was clear this was the non-talking variety. He didn't climb up onto its back, instead deciding to walk alongside the pair of youngsters, leading the horse by its reins.

As they walked, Joshua told them about the isle of Terminus. As the Frontier Isle, the people here lived as pioneers. They travelled to new areas and created settlements in the wilderness. They lived off their wits and in harmony with the land but always with an eye to boldly exploring yet more lands that no-one had been to before.

When the subject of the war came up, Joshua explained how Terminus had been hit hard.

"The crownies haven't come here directly but a lot of our young folk left to go join the Resistance," Joshua said. "Our idea of exploration and livin' on the edge of civilisation don't go too well with what the Queen wants. She wants us all

200

to be doin' simple and safe things but that's just not our style out here."

Pretty soon, the town of Reliance came into view, still far off. As the sky darkened, the glow of a few street lamps started to scatter across the town.

"Do you get problems with Raiders or pirates or the like?" Seb asked. "I know a lot of these kinds of border towns do." Teresa flashed him a glare and he quickly added "Erm, so I hear..."

"Used to," said Joshua. "Just before the war, we were constantly being hit by this one group of Raiders. Then along came this strange little band of characters from outta town. Ended up helpin' us get rid of the Raiders permanently. Changed the town for the better, really. The oddest trio you ever saw."

At the mention of an 'odd trio', Teresa couldn't help but laugh. "Did one of them wear a tweed jacket and think way too much of himself?"

"You know the Professor?" Joshua said, astonished.

Teresa stared in shock. "What? I was just joking! Are you telling me the Rogue's Run Trio were actually h-"

Teresa froze.

A quiet, guttural growling floated out of the calm evening air.

Surely not. That noise. Surely it can't be *them!* How could they be here?

"Teresa? What is it?" Seb asked, concerned.

Teresa jerked her head as the growl emanated again from the semi-darkness. It came from the sunward direction. But then it switched, coming from darkward as well. They were being penned in.

"Dog-Men," said Teresa. "They've found me here. But how? How are they managing to-"

"What are Dog-Men?" Joshua said but his voice was drowned out by the sound of a harsh growl in Teresa's ears.

"Run!" she yelled. Seb and Joshua ran alongside her, Joshua's pistol drawn even as he clung to his horse's reins.

Teresa headed for the lights of Reliance, tantalisingly close now, pumping her legs and arms as fast as she could. This is what she could feel when they landed, she realised. It was the Dog-Men watching her. They were on Oblivia and now here? How were they following her? More importantly, *why?*

The pounding of feet and the terrifying yelps and growls grew louder from both sides. The low light was turning the surroundings into a deep, endless grey. It was a little bit like being out in the NothingSpace where something would only become visible when it was close to you. She could hear them, hear their feet thumping rapidly on the ground and their heavy, laboured breathing. They were keeping up with them but so far, they were hidden from view. The trio were now running through a small smattering of trees, which only ratcheted up the dread even further.

"Where are they coming from?" Seb shouted, drawing his sword, trying to spy them himself.

"Let me get a better view," said Joshua and he vaulted expertly up onto his horse. Teresa watched as he swept his gaze left and right through the dark trees, pistol held close, ready to point as soon as a target was spotted.

Then she saw it.

It was the one to the left of them, running so fast, easily keeping pace with the trio. It was moving faster than Teresa had seen them move before. The man-portion of the creature was as tall and lean as she remembered. His head was turned toward her and his lack of eyes made the image even more ghastly. The man-creature's arm stretched out in front of it and eventually became a huge, slavering dog-creature. The man was blind but the dog could see and smell just fine. Its eyes shot over to the group and it snapped and snarled with the threat of imminent bone-crushing.

"There's one! Over to the left!" Teresa shouted.

Joshua emptied a bullet into the trees and the Dog-Man yelped, jumping to avoid the suddenly exploding tree bark. The shot didn't deter it, though, and it kept running.

"There's the other one!" Teresa said. "On the right, look!"

Joshua let off another shot, to the right this time, at a second Dog-Man that had come into view. The bullet seemed to skim a nearby rock and ricochet into the trees with a high-pitched zing. The Dog-Man roared defiantly and refused to back off. In fact, it started to move in - as did its partner.

Focusing through her fear as best she could, Teresa swept her hand at the one on the right, summoning the Threads to toss the creature away. It worked. The dual being was launched into the air as if hit by a giant cricket bat and crashed to earth with a tumble of dust and growls.

"Come on, we're nearly there!" Seb cried. Sure enough, the town was no longer just lights in the distance. A wooden archway was set over a main road that ran in between two rows of wooden buildings. A battered, handwritten sign was nailed to the top of the archway - *Welcome to Reliance*'. Instinctively, she felt that the Dog-Men wouldn't follow them past it.

With a final burst of energy, and feeling like an Olympic athlete crossing the line, Teresa dived through the archway and inside the town boundary. Her gut-feeling was proved right as she turned around to see the nightmare creatures bounding away into the darkness, their snarling fading into eventual silence.

Teresa bent over double, air trying its best to get back into her lungs in huge, desperate gasps. It didn't help that her heart was thudding violently against her chest. Seb looked to be in the same situation. Joshua, astride his horse, moved quickly back and forth across the town entranceway, gun still out, trying to spot the creatures in case they suddenly came back. But Teresa knew they wouldn't. Not tonight.

"That was close," Teresa said. "I don't know how we managed to escape them."

"Neither do I," said Joshua, coming over to them and hopping off his horse. "Especially as I didn't see anything."

Teresa glanced up at him, her breath suddenly frozen in disbelief. "What are you talking about? They were right there on either side of us. You shot at one!"

"I shot where you pointed," he said. "But I didn't see what I was shootin' at. I just followed your lead and trusted somethin' was there."

Seb shook his head. "Gotta say, I didn't see them either," he said.

"So why were you running?" Teresa asked, incredulous.

"Because you said to!" Seb said, regaining his breath. "I know enough that if Teresa Smith runs from something, then you run from it too! But…" he shrugged, "…I just didn't see it myself."

Teresa couldn't believe it.

Was she actually going mad?

CHAPTER TWENTY
UNDERWATER TREES

- ARTHUR -

Arthur did not like the way this trip was shaping up.

"Everybody ready?" Rackham asked, his voice reverberating around the dome that was the underside of the overturned boat. The scientist and his three visitors held tightly to upside-down seats as the water lapped around their ears. Arthur spat out the salty seawater that kept finding its way into his mouth while trying his best not to shiver as they bobbed up and down in the freezing water.

"Can I just ask if you're 'specially knowledgeable about how boats actually work, sir," said Stick, trying not to hit his head on the 'ceiling'. "Cuz I gots to tell you, they tend to be th'other way up…"

"That's when you're travelling above the water," said Rackham. "When you're going underwater, the boat needs to be upside down. That's just pure logic."

Arthur wondered if Rackham was pulling everyone into his world of crazy because that comment actually made sense.

"Anyway, no more talking," the scientist said, "You'll waste the air. Here we go!"

By Rackham's head, attached to the prow of the boat there was a ratchet wheel and a locking lever and another matching one at the stern, next to Arthur's head. A chain came up out of the water at one end of the boat and wrapped around the wheel next to Rackham. The wheel next to Arthur had an identical arrangement. Rackham pulled out the lever next to his wheel and immediately, both wheels began to spin extremely fast.

The *clack-clack-clack* noise assaulted the ears of the assembled travellers but the most disconcerting thing was the sudden, sickening motion of the boat as it abruptly plunged downwards under the sea.

Not wanting to appear too scared in front of Ami, Arthur did his best to hold back his cry of shock. It didn't work. Fortunately for Arthur's ego, he wasn't the only one crying out in fear.

"Stop doing that!" cried Rackham in consternation, "You're using up all the air!"

Arthur really wanted to be calm but the constant downward motion and the deafening clacking noise of the ratchet wheel in his ears had other ideas. Both wheels were spinning and more chain was coming out of the water and winding around each of them. Some kind of automatic pulley mechanism, a part of Arthur's brain realised. It was reeling the upside-down boat down towards the sea bed. *That's great*, he thought. *I'd be fascinated if I wasn't so terrified.*

All this was so overwhelming that it was several seconds before Arthur noticed the most important aspect of what was happening.

The air pocket under the boat wasn't disappearing.

Well, that made sense, he thought. It was like an upside-down glass or bowl in the washing-up sink at home. If you pushed it down into the water, the air bubble would remain in the bowl, trying to push it back up to the surface. If you weren't going to go to the trouble of actually building a submarine, Arthur supposed it was quite a clever way of doing it. But, Arthur also knew the water pressure would increase the further down they went, which meant the air bubble would get squeezed out, little by little, until...

With a deafening *clang* and a boneshaking shudder, the descent stopped and the boat was still once again.

"Well... that was fun!" Ami gasped as she smiled at Arthur. Arthur couldn't tell if she was being sarcastic or not.

"It's even faster going back up!" Rackham grinned. "Right, next stage. Deep breath. And don't lose sight of me. This is the dangerous bit."

Stick's eyes widened in shock. "It gets *more* dangerous?!"

"Don't worry, this next part won't last long. Either you'll arrive with me at our destination or you'll drown and float away. Either way, it'll be quick. Ish. Come on! Lots to do!"

With that he took a deep breath and pushed himself under the water. Not pausing for another second, all three of his visitors did the same and the little air-pocket under the boat was left on its own, empty and silent.

The water pressed in all around Arthur and the sudden loss of sound made it feel even more constricting. He'd expected it to be freezing but it actually felt quite warm - his brain was probably playing tricks on him, he decided, on account of it being utterly terrified.

Fortunately, they weren't that far out to sea, so the seabed wasn't as far down as it might have been. Also, the surroundings weren't as dark as they would have been in deeper waters. Shafts of sunlight lanced down from above, illuminating the scenery in stripes of soft blue. The landscape- or, seascape - was like a ghostly version of the world above. There were hills and valleys and vegetation that looked like trees, their leaves slowly waving hello to the visitors. And then, of course, there were all the fish. And in this weird, underworld, the fish flew around as if they were birds. Splashes of red, blues, yellows and silvers darted around, this way and that.

With a start, Arthur remembered he wasn't here to take in the beauty - he was supposed to be keeping track of Rackham. Stick and Ami were just ahead of him and Rackham's feet could just be seen in the murk ahead. Arthur was never much of a swimmer but he found moving forward underneath the water relatively easy compared to trying to keep yourself afloat on top of it.

He forced his arms to repeatedly sweep backwards in strong breaststroke strokes and his legs pumped in wide frog-kicks like the others. And all the while, Arthur tried to ignore the fact he was running out of breath. Where exactly were they going? If they didn't get there soon...

Arthur's prayers were suddenly answered. A sprawling, dark shape resting on the sea bed began to emerge from the murkiness ahead of them. It slowly came more into focus as they drew nearer to it and Arthur quickly identified it as a massive, sunken ship.

It must have been there for ages, he thought, because it was covered in endless strands of seaweed and vines. It almost looked like some giant plant-beast had wrapped its tentacles around the passing ship and dragged it down to its watery grave.

Arthur felt there was something strange about the submarine vegetation, though. The branches formed an intricate pathway all over the vessel's hull, criss-crossing, splitting and re-joining in so many ways, it boggled Arthur's mind. It made him think of roads - a complicated collection of paths and junctions, so numerous that if you tried to follow one route, you would get hopelessly lost. And yet... if you could focus on it, you could find multiple alternative paths to get from one place to another. Arthur found the longer he looked at it, the more it was starting to make his head hurt.

But then, he thought with sudden panic, that might be down to the fact he really, really needed to breathe.

Arthur had initially thought Rackham was going to bring them down here, show them something important and then return to the boat before they ran out of breath. But they were just going further and further down. With Rackham not quite being all there, Arthur was seriously beginning to consider the possibility that following him so far underwater had not been the wisest course of action.

Pumping his arms and kicking with all the energy he had left, he followed Rackham as the man swam into one of the ship's windows. The entire vessel was on its side so that meant they were swimming straight down. They were immediately following one of the ship's lower-deck corridors. As they descended, they passed several doorways, revealing cabins whose water-entombed interiors were covered in barnacles and seaweed.

Arthur's chest was starting to really throb and his mind was screaming at him to take a breath, even though it also knew that if he did, that would be the end of him.

Rackham darted to the right, into a doorway and the trio followed him. Arthur's vision was starting to blur and all he could see were dots forming in front of his eyes. He fought to keep Stick's feet in front of him and realised they were now going upwards. But they were still so far under the water they were never going to be able to-

Air!

With simultaneous shock and exaltation, Arthur's head broke the surface of the water and he suddenly emerged into sweet, sweet air. His lungs immediately drank in huge gulps, refilling his body and muscles with the oxygen they'd been too-long denied. Stick grabbed Arthur to stop him falling back under the surface and helped him clamber up onto the floor.

Actually, Arthur realised as he continued to gasp, reclaiming his air, it wasn't a floor. It was the wall. The entire room was rotated on its side by ninety-degrees. The boat was on its side, of course, Arthur remembered.

"The entire room is an air pocket..!" exclaimed Ami, catching her breath. "Like under our little boat, but bigger."

"Of course, of course! We're not fish, you know! The Threads told me it was here, months ago," said Rackham. Then, he shrugged. "Well, that's not strictly true. The Threads actually told the pixies. It was the pixies that told me."

"Threads…" Arthur clambered to his feet, his brain slowly getting back to normal speed. "I thought you were a scientist?"

"Specialising in plants and living organisms, yes," said Rackham as he made his way over to a table in the middle of the room. It was strange to see a table on the wall, not to mention walking along the wall himself. Arthur wondered if this was what it was like being a spider. "In Arilon, the Threads form the fabric of everything. Despite what the stupid Primacy used to say, you can't be a proper scientist if you don't understand them. They're not magic." He turned to Arthur with a conspiratorial smile, "The pixies… now, *they're* magic."

Arthur cast a sideways glance at Ami and Stick whose mystified expressions told him what he wanted to know - even in Arilon, there were no pixies.

The group arrived at the table and it was covered with a mass of papers and pencils and ink pots.

"How did you get all these things down here?" Ami asked.

Rackham grinned. "Wasn't easy!" He hurried over to the table. "Come! Come, come, shove your eyes in this direction."

Arthur stood next to Stick and Ami as Rackham shuffled and arranged the papers. Each one was covered in countless unintelligible scribbles - lines going back and forth and crossing over each other. Some were in pencil, some ink, some scratched in what looked disturbingly like dried blood. Not for the first time, Arthur wondered if this fellow even had anything serious to show them.

However, Arthur soon realised that the images on all the pages actually did show something interesting. Each page matched up with the ones around it, eventually joining to form a huge mosaic. It was the image of a complex web of pathways and roads. Suddenly Arthur realised what it was he was looking at.

"It's the vines around the ship!" he exclaimed.

"Yes, yes, apple for you. Ten points to Alan."

"My name's not Alan, it's-"

"I don't care. Another ten points if you can tell me what this picture really is."

"You mean it ain't a bunch of underwater trees?" Stick asked.

Arthur felt like the answer was on the tip of his tongue but he wasn't completely sure. And anyway, he didn't want to say the wrong thing and look stupid, especially in front of Ami.

"Underwater trees!" Rackham laughed. "And they call *me* crazy!"

"Underwater trees would suggest underwater birds to sit in the branches," Ami grinned.

"Exactly, and there are no underwater birds!" said Rackham. "The pixies ate them all. Come on Alan, look closer, what do you see?"

Rackham moved and shuffled the papers as he talked, carefully making sure they were joined correctly and occasionally moving one that was in the wrong place and inserting it into its proper location. Still, the answer seemed to lurk just beyond the edge of Arthur's thoughts, annoyingly teasing him but staying just out of reach.

"The path to the Engine, that's what the Cat sent you here to find," said Rackham, moving on. "That's what he set me to finding, all those months ago when he rescued me."

"How exactly did he do that?"

"Oh, it was exciting! There was a boulder, running down a hill and some very angry mercenaries from the island of Seditia. Oh, and a giant wedding cake. But wait till I tell you how we escaped…"

Someone's been spending too much time with the Cat, Arthur thought, somewhat amused.

"No, no, stop asking, I can't tell you about it now! There's no time," Rackham protested, even though nobody had spoken. "So, the path to the Engine. Bit tricky. You see, it's not a geographic path."

"Geographic?" Arthur said.

"Yes, it doesn't follow a set of physical points. It's not like - turn left at the forest, turn right at the lamppost, go forward a hundred paces and wallop, you have arrived at the Agency Engine."

"No, that would be too easy…" Arthur muttered.

"It's hidden in a particular place. I know the place, I know it very well," said Rackham.

"Well, then send us there!" said Stick. "Why, that does sound easy after all!"

"I know the place," said Rackham, "but I don't know the time. It could be a thousand years ago or it could be a thousand years from now. Or anywhen in-between. I mean, I suppose I could just send you to the place and have you wait for a thousand years, just in case. Buuuut, I'm not sure that would be making the most of your various abilities, do you?"

"Such as our ability to only live around eighty years," Arthur nodded. "Yep, not the best plan."

Arthur made himself comfortable, leaning against the table edge but was careful to avoid dripping onto the papers as he was still sodden from their little swim. He tried his best to concentrate because he had the distinct impression this was not going to be an easy conversation to follow.

"So we know the *where* but not the *when*," Arthur confirmed.

"Exactly. What we need is a path that leads us to the right *place* at the right *time*," said Rackham. "Preferably with lots of pretty lamps sitting along the edge to show us the way, okay?"

"So, it's a path of events rather than places," Ami guessed.

"Excellent! Ten points to Janine. Well done, Janine."

Ami smiled and shrugged. "Thanks."

Rackham motioned at Stick. "Come on Ferdinand! You don't have any points yet."

"I'm bidin' my time," Stick assured him.

"Okay," Rackham continued, "So, as Janine says, the path we need is a path of events, not places. A million different people, making a million different choices. All I need to do is track those choices and the events that come from them, and I can trace anything back to its source."

Arthur nodded. "Like the Queen did with me. She needed to find the most scared person she could to kick-start the first piece of the Agency Engine - and she came up with me. Then she traced backwards through all the choices and all the people who needed to make those choices in order to have the outcome she wanted - me being evacuated to Waterwhistle."

Suddenly it hit Arthur.

"These drawings, I know what they really are!" Arthur gasped. "They're-"

"Arilon," said Stick. Everyone looked at the bartender in shock. He stared back. "What? I said I wuz bidin' my time."

"Ferdinand the Tall is absolutely correct!" Rackham cried. "Ten points to House Ferdinand! Yes, this picture is indeed Arilon. Not the places within Arilon but…"

"It's the Threads," Arthur said. "It's what I saw when we were up in town earlier. The energy that underpins everything in Arilon. A billion different pathways to a billion different outcomes. And the vines around the ship look the same."

"So… those vines…" Ami said, the pieces falling into place for her as well, "they mirror the pathways through the Threads? They allow you to read the different things that might happen in the future?"

"Past, present and future, actually, but yes, you've got it," said Rackham.

"I've heard of people that can read the future in the Threads," said Ami. "Are you saying you can do that?"

"Charlatans and con artists," Rackham actually spat on the floor. "Reading the future takes immense skill and power, the likes of which most people in Arilon simply do not have. Yes, Janine, I can do it but most people can't, no matter what it says on the sign outside their circus tent. And the ones that actually claim to be able to *change* the future…" The scruffy man shook his head in obvious distaste at such fraudsters.

"The future can't be changed?" Arthur asked, alarmed.

214

"Well, let's just say that you can *make* the future, but you can't *change* it," Zane Rackham said with an air of both mystery and nonchalance. "Not unless you want to deal with some very annoyed Threads, anyway…"

Arthur tried to process what Rackham meant by that. You can make it but not change it? Maybe that meant that your actions shaped the future, which made sense. But if you somehow knew the future and wanted to alter it, that wasn't such a simple task. That wasn't good news for Teresa, nor for the request made by his old self all those months ago, Arthur thought.

And how the heck did you get 'annoyed' Threads..?

"So, how did it grow like that?" Ami asked.

"Oh, the life force that powers Arilon is too powerful to stay hidden. It's always making itself known, constantly manifesting itself physically all around us, if only we take the time to see it. The swirl of a leaf in the wind perhaps. Or the pattern of pebbles lying on the ground. Nothing is ever truly random, it all follows the path of the Threads - it's just that the Threads are too complicated for us to comprehend, so it *seems* random. But in a few places, the power of the Threads comes through so forcefully, it affects the environment in a much more direct way. And in those places, you can read the environment and hence read the Threads. But even then, it's much easier to do so if you have an affinity with them. You need skills, see? Skills!"

"Like the Queen, or Bamboo," said Arthur. "Or, you I suppose."

Rackham went silent for a moment and his face suddenly lost its manic animation. When he spoke, it was with a crushing regret that he obviously carried with him all the time. "When I designed the Agency Engine, I was trying to figure out how something could sit on top of the Threads and access all the things the Threads could access. The Threads carried life and energy and choice and outcome, so what if I could somehow interact with that energy? Maybe even influence it - you know, a nudge here or a shove there. Or maybe... I could take full control of it. A machine that could fully control the Threads could do-"

"Anything," said Stick, dread filling his voice.

"Indeed," Rackham nodded. "So yes, Alan, I have some skills, more's the pity. But my skills lie in understanding *how* the Threads work rather than actually making them *do* stuff like you."

"You're like a race car mechanic," Arthur said. He recalled watching the newsreels of the Indianapolis 500 race at the cinema. "You know how to fix and tune the car but you need a driver to actually take it out and race it."

Rackham looked confused. "What's a 'race car'?"

"Oh, it's a kind of-"

"I don't care. The point is the Agency Engine sits on top of the Threads, following their winding paths through Arilon. And my maps of this place can help you track back to where - and when - the heart of the machine is."

"Okay, so its connection to everyone and everything is what makes it so powerful," said Ami, "but it's also what will allow us to track it down, right?"

"Correct, Janine!" said Rackham. "Though I've run out of points. Sorry. So, all I have to do in order to track it down is sift through a billion different people and a trillion different decisions and a bazillion different events."

Arthur shrugged. "Well, okay, that sounds easy..."

"Oh, no, Alan, it's basically impossible," said Rackham.

"Yes... I know... I was being sarcasti-"

216

"Fortunately," said Rackham, producing a huge, two-handed broadsword sword from under the table, "we currently have a biiiig modifying factor to help us."

"Woah!" Stick gasped as all three visitors took a step back, "what you plannin' ta do with *that?!*"

"Oh, this? Don't worry." Rackham turned the sword point-down and leaned on the blade while flicking his long hair out of his face, nonchalantly. "It's just my walking stick. I'm getting on a bit, you know?"

The three youngsters warily stepped forward towards the table again, each with one eye on the crazy person's weapon.

"Ferdinand, my unfeasibly tall friend," Rackham gestured at Stick and then at three of the stone paperweights on the table. "You see those three stones? The ones closest to you? Choose one and pick it up, please. Any one, I don't mind."

Puzzled, Stick looked down at the three rocks. They were all smooth and grey but one of them was twice the size of the other two. Arthur watched as the bartender tried to decide which one to go for, probably trying to figure out the point of this exercise and hence which one Rackham wanted him to pick up and whether he should try to outfox the man. All the things that Arthur would think if he were doing it. In the end, Stick resorted to a bit of eeny-meeny-miney-moe and picked up the small stone on the right. He held it up to show Rackham.

"Very good!" said Rackham. "Put it back."

Stick did so.

"Excellent. Now do it again. You can pick up the same stone or another one, I don't care."

Exchanging confused glances with Ami and Arthur, Stick eventually shrugged and went back to eeny-meenie-min-

"Yaaaaargh!" Rackham suddenly yelled, the massive sword suddenly whirling above his head. "Pick one up now or I'll chop your whole arm off!"

Arthur and Ami leapt in fear as did Stick but the bartender quickly reached forward and grabbed the large, central stone. He quickly held it up.

"I picked one, see? Please stop bein' crazy now, Mister Zane!"

Rackham smiled and lowered the sword, returning it to its walking-stick position.

"Excellent, Ferdinand," he said as he picked up a small tin that had been sitting on the table the entire time. He opened it and removed a piece of paper, handing it to Arthur. "I wrote this ages ago. Been hoping to try this out on someone for ages. Go on, Alan, read it out loud for the whole class."

Keeping one uncertain eye on the madman, Arthur read what was written on the paper. "*No idea what the first choice will be. The second choice will be the big stone in the middle.*"

Suddenly the penny dropped for Arthur what this was all about. "You knew which choice Stick would make when he was scared."

Rackham clicked his fingers and pointed at Arthur, smiling.

"The modifying factor you mentioned just now," Arthur went on, "the one that we have in our favour to help us predict our way through the Threads… it's fear."

"Ta-da!" Rackham said, pushing the sword away and letting it clatter to the ground with a deafening, metallic clang.

"Yeah, we already knew that, actually," said Stick, still rubbing his chest to bring his heart rate back to normal. "You could've jus' asked us rather than tryin' to chop my hand off."

Rackham looked slightly crestfallen. "What..?"

Ami shrugged and smiled sympathetically. "The Cat kind of already mentioned it."

Rackham looked very crestfallen.

"But, no this is still good," Arthur said, hurriedly, trying to cheer him up again. "The Cat said the fear coming from the war was helping you track the machine down but now I understand what he really meant." Arthur turned back to the papers and the giant picture of the interconnecting pathways. "While the war is going on, the primary emotion people feel is fear. It's everywhere, infecting every decision. When you're that scared, you don't think of all the choices you might normally think of. It reduces the things you think and feel and do. Suddenly, a million choices become ten thousand choices. Or a thousand. Or a hundred." He looked over at Stick, still holding the big rock. "Or one."

Rackham darted forwards, straightening the pages of the drawing once again. "Aided by the fear from the war, I have been memorising the vines around this ship and sketching them, tracking all the choices and events that pertain to the Agency Engine. Random people, random choices, random events…"

"Except not random," Arthur said, "just really complicated."

Rackham smiled. "Precisely! Like a hundred thousand dominoes falling in different directions, each choice affecting the next, one person to another…"

"Sounds exhausting," said Ami, sympathetically.

219

"I really need a nap, Janine, I'm not going to lie," Rackham agreed. "But I think I have finally figured out the final sequence of events that will lead you to the Agency Engine."

He drew their attention to one line that stretched over several sheets of paper. The line had been drawn and redrawn so many times it stood out over the others. It was taking a definite, specific path through the forest of possibilities. Along the line, there were several large circles showing specific junction points on the path. Each point had a word written next to it - *Place, Event, Person.*

Rackham pointed to the first circle. *Place.*

"In a place with no rules," he said, "you must figure out your own rules, using only your sense of right and wrong."

"A place? A lawless place?" said Arthur. "Where people have to come up with their own laws. Their own rules of how to live."

"Terminus," said Ami. "That sounds like Terminus, the frontier isle."

Arthur's eyes opened wide in surprise. "But, that's where Teresa's gone!" he exclaimed.

Rackham's eyes narrowed. "She's not still a Needleman is she?"

Arthur shook his head. "No, no, we fixed that."

Rackham breathed a sigh of relief. "Oh, that's good then. But if your sister has gone there, that isn't a co-incidence. Everything in the Threads means something. Tick and tock. Cause and effect."

"What's special about Terminus?" Ami wondered. "Did Teresa go there because it's important? Or is it only important because she's gone there?"

Stick shrugged. "Maybe it's both."

"Yes, yes, listen to Ferdinand the Lanky," said Rackham. He moved his finger along the line to the next circle. 'Person' scribbled next to it. "Next we have a person who is in this place without rules. They are usually very sure of themselves... but when someone like that finds themselves bereft of rules, they begin to struggle. They need the rules to help them know who they are. Without them, they are lost."

Well that definitely sounded like Teresa, Arthur thought.

Rackham moved his finger to the next circle. *Event.* "This person will be surrounded by a swarm of darkness..."

Arthur leaned forward. "She's going to be attacked..?!"

"I didn't say 'attacked', I said 'surrounded'. There's a difference."

"I got s'rounded by a swarm of angry bees once," said Stick. "Sure felt like the same thing ta me..."

"But look!" Rackham said, jabbing a finger on the next junction point. "Another person! A knight in shining armour."

"A knight?" Arthur said, hopefully. "Maybe Iakob or Iosef show up. They're good at swooping in and saving the day..."

"But they're fighting on Phobos," said Ami.

Arthur shrugged. Maybe they up sticks and head to Terminus. Who else could it be talking about?

As Rackham moved his fingers to the next circle, his eyes looked up at the trio, more solemn than he'd been at any point so far. He said just one word.

"Death."

The three guests stared at him. Ami spoke, but it was a hoarse whisper.

"Whose?"

"Impossible to say," said Rackham. "Look at all the lines going through this circle. Too many possibilities. Different people, different deaths. But they all flow through the circle, which means any further progression on the path has to be paid for with life. Sorry about that one - it's a downer for sure."

Arthur felt a cold blanket drape over him. It matched the next circle Rackham pointed to. One marked 'place'.

"A cave of despair."

"Is the cave on Terminus? Arthur managed to ask eventually.

"It might not be a physical place," said Ami.

"But I thought 'place' meant a place," said Arthur. "A real place."

"A cave in your mind is just as real as a cave in the forest," said Rackham. "You can get lost in either."

The next circle was an event. "The return of something you didn't realise was lost."

Stick took out his tin of badges from his jacket pocket, checking its contents. Ami and Arthur looked up at him and he gave the tin a satisfied rattle. "It ain't this. All the badges are still here."

Ami smiled at her friend and everyone's eyes returned to the page.

He jabbed the second to last circle. "The hand of an enemy," the man said. "You have to take it or the road ends right here."

Arthur's breath caught for a moment - didn't his old-man self say something about the Queen extending a hand of help to him? Was this to be that moment? The moment where he'd been warned he had to kill the Cat?

Rackham moved his finger to the final circle. The multitude of lines on all the pages eventually funnelled down into this one circle.

"The Agency Engine," he said finally.

All the hope and optimism Arthur had felt throughout the conversation had left him now. He could see a path to the Agency Engine, which is what he'd hoped for. But the road that took them there seemed laced with darkness and tragedy.

Terminus.

Teresa.

An attack - or rather, a swarm - of darkness.

A knight in shining armour.

Death.

A cave of despair.

The return of something you didn't know was lost.

The hand of an enemy.

The Agency Engine.

Rackham placed a hand on Arthur's shoulder.

"I'm sorry," said the man. "That's the road. You can choose not to follow it - that's your right, your choice. This is all just probabilities. None of it's fixed in stone yet. Step off the road now, go home. Maybe things go differently. Maybe nobody dies."

"And maybe lots of people do," said Arthur. "You say I have a choice. But Teresa's in danger. There's no version of the future where I don't help her."

Rackham looked down at his scribbled pathways. "Nope," he shook his head. "There actually isn't."

"So, in truth, how much of a choice do I really have?" As he spoke, Arthur's mind went back to his argument with his sister. Not even a falling out like that would keep them apart for long. The Threads - the universe - wouldn't allow it. "Seems like the future is pretty fixed to me."

Rackham put a hand on Arthur's shoulder. "The Cat chose well. The three of you, your sister. And others too. You'll all play your part in the future of Arilon. But you just have to

223

keep remembering one thing above all else." He looked Arthur in the eye, sadness welling out of his own.

"Nothing lasts forever."

CHAPTER TWENTY-ONE
THE THING ABOUT PIES

- TERESA -

"You know what's interesting about a pie?" said Seb, his fork hovering above his plate and the round, hot, baked circle on it. "You look at the outside of the pie and it looks like any other pie. But it's not until you take your fork and dig into it that you actually find out what's inside."

"Meat. Meat's inside. That's a meat pie," said Teresa.

"Yes, I know."

"You know it's a meat pie."

"Yes... I-"

"You know it's a meat pie because when the nice lady came over and said 'what would you like to eat'..."

"Teresa, you're missing the-"

"...you said to her 'I would like a meat pie please'."

"It's just the... you know, the mystery of... something that looks one way on the outside but... but inside it's..." Seb sighed and gave up. "Doesn't matter, you've killed the moment."

He dug his fork in and shoved a piece of meat pie into his mouth.

"You're not eating?" he said through a mouthful of steaming hot food.

Teresa's own pie and fork remained untouched. "I don't know, there's just something about being chased by apparently invisible dog-monsters that kind of takes a girl's appetite away."

Seb shrugged as he cut into the pastry again. "Funny. Has the opposite effect on me."

Sighing, Teresa looked out of the window at the town of Reliance - the sun was up and people were out and about, going about their morning business. For the first time, Teresa got a good look at the place they'd stumbled into.

Reliance looked like it had been taken straight out of the pages of a cowboy movie, the type of films she wasn't interested in but Sam loved. There was a main street which was flanked on both sides by a long palisade of shops and stores - everything from weapons to clothes to food was on sale out there. Not to mention the Sheriff's office, the blacksmith and the undertaker. Following the direction of the street was a Travel Line, several yards higher than the tallest building. It seemed to be the only one anywhere near - the town was probably specifically built underneath it, Teresa thought. A wooden platform had been built in the centre of the highway that reached all the way up to the Travel Line and allowed people to embark or disembark from ships and then walk down some very rickety stairs to street-level. Men and women, on foot, on horseback or in carts were trekking back and forth past the platform as Reliance began to wake up.

Looking around the room the pair were now sat in, the old western theme continued. Their new accommodation was an old saloon and looked like any number of such places in cowboy movies Teresa had been forced to watch over the years. Their father had once taken all three of them - Sam, Teresa and Albert - to the movie house in Nottingham for Sam's birthday. Knowing Sam's love of cowboys, they were going to see a western called *Three Men From Texas* starring William Boyd. However, when they'd arrived, there'd been some kind of mix-up and the only western the cinema was now

226

showing was a film called *Go West*, a comedy cowboy movie starring the Marx Brothers. Sam had been extremely disappointed and had burst into tears, refusing to even go in. Teresa would have been perfectly happy to give silly cowboy movies a miss altogether but it was Sam's birthday. Putting her own feelings to one side, she'd managed to calm her brother down and convince him to give this film a try. The four of them had all gone in and the film had actually turned out to be hilarious. They'd all really enjoyed themselves. Teresa remembered her and Sam laughing so much, their faces literally ached for hours after.

This saloon, unfortunately, did not look like a place of laughter. From the moment Joshua had brought them here and arranged rooms for them with Sally, the proprietor, Teresa had felt it. Sally had been kind enough but the other patrons all had an air of quiet suspicion and wariness. Even now, the saloon's smattering of other customers sat at their tables or at the bar, nursing their drinks and occasionally glancing over their morning coffees or newspapers at the pair of strangers.

Having said that, she couldn't blame them for being suspicious of these two strange individuals who'd drifted into their town. Right now, Teresa was even suspicious of herself. Had she really seen the Dog-Men? Or was she actually beginning to lose the plot?

"I just don't understand how you couldn't see them," she said for the million-and-first time, just as exasperated as she was the first time she'd said it.

"Perhaps they have some kind of ability that only allows one person to see them," Seb shrugged. "Like… I don't know, like a defence mechanism."

"But now I think about it," said Teresa, her eyes briefly closed in recollection, "I don't think Kia could see them, either.

I mean… I thought she could, but now I really think about it… perhaps she was confused, wondering what I was talking about. Just like you and Joshua."

"Who's Kia?" asked Seb.

"Oh, one of the Painted Ones."

"The… Painted Ones?" Seb said in disbelief, forkful of pie temporarily frozen halfway to its destination. "The… *extinct* Painted Ones?"

"I haven't told you that story," said Teresa. "I don't tell you everything, you know."

"Clearly," Seb said as the fork resumed its journey and deposited the pie into his mouth.

Teresa sighed and finally gave in to the tiny part of her brain telling her she needed to eat something. She began to cut up her pie - vegetable and potato. As soon as she broke the crust, the aroma escaped and teased her nose, making her realise how hungry she really was. It reminded her of what Seb had been wittering on about before and she thought perhaps he actually had a point. Before, it had simply been a round piece of pastry - but now, once she'd actually dug in to it, what was on the inside was finally discovered.

"Afternoon Mr Feeney, Mrs Feeney," said Sally over at the bar as an elderly couple entered the saloon. "Any word from Karl lately?"

"Not for a couple weeks," said Mrs Feeney, resting herself against the wooden counter-top. "He said somethin' about going to some big base and that was the last we heard from him."

"I'm sure he'll be fine, the damn fool," grumbled Mr Feeney. His gruff exterior was severely failing to hide his extreme worry.

Teresa felt cold and numb from her head to her toes. If that base they were talking about was Titanium, there was a good chance Karl Feeney was not coming home. And that would be all because of h-

"Not your fault," Seb whispered to her. She looked up at him in surprise. He was staring at her as though reading her mind. "I know you take the attack on Titanium personally for some reason, but if their son was killed there, it's not your fault. And, anyway, he may well have survived."

"Long enough to take part in the attack on Phobos," Teresa said, darkly. Seb's expression darkened and he had no answer for that. He returned to eating his pie.

The pair sat in silence for a while as Teresa stared out of the window at the sight of the town waking up. People loading up horse-drawn carts with shovels and tools, presumably heading out into the wilderness to do who-knew-what. Others were opening up their stores and putting chalk boards out front, telling of the day's deals on clothes or nails or guns. She focussed on all of this because it helped her to not worry about Arthur.

Seb looked around as he munched. "So, what do you think of this place? Reliance?"

"It's quiet," said Teresa. "And I don't know where we're going to start looking for the Dressmaker."

"It is quiet," Seb agreed. "According to Joshua - not to mention old Mr. and Mrs. Feeney over there - that'll be because so many of their young ones have gone off to fight for the Resistance."

Teresa nodded as she chewed. She knew that feeling - Waterwhistle was exactly the same.

"But, I don't know," Seb continued. "I think there's something else going on too. Something I can't quite put my finger on."

"I know exactly what it is," said Teresa. "I've seen it before, back home in my village. We were infested with Yarnbulls and everyone behaved like this."

She looked around at the people. Almost nobody shared a table with another person. Almost like they didn't trust each other.

"It's fear," she said. "Everyone here is very, very afraid."

Seb glanced around them, his expression showing that now he was seeing exactly what Teresa was talking about. "Well then, that beggars the question," he said slowly, looking back at Teresa. "Afraid of *what?*"

The doors to the saloon opened and Joshua entered with a woman by his side. After dropping them off earlier, the Deputy had promised to return after discussing their situation with the Sheriff. Teresa had assumed the Sheriff was a man but from the authority with which this woman entered the saloon - not to mention the gold star on her jacket - it was clear Teresa's assumption had been very wide of the mark.

As the Sheriff walked over, nodding hellos to the assorted townspeople present, Teresa couldn't shake the feeling she'd seen the woman somewhere before.

"Enjoying supper?" Joshua smiled to see them eating. "Miss Sally sure does make a good pie."

"She sure does," said Seb. "You know what's interesting about pie? You look at it on the outside-"

"Seb," Teresa interrupted him.

Seb sighed. "Doesn't matter, I'll tell you later."

The Sheriff wasn't as tall as Joshua but she put out a much more powerful presence. She had steel blue eyes that were somehow both intense and unhurried at the same time. Short auburn hair hung down from under her hat. Joshua gestured toward his boss. "Folks, this is Sheriff Grace. She's in charge around here."

The Sheriff tipped her hat. "Nice to meet you both," she said. "Join you?"

"Of course," said Teresa. The pair pulled out chairs and removed their hats, placing them on the table. Sally called out from the bar, asking if the pair wanted coffees.

"No thanks, Miss Sally," the Sheriff called back as she sat down. "Already had two, it's not even ten o'clock. There's only so much 'awake' I can take this early."

"I'll have a cup, please Miss Sally," Joshua called over.

"One hot bean juice comin' right up," she smiled. The Sheriff turned back to Teresa and Seb. "You folks tried the cake here? Miss Sally does a mean chocolate sponge."

Taking herself by surprise, Teresa suddenly found herself grinning. "My brother would be over the moon to hear you say that. He loves cake."

"Oh, well then you bring him by sometime," said the Sheriff. "He certainly won't regret it."

The smile faded from Teresa's face as the memories of her and Arthur's last conversation replayed themselves in her mind.

"I'll be sure to do that…" she said softly.

"Anyway," the Sheriff said, getting down to business, "I hear you folks had some trouble over on the outskirts."

"We did but we sorted it with your deputy's help," said Seb, smoothly.

"Well, my deputy said there weren't nothin' out there."

"That's not exactly what I said," Joshua jumped in. "I said I didn't *see* anything. But I think there was definitely

231

something there. Due respect, but Miss Teresa don't seem like the kind to spook easily and she was terrified. I hope you don't mind me sayin' so, Miss Teresa."

"Nope," Teresa held up her fork for emphasis and gave an exhausted smile. "I was definitely terrified."

"So if she said there was something there, then I reckon there was something there," said the deputy.

"Uh-huh. Something... invisible," said Sheriff Grace. Teresa couldn't tell if the Sheriff was being sceptical or just trying to run things through her mind.

"I... well, I guess so, yeah," said Joshua, eventually. "Invisible'd be the word."

The Sheriff picked up her hat and turned it over and over in her fingers. This was obviously what she did, Teresa realised, when she was turning something over in her head.

"Well, these are strange times an' no mistake," she said, eventually. "Invisible monsters probably just fits right on in."

Teresa found it interesting how quickly the Sheriff accepted the strange story. Joshua had stood up for Teresa's account of things but she could tell that was just because he trusted Teresa herself, not because he believed in things like invisible dog-men. The Sheriff, on the other hand, didn't seem especially disposed toward Teresa - and yet, she seemed ready to accept the strange event on its own merits. Teresa wondered if maybe some of Arthur's Seer stuff was starting to rub off on her because she was getting the distinct feeling that Sheriff Grace was not originally from around here.

Sally came over to the table, all smiles and sunlight - unlike the majority of her customers - and delivered Joshua's coffee.

"Thank you kindly," he said, reaching gratefully for the hot, metal cup.

232

"You kids want anything else?" she asked them with a kind smile. They both thanked her and said no. "Well just holler if you change your minds," she replied. With that, she bustled away to go and clear some glasses that a patron on the next table had left behind.

"I hear you're lookin' for the Dressmaker," the Sheriff said once Sally was gone. "You know her?"

"We were advised to see her," Seb jumped in before Teresa could speak. "Personal family issues. Apparently, she's a good person to talk to."

"That's for sure. She definitely does more'n just make dresses," said Joshua, putting the coffee on the table, untouched. "She's like the town's surrogate mother."

"It's true," the Sheriff nodded. "You got an ache, she knows the plant to rub on it. You got a problem, she always has a story that'll help you figure it out. And she makes a heck of a midwife. Half the town's babies were brought into the world by her."

"She sounds... amazing," Teresa said, staring at what was left of her pie. "I was really counting on her being able to help me too. I risked a lot to come here."

"So you've never met her before?" the Sheriff asked again. "Got no idea why she might've disappeared?"

Teresa shook her head, eyes still on her pie. "Nope. Sorry."

Sheriff Grace nodded. "Well, don't worry. Like I said, she's a big part of this town. We ain't gonna rest until we've found her. You'll get the chance to ask her your questions, don't you worry none."

"Oh, hey," Joshua said, suddenly remembering something. "I been hearin' some chatter on the grapevine this morning. Apparently, the Resistance is makin' a play for

Phobos today. Head on attack. Everyone's talkin' about it." He kept his voice low, in case anyone in the saloon had relatives who'd gone off to fight.

Sheriff Grace whistled a low, soft whistle. "Head on? Why, they'll be cut to shreds."

"Well, it sounds like a good thing we're well away from it, then," said Seb, glancing at Teresa.

"Those people are heroes," said Joshua. "Putting their lives on the line so the rest of us can be free."

"Yup, no argument from me," said the Sheriff. "Let's hope we don't forget it. Be a heck of a thing if a hundred years from now, we forgot everything we learned and end up makin' all the same mistakes. Throwing away all their sacrifices like yesterday's newspaper. Some tyranny don't look like tyranny at first, that's what we need to remember."

Teresa couldn't figure the Sheriff out. On the one hand, she was quite cold and businesslike. She reminded Teresa of General Kingsley, in that way. Focus just on what's in front of you and get it done. And then, suddenly she stepped back and was able to look at the big picture, too. Almost philosophical. It seemed to Teresa that she was hiding a secret well of feelings below that gruff exterior.

Right now, she was pointing her hat at the coffee cup sitting in front of Joshua's. "You know how I said I didn't want one a' those…?"

The deputy smiled. "I knew you'd change your mind. That's why I got this one for you."

"Well, if you ain't the best deputy a Sheriff ever had," she smiled, picking up the tin cup. It was still steaming hot but she drained the whole thing as if it were cold water. She sat back for a moment, eyes closed, savouring the taste and presumably feeling the heat go down, Teresa thought. Looking at the woman sitting back like that, her eyes closed, she looked almost asleep.

Realisation suddenly hit Teresa like a truck. She knew now where she'd seen this woman before.

"Well, I guess we better get back to payin' off our sins." The Sheriff snapped her eyes open and switched back to business mode. "Work to do, people to see."

The pair rose, putting their hats back on. "Nice to meet you both," said the Sheriff.

Teresa nodded, her mouth unable to open. Seb replied, "You too, Sheriff. Please let us know if you find out anything about the Dressmaker."

"Will do," said Joshua. "I'll drop by later to check up on you both."

And with a tip of their hats, the pair left.

"Do you know who she was?" Teresa hissed at Seb, as soon as the pair had disappeared through the swing-doors.

"Yes, Teresa, she was the Sheriff of this town," he rolled his eyes. "Please keep up."

"No, I mean, I've seen her face before," said Teresa. "On Needlemen island. One of the Sleepers."

Seb pointed a fork at the doorway in disbelief. "You mean she's-"

Teresa nodded. "Reliance's Sheriff is a Needleman."

CHAPTER TWENTY-TWO

TIN STAR

- TERESA -

"So, remind me again why I decided to come here with you?" asked Seb.

"Because we're going to find out what that Needleman is up to," said Teresa as they walked down the Reliance main street under cover of night.

"No, no, I meant, why I decided to come with you to this damn island," the young pirate clarified. "Right now, I could be kicking back and joining in the fun of a devastating attack on a heavily fortified city full of soldiers and Yarnbulls. All of which would be preferable to breaking into the office of a Needleman, let me tell you."

Teresa sighed, her breath making clouds in the cold, night air. "I was a Needleman, in case you'd forgotten. Are you so scared of me?"

"More than anyone," Seb nodded.

The main street stretched the length of the town with palisades of building frontages lining both sides of the highway. It was supply stores and food shops and a doctor's office and even an undertaker - but everywhere was cloaked in darkness. This late at night, everyone in Reliance was at home. There were small lanes and by-ways that branched off the main thoroughfare and these led to the actual houses and cabins where the people of Reliance lived. The abandoned main street was perfect for the clandestine activities that Teresa had brought them here to carry out. Nevertheless, they kept to the shadows as much as possible while they picked their way down the street. One stray pair of eyes and the game was up.

Very quickly, they arrived at the door to the Sheriff's Office. Like the rest of the nearby windows, there were no lights on inside and no sign of life.

"Come on," Teresa tried to hurry her partner along. "We saw the Sheriff and Joshua go riding off but we don't know how long they're going to be. We need to get in and out as fast as possible. Time to exercise your piratey skills for the greater good."

"You realise this is about as hare-brained a plan as you could have come up with," said Seb, taking out his lockpick tools and getting to work on the front door. "In fact, it's not even a plan. It's a scheme. A fancy. A notion, even."

"Look," said Teresa, glancing nervously up and down the deserted street, "I appreciate we don't have a lot to go on. All we know is we have a missing Dressmaker and we have a Needleman. Now, that doesn't sound like co-incidence to me. And in the absence of any other ideas, I say we break into her safe and see if there's anything stashed away in there that can help us figure out what's going on."

"And you know she has a safe because of the movie thing."

"The Sheriffs in cowboy movies always have a safe," Teresa shrugged, her apologetic expression betraying how much of a stretch she knew this was.

"And does the evil villain always write out their nefarious plan and then conveniently put it in the safe?"

"More often than you'd think," she said.

Seb glanced up at her, his expression unimpressed.

She shrugged again. "You said it was a scheme."

237

"I said it was a notion." The lock clicked and the door popped backwards a couple of inches. "But it's all we have and I do love a good break-in." He grinned.

Teresa allowed herself a quick smile of triumph. "Okay, hurry up. I'll keep watch."

With a quick salute, Seb disappeared inside, silently closing the door behind him and Teresa turned her attention back to the street.

A gust of wind blew past and Teresa hugged herself, briskly rubbing her hands up and down her arms. This was a long shot, she admitted to herself. But what else could they try? If the Sheriff was a Needleman, their main authority option was taken away.

Teresa didn't believe Joshua was a Needleman - partially because it would be a waste of resources (they didn't need both Sheriff *and* Deputy to take control of the town) but mostly because she just didn't get a feel of it from him. It had been a while since she'd been purged of her Needleman self but she still had the memories from that time. Your memories make you what you are, she had learned. And her memories of being a Needleman gave her an insight into that breed. Maybe it was wishful thinking, but she just didn't get a Needleman sense from Joshua. Nevertheless, they couldn't go to him without proof - he'd never believe them. If they found something in the safe, then maybe. But not until then.

The Arilon sky at night was the deepest black Teresa had ever imagined. On Phobos, it felt claustrophobic and smothering. And yet out here - despite being the exact same blackness - it felt open and expansive. Kind of inviting. Maybe each island influenced how you felt about it, Teresa thought.

Thinking of Phobos and recalling Seb's comment about the attack on Gast, Teresa looked up into the sky and wondered how the battle was going. It was strange to think somewhere out there, thousands of miles away, would be a deafening clash of steel and booming cannon-fire. All that shouting and fighting and dying. Yet here, it was cold, dark and silent. She sent out prayers to all the people she'd come to know - the Cat, Iakob, Iosef, Grom... even Captain Thrace, she smiled.

And Arthur.

Right now, she really wanted to know her brother was alright. She just wanted to talk to him and-

"Teresa?"

The sound of the Sheriff's voice made Teresa jump out of her skin. She turned to see the woman walking toward her along the wooden promenade. How was she not even making a single sound?

"To what do I owe this late-night visit?" the Sheriff asked. The woman seemed really tall as she looked down on Teresa and her hat suddenly took on a distinctly Needleman-type feel.

"Sheriff Grace!" Teresa greeted her loudly - loud enough for Seb to hear, she hoped. "I, er... I hadn't heard from you or Joshua yet and I came by to ask if you'd made any progress tracking down the Dressmaker?"

"You came here at this late hour?" the Sheriff took a step closer to Teresa. "It's dangerous out, you know. All kinds of critters can come prowlin' around town."

Teresa looked the woman in the eye. "I can only imagine."

Abruptly, the Sheriff yawned and exhaustion seemed to take over. She took off her hat and ran her fingers through her auburn hair. "Truth is, me and Joshua just took a ride around town, looking for these Dog-Men of yours. Figured they may have something to do with the Dressmaker goin' missin'. Co-incidence seemed to be too much to ignore. If we could catch one..." she shrugged and put her hat back on. "I don't know, I kind of hoped we'd be able to get some information from it."

"Well, perhaps you're just looking in the wrong place," Teresa said, a sudden idea coming to her. "You need to try outside the town. That's where we saw them."

"Tell the truth, it's been a long day," said the Sheriff beginning to move to the door. "I got some paperwork I need to finish off and then I need to hit the h-"

"Or..." Teresa quickly moved in front of the Sheriff, blocking her off from getting to the door. "Or... I could come out with you, right now. On patrol."

"You?"

"They seemed drawn to me," Teresa said. "Perhaps my presence will tempt them out."

The Sheriff looked Teresa up and down for a moment. Teresa wondered what thoughts were running through that brain of silver and shadow.

"Okay, fine, that might work," she said. "You know you're pretty brave for a-"

"Girl?"

The Sheriff laughed. "I was goin' to say 'kid'. Come on, horses're this way."

The only thing Teresa found more exciting than riding a horse, was how quickly she picked it up.

"Look at you," said Sheriff Grace as the pair trotted out past the town gate. "You're a natural."

Teresa smiled at the compliment - before remembering the person giving the compliment wasn't a person at all.

They rode in silence, calmly trotting through the dark wilderness. Oddly, having a companion made Teresa feel safe, despite the fact her companion was more dangerous than anything else out there.

"Tell me about your brother," said the Sheriff, eventually.

Oh, here we go, Teresa thought. *Now it shows its true colours. Trying to get information from m-*

"When you were growing up, what was it like? Having a brother?"

The question stunned Teresa for a moment. She was so confused as to why a Needleman would ask such a question, she actually found herself answering it.

"Well, the brother I was talking about - we didn't actually grow up together. I have two other brothers. I loved them, we had a great time… But I always felt like something was missing. Something I couldn't put my finger on. I mean, at the time, I don't think I consciously realised it. It was just a feeling that I didn't properly notice until a couple of years ago."

"Is that when you met him?"

Teresa nodded. "We were twins but we'd been separated at birth." Teresa half-smiled at the sound of it. "It sounds like something from a dramatic novel, doesn't it? But from the moment we met, we both knew we'd found the missing part of ourselves. He instantly became everything to me, and I became everything to him. When we were apart, we both felt… I don't know, lost. Directionless. But together, we could achieve amazing, unbelievable things." Teresa suddenly found herself faltering. "Lately, though…"

The silence hung in the air between the two. The only sound was the soft clopping of the horses' hooves on the stony ground.

"You've begun to feel smothered," the Sheriff said eventually. Shocked at the creature's insight, Teresa looked around to see the Sheriff looking away into the darkness as she spoke. "Resentful. You want to be your own self but your mind is filled with the other person." She turned to Teresa. "Somethin' like that?"

Teresa nodded, wordlessly. She'd been afraid to say it out loud, but she was now hearing it from someone else's lips and it was exactly how she'd been feeling. "I just need to figure myself out. I need to be on my own to do that but… but I also want my brother here with me. We're one. I love that feeling. But… but I hate it as well." She swallowed down the feelings the words were threatening to bring up. "Does that make me a bad person? Selfish?"

The Sheriff smiled. "Confused, maybe. But then, we're all that. Look…" she brought her horse to a stop and turned to Teresa fully. "Each person is created as a particular thing. Forged, like a… like a horseshoe in a fire, right? You're a particular shape. But then life happens and you learn things, experience things. And those things add extra stuff to you. Change your shape. Sometimes for the better, sometimes for the worse. But underneath it all, you're still the same old horseshoe. Not good, not bad, just you. But you can be hard to find under all that extra stuff. When it comes to chippin' away, trying to discover your original shape… well, if you can do it on your own, then fine. But if you need help, you shouldn't be afraid to take it. Figurin' out what you really are… it can be real difficult."

As the Sheriff spoke, Teresa noticed her fingers brush involuntarily against her badge. All of a sudden, the small, scratched, piece of tin on the woman's chest seemed to shine in the darkness, like an actual star. Perhaps guiding weary

242

travellers to their destination. To the truth they were looking for. Amazingly, Teresa felt, in that moment, that it was the Sheriff that was trying to follow that star and figure out who and what she was. She found herself smiling.

Sheriff Grace looked at Teresa, her brow furrowed, sternly. "What's so funny?"

"It's just something Seb said to me today about pies."

The woman's confusion deepened, but a shadow of a smile crept onto her face as well. "Well, that's about the most random thing I've-"

Teresa suddenly stiffened.

"Don't move," she said to the Sheriff. "It's behind you."

CHAPTER TWENTY-THREE

CONFRONTATION

- TERESA -

The unmistakable shape of the predator was hiding in the bushes off to the side of the road, the dog's eyes and malicious-looking teeth clearly visible through the leaves.

The sheriff began to move her hand down to the holster at her hip.

"No, wait," Teresa whispered. "Circle around behind it."

"What..?" the sheriff clearly wasn't a fan of that idea. "Let me just plug it now. I'll hit it in the leg or-"

"I need to do something first," Teresa hissed through gritted teeth. Her eyes flitted to the sheriff, briefly. "Please."

For a long moment, the sheriff that was a Needleman that was a sheriff sat, her hand on the hilt of her pistol. The shape in the bushes shifted slightly. There was the barest suggestion of a growl. Teresa was convinced the law-woman was going to spin around, guns blazing...

...right up until she released her grip on the gun and turned her horse away.

"You got sixty seconds," she said and trotted briskly into the darkness.

Teresa turned back to the indistinct shape in the bushes. She couldn't see it properly with her eyes but her fear could make it out, clear as day. She had one minute while the Sheriff took in a long, wide arc which would bring her back around behind the Dog-Man. The creature would soon be trapped between the two of them and the Sheriff would then hope to incapacitate it with a carefully placed shot. Before that happened, Teresa wanted to have a word.

Her eyes remained locked on the dark bushes as she climbed down off her horse. She stepped slowly toward the still not-quite-visible-but-definitely-there shape. Every part of Teresa wanted to turn and run. It was like holding onto a burning hot piece of metal. She just wanted to drop it. But she held on as tight as she could.

"So, you've been chasing me for a long time," Teresa said into the darkness. "All those months on the island. And even after I left, you keep popping up. Invisible to everyone but me. I know I've been a bit slow but I think I've finally figured you out."

She stepped around the bush and there it was. So much taller than she remembered and so much more angry-looking. The teeth were big, the growl was murderous and the anger rose off it like steam.

Her heart-rate immediately kicked up another gear and icy fear froze her skin. But she remembered Arthur's story about forcing himself to see the Yarnbulls for the first time - and how it was the thought of her that gave him the bravery to do it. Ever since then, they had both inspired each other to boost their nerves and find that extra scrap of bravery when they needed it. She filled her mind with Arthur now and somehow, her feet kept creeping forward, inch by inch.

"I've known for ages that I have a darkness in me. My ruthlessness. My fierceness. My single-mindedness. My whole life, I've always known that when I try to be a good person - the person I want to be - I have to constantly fight against those unsavoury parts. And now I know why - to keep from becoming the Queen."

The creature stood there, both faces fixed firmly on Teresa as she slowly advanced. It looked like it was about to attack at any moment but at the same time, she could tell it was listening to her. And she was sure it understood what she was saying.

"I've always done my best to keep those demons at bay," she continued, slowly, "but here's my problem… it's those same demons that saved me on Needleman island. My ruthlessness kept me alive. My fierceness kept you at bay. My single-mindedness thwarted you and the Needlemen. So can I really get rid of those things if they're so important?"

She took another step towards the Dog-Man. Being closer to it should have made her more scared of it, but somehow, the opposite was true.

She took another step.

"I've spent so long running and hiding from you but all that's done is make me scared. It made me fall out with Arthur. It made me think I had a real chance of becoming the Queen. But after talking with our Needleman Sheriff, of all people, I finally realised what you are."

She took a deep breath.

"You're me, aren't you?"

As soon as she said those words, both halves of the creature seemed to change, slightly. The dog's fierce features relaxed slightly and the man-creature's mouth - usually snarling with rage, softened just a little. Both their sets of legs straightened and the man stood up tall. No longer ready to pounce, they were now simply standing. It was as though the entire creature had been relieved of some burden. Like the lifting of a curse in some old fairy tale. The change confirmed to Teresa her suspicion had been correct. She was both elated to have figured it out but also terrified of what it actually meant.

"Yes, some part of me," she went on. "Something angry. Something that wants to lash out. All those dangerous parts of myself wrapped up into a physical form. And what's your purpose? To torment me? To somehow drive me into being that bad person? To scare me? Well, I'm not scared anymore. Here I am, facing you. I'm here to tell you to get lost. I'm not a bad person. I'm a good person. I will always overpower you. I will always keep you down. You will never win, never take over. You will never make me into *her*."

The man-creature, towering over her, looked down on Teresa. Even with no eyes it somehow held her fast in its gaze, even as the dog was looking up at her, doing the same. They held her like a stricken butterfly in a pincer. But as close as she was, Teresa saw something in their faces that she had never seen before. It wasn't a new expression, she realised with shock, it had always been there. She'd just been too terrified to notice. It lurked in the recesses of their eyes and the set of their mouths, and Teresa now saw it so clearly, she wondered how she'd never noticed it before.

Fear.

"Mmmm…"

Teresa froze. The noise was coming from the man-creature. It was trying to speak!

"Mmm.."

It leaned in closer to Teresa's face. The smell of despair was overpowering.

"Mmmother…"

The blood ran cold through Teresa's veins.

"Mmmother…."

Teresa shook her head. It stepped forward and this time she stepped back. "No, what are you-"

"Motherrr..." it reached a withered hand out toward her.

Suddenly the Sheriff galloped into the clearing, gun out. "Damn!" she exclaimed. "Did I miss it? Is it still here?"

Teresa stood there, staring at the Dog-Man standing right in front of her - between her and the Sheriff. It's hand was reaching out to her, still.

"Yes..." she said, eventually. "You missed it." She stared into the man's face and then the dog's eyes. "It's gone."

She turned around and headed back to her horse. Grasping the reins, she heaved herself up and swung her leg over, seating herself back in the saddle. She looked back to the spot she had just been standing in but the Dog-Man really was gone now. Except it wasn't, was it? It was right there within her and it had been all along. Except now it was speaking to her.

"Dammit..." the Sheriff sighed. "Well, worth a shot, I guess. It's late, though. Let's get back to town."

Wordlessly, the pair of them turned their horses toward Reliance and started the trip back. In the distance, the wolf-howl rose again. Teresa was no longer thinking about the creatures out there, though. And she now realised the most dangerous thing out here wasn't the Needleman riding next to her.

The most dangerous thing out here, or anywhere, was Teresa herself.

CHAPTER TWENTY-FOUR
THE JOURNAL

- TERESA -

Mother.

Teresa sat on the end of her bed, hot cup of tea in her hand, staring at nothing in particular. All she could think of was that one word.

Mother.

"Hey, are you in the room?" Seb waggled his fingers in front of her eyes.

Teresa didn't look up at him but responded. "Yes, I'm in the room. Thank you for my tea."

The room itself was located above the saloon and all the noise from downstairs rose up, unimpeded, through the floorboards. The sounds of drunken babbling, jaunty piano-playing and the clatter of occasional fights breaking out over card games could all be enjoyed from the saloon's upstairs accommodation. The rooms were quite sparse and pretty much everything was made of wood - but it contained all the furnishings a visitor to an out-of-the-way frontier town might need. A bed, a tin bath and a horizontal bar attached to the wall to hang your clothes on. Teresa decided Sally must have given her a deluxe room because she also had a table pushed up against one of the walls. It was for this reason that Seb had decided they would use Teresa's room for their little strategy meeting.

"Again, thanks for a first-class diversion," Seb said, gesturing at a pile of old, worn notebooks on the table. "Thanks to you taking that Needleman away, I was able to lift this little lot from the safe but..." The young quartermaster took a step back and looked at his companion. "I don't know what you both got up to out there but since you came back you've seemed... not quite yourself. Are you okay?"

Not quite myself, Teresa thought. That's about right. What exactly is 'myself'?

"I'm..." Teresa shook her head. What did the Dog-Man mean? Why was it saying 'mother'?

"Nope, I've lost you again," Seb said, waving his hands again. "Hello? Anybody home?"

Teresa looked up at him, this time. "Sorry, Seb. I'm here. I just had to figure some things out. I just... I really need to speak to the Dressmaker."

"Well, these journals might just hold the clues we need to track her down," he said pointing at the collection of battered books and pads on the table in front of them.

Teresa focussed on the haul for the first time since her return.

"They're all diaries?" Teresa was puzzled. "Who do they belong to?"

"Well, that's the interesting thing..."

There was a knock at the door. Teresa looked up in surprise but Seb held a hand out.

"Don't worry, I invited someone."

Seb opened the door and Joshua stepped in.

"What are you-?" Teresa stood in shock and embarrassment. The evidence of their crime was laid out all over the table and the town's deputy was standing right there, looking at it.

"Joshua, I-" Teresa didn't know what to say.

"It's okay, Seb told me everything."

Teresa turned to Seb, her confusion growing even deeper. "What..?"

Seb shrugged. "On my way back here after I left the office, I saw Joshua. My gut told me something was weird with the Sheriff keeping so many journals in her safe but I didn't know exactly why. You'd said you didn't think Joshua was a Needleman so I went with your instinct and told him about Sheriff Grace being one and what we'd done."

Joshua took over. "There's been somethin' off with her for a little while now. And actually, terrifyin' as Seb's story was, it made sense. And when he told me the names on some of the journals, that clinched it for me. Given who those books belong to, I knew I had to come because I realised this town's in even bigger trouble than I thought."

Joshua moved over to the table and started sifting through the various tattered books and notepads. He lifted them one by one, reading off the names on the cover or the first page. "Marla Crook. Anders Rykard. Ana Briggs."

Teresa glanced at the deputy. "What is it? Are they all... you know..."

"Dead? Missing?" Joshua smiled. "Nope. Marla's looking after her mother. I saw Ana in the hardware store this morning. Anders - I just passed Anders downstairs in the saloon."

Teresa was puzzled. "So what's the problem?"

"People here, on Terminus, we keep journals in the same way other people breathe. They're real important to us. There's no way Marla or Anders or Ana or anyone in this town would just leave 'em sittin' in the Sheriff's safe for no reason. Unless..."

Teresa finally saw what Joshua was getting at. "Unless, the Sheriff isn't the only Needleman in town."

"So what do you think?" Seb said. "Because I think we just found our kidnappers."

Teresa shook her head. "I'm not so sure. The Sheriff, I was talking to her while we were out and…" Teresa wasn't sure what exactly to say. "I think there's something more going on. I don't think they're regular Needlemen. Also," she pointed at the journals, "why would they be gathering up the journals? Needlemen get all your memories when they replace you. But, apparently, not these ones."

The deputy shuffled in obvious discomfort as Teresa spoke. He was clearly very uncomfortable with all this talk of Needlemen, as anyone in Arilon would be. And to hear Teresa speak so knowledgeably about them was obviously making him very nervous. Teresa ignored it and pushed on.

"I think there's something different about these Needlemen. I think they've gathered all the journals of the people they've replaced so they can use them for the same thing we want to use them for."

"To find clues as to the Dressmaker's whereabouts," Seb realised. "They're looking for her, too."

"Okay, it may only be a matter of time before the Sheriff-" Joshua stopped himself, "-I mean the Needleman figures out the journals are gone. So we'd better get reading."

"Ooh, the very reason I became a pirate," said Seb. "So I could read more."

Joshua suddenly turned to Seb. "You're a pirate?"

Seb suddenly froze, caught out by his slip, and stared the lawman in the face. "Um. No…"

"It's okay," said Joshua, holding up his hands. "I'm not going to arrest you or anything. It's just… my brother ran off and took up with pirates. We haven't spoken in a long time. We… didn't part on the best of terms."

252

"Well, wherever he is, I'm sure he's very rich by now," said Seb. "And almost certainly not doing all the reading I'm about to be doing. Anybody want a coffee? I have a feeling we're in for a long night."

Both Teresa and Joshua said they would have some and Seb headed down to the bar to acquire a pot. As the pair began to sort through the books, Joshua turned to Teresa.

"You seem to know all about Needlemen. I ain't gonna ask how, but... the Sheriff... do you know if she...?"

Teresa put a hand on the deputy's arm. "I'm pretty sure she's fine. The person getting replaced is sent to a... far away place. But I saw Sheriff Grace there and I brought her back. She's safe and being looked after by someone I trust completely. She'll be back here eventually, I promise."

The relief flooded Joshua's face and Teresa realised how much of his earlier apparent anxiety was actually worry for his boss and friend. Teresa decided not to mention the fact that, in order for the real Sheriff Grace to wake up, they would need to kill the Needleman pretending to be her. She wasn't sure it would benefit anybody for Joshua to go rushing off into a fight he would almost certainly lose - perhaps along with his life. Besides, there was something very out of the ordinary with the Needleman Sheriff and Teresa felt that she was going to be an important element in the bigger picture, somehow.

"Come on," she said, "we'd better make a start. No point waiting for Seb, he'll probably go to another island for the coffee just to get out of doing this."

In the end, Seb wasn't quite as long getting the coffee as Teresa feared. The three of them made good progress, scanning through the journals looking for any mention of the Dressmaker or Needlemen or anything out of the ordinary. It

253

didn't take the trio as long as they feared to make a breakthrough. It was less than an hour when Seb jumped out of his chair.

"Here! Got it!" he exclaimed, handing the book to Teresa, pointing to the relevant page. Teresa saw the words scribbled in elegant handwriting.

The Dressmaker came to my door.

Excitement washed over her as she flipped backwards through the pages, quickly finding the first mention of the enigmatic local celebrity. Before starting to read it, Teresa checked the diarist's name at the front of the book. "Eva Torres."

"Eva? She runs the local paper. Hell of a writer, far as I know such things. Does like to get herself into trouble to uncover a story," he smiled, sadly. "Is she gonna come back, like the Sheriff? Are all of them?"

"I think so," Teresa said. "I hope so."

Joshua nodded and gestured at the book. "So, what did Eva have to say before she was spirited away?"

Teresa cleared her throat and began to read.

12/4/27RE

My, what an odd surprise! The Blind Dressmaker came to my door in the middle of the night! She said she sneaked into town under cover of darkness - specifically to find me! Apparently, I'm one of the few people in town she can still trust. She won't explain what she means. I'm safer not knowing the details, she says. She just needs somewhere to stay for the night while she figures out her 'next move'. Like I said - odd!

But me and the Dressmaker, we go way back. We've known each other for years. She's always been very secretive about her past but I do trust her. So, of course I invited her in immediately. She seemed distressed which is most unlike her. Anything I can do to help her, I'm obviously going to do.

After I'd gotten her settled, my journalist's instinct drove me to keep pushing for details and eventually she did mention one or two little morsels. However, hearing them did make me understand why she wanted to keep the full details to herself. Even just these little bites were enough to set my nerves on edge... She mentioned that she was hunting something. Something dangerous and powerful. But it had noticed her spying on it and now the tables had turned and it was hunting her. She said I shouldn't worry none as it didn't yet know where she was.

She promised she would be gone by the time it did.

13/4/27RE

The Dressmaker spent most of the day holed up in her room, keeping out of my way. Said the less she sees me, the safer I'll be. Whatever that means!

I took her some food, which she was very grateful for, although she said she didn't need much. Apart from that, I've barely seen her.

However, there was one incident that was very strange which I had to record here. It was a moment where, I guess, it reminded me what a strange and mysterious individual my visitor is.

I was passing by her room and I heard her talking. At first, I thought she was talking to herself. Bit odd by itself, of course, but not unheard of. My Aunty Maeve used to talk to herself all the time. But then, she also used to dance around the street naked every thirtieth night so, perhaps she's not the best example I could have chosen.

I'm ashamed to say I didn't pass by as quickly as I should have and I lingered a little outside her door. Terrible of me, I know, but I blame my journalistic instincts again (they have gotten me in plenty of trouble over the years, it's true).

Standing outside the room, I quickly realised the Dressmaker wasn't talking to herself, at all. She was reading a story. Or maybe a letter? I'm not sure. From the slow and stilted way she was reciting the words, I could tell she was actually writing it as she was reading it. I could tell because I often do the same thing when I'm writing something up for the paper.

The story itself was strange - not like any story I've ever heard before. It seemed to consist entirely of a conversation.

One side of it was meant to be the Dressmaker herself, I reckon. I thought this because she was saying she couldn't talk long due to this thing that was chasing her. This method of communicating was extremely disruptive and loud and the entity was bound to notice if she went on too long.

Then there was a pause. Then I heard her talk again as she wrote the reply to her own words. The character replying said they were kind of busy fighting in Gast (which I'd heard tell was happening right now - note to self; I need to finish the piece for tomorrow's paper about the Resistance attacking Phobos).

Then she asked about the children. She wanted to know if they were in danger. She paused again, like last time, as if she was actually waiting for a response to come out of the page.

Then, wouldn't you know it, someone knocked on my door! I quickly went to go and see who it was. It was Alma. I love her and all but I'd have given everything for her not to have come along at that moment!! She started prattling on about some things she'd bought at the market and what a good deal she'd managed to get. She said she'd purchased some new garden tools from Mr. Arshavin and I could have mine back that I kindly lent her. She was going home now so I could come round and pick them up later, if I liked. I hurriedly told her yes, yes, I'd be round in a while and I shamefully admit that I closed the door before she'd finished saying goodbye. I rushed back to the corridor, stepping as quietly as I could around that stubborn, creaky floorboard.

I couldn't hear any talking anymore. She seemed to have stopped whatever she was doing. However, I did realise that there was a soft sound coming from the room.

The Dressmaker was crying.

I raised my hand to knock on the door and go in to comfort her but I felt like I'd already invaded her privacy enough. Anyway, I got the sense that she wouldn't want me to see her like that so I decided to leave her to it.

I'll cut her an extra big slice of cherry pie later.

13/4/27RE (later)

I went round to Alma's later as promised to pick up my tools. I knocked on the front door but there was no answer. I looked in the window and I couldn't see much at first. But then I saw some man in a suit. Well, I thought that was strange seeing as you don't get many suits on this island. But I looked again and the man was gone. I got to wondering if I'd just imagined him. Suddenly, the door opened and Alma was standing there. She seemed a bit odd to begin with. Her face didn't look the same. I mean, it did, but it didn't move the same as normal. Her smile was a bit crooked and Alma normally has such a wide smile. But a few seconds later, the smile was just as warm as normal. She invited me in and I got my tools after having a nice pot of coffee and a chatter, to make up for rushing her away earlier.

<u>13/4/27RE</u> (later)

I had a visit from Sheriff Grace today.

I'd managed to tempt the Dressmaker out of her room with the promise of warm cherry pie and we were having a nice chat about nothing in particular. I was just cutting the pie when there was a firm rap at the door and the Sheriff called out to announce herself. Nothing too strange in that. She's always liked to make impromptu personal visits - make sure everyone is okay and suchlike. It's one of the reasons why we've kept her on as Sheriff way longer than the rules normally allow.

The odd thing was, though, that the Dressmaker immediately hid and told me not to say she was here. Now the weird thing about that is the Dressmaker and the Sheriff have known each other donkeys years. They're real close friends. Between the two of them, they've probably helped this town more than anyone else. So, why was she hiding? I got to say, it kind of made me a bit scared myself.

I answered the door and the Sheriff told me the Dressmaker had gone missing and had I seen her? I told her I had not. I'd never lied to the Sheriff before. Well, okay, I might have told a couple of little curved truths (as my momma used to call them) in order to get access to some place for a story for the paper. But this was a barefaced lie about something real important. And I didn't even know why I was telling it.

I guess in that moment, I trusted the Dressmaker more than I did the Sheriff.

She asked me if I'd seen anything out of the ordinary at all. I said, only that new dress Mrs. Mason had decided to wear. The Sheriff laughed and admitted that she was probably going to have to arrest Mrs. Mason on account of crimes against fashion.

She advised that I keep an eye out and let her know the second anything strange happens. Then she left.

I think I just about got away with it - but you can't really ever tell with the Sheriff. She plays her cards real close to her chest, that one. Always has.

After the Sheriff went, the Dressmaker thanked me and said she would be leaving this very night rather than put me through any more strangeness or potential danger. She wouldn't tell me where she was planning on going but I got the impression it wasn't far. Assuming she's heading out of town, the most likely place would be the old Raider fort, I guess.

I insisted on giving her some fruit and some sandwiches I had made up. And I gave her the whole cherry pie, too. She thanked me profusely and then, just like that, she was gone.

As a journalist in Reliance, you don't get many strange or interesting things to report on. This last day had been among the most interesting things that had happened to me in quite some time - and I couldn't write a word about it. Maybe I need to go and talk to the Sheriff. Ask some subtle questions, see if I can dig anything up. You never know, there might be a wider story in it after all. At the very least, I'm going to have to figure out how to write a story about the Dressmaker going missing while knowing all the time that she'd already been by for a sleepover.

Yes, that's what I'll do. There's something strange going on here and the Dressmaker certainly didn't trust the Sheriff. So I think a trip over to the Sheriff's office in the morning is on the cards. See what I can dig up.

There may be a story there after all!

Teresa turned the page.

"That's the last entry," she said. "She went to see the Sheriff and whatever came back was no longer interested in making journal entries. And that was a few days ago."

"I was talking to Eva just yesterday..." said Joshua, almost to himself. His tone was fearful because he now knew that it hadn't been Eva at all.

Teresa closed the diary softly.

"No wonder the townspeople are scared," Joshua said, quietly. "They can feel somethin's wrong, just like I could with the Sheriff. Half the town's probably Needlemen."

"What was she hunting for?" Teresa wondered. "The Dressmaker, I mean."

"Something so terrible, it started hunting her back," said Seb. "Hands up who wants to mess with *that* thing."

Teresa tried and failed to suppress a shudder. The Dressmaker was certainly a capable individual from what they'd seen. Anything that could get her running for cover was something they could do with giving a wide berth.

"Still," Seb continued, "at least we know she wasn't abducted. She's at the Raider fort…"

Seb and Teresa both glanced at Joshua, since this was his neighbourhood.

"It's close by," the deputy admitted, "but do you think she'd hang around here? She seemed pretty spooked."

"Yes, and that suggests that she would have wanted to get away from here altogether," said Teresa. "But she stayed in town. That means she's trying to stay local, for some reason."

Joshua nodded, rubbing the back of his head as he ran things through his mind. "Okay, well if that's the case, the old fort's not far away. Maybe a ten minute trek up into the hills."

"I take it that's the same set of Raiders that the Rogue's Run Trio helped you get rid of?" Teresa nodded. "That would be a good shout. It's nearby, at least. But wouldn't the Needlemen have looked there for her already?"

Joshua shrugged. "Maybe. It's big but not that big. If they'd looked for her up there, I'm pretty sure they'd have found her. But if that were the case, why's the Sheriff still lookin'?"

"Maybe she's just pretending," said Seb. "To hide the fact they already found her."

Joshua shook his head. He wasn't convinced.

"There's only one way to find out," said Teresa, grabbing her shoes and beginning to pull them on.

"I know it's a short trip," said Joshua, "but I wouldn't recommend going up in those hills in the middle of the night with all the rock cats and such. It's too dangerous."

Teresa briefly looked up from her boots. "Would you say it's more or less dangerous than facing down an enraged Needleman who's just discovered someone emptied its safe?"

"Good point," Joshua clicked his fingers and pointed at Teresa.. "Middle of the night it is…"

As she tied up her laces, Teresa couldn't help but wonder - what exactly had the Dressmaker been doing? If the Needlemen were after her, why was she hanging around town? What else was hunting her aside from the Needlemen? What had she been looking for?

What on earth had she been up to since they'd last met?

CHAPTER TWENTY-FIVE

RECOLLECTION I

- THE BLIND DRESSMAKER -

"You would not believe what we went through to get here," said the feline creature at her door. The Dressmaker smiled.

"I'm sure," she said. "Please come in."

Her first meeting with the Cat and with Arthur and Teresa. This was the moment things started happening. A series of events that had led her ultimately to this present moment, sitting in the dark, waiting.

It had all started on that day.

The creature known as the Cat entered the shop along with the two Valian knights, Iakob and Iosef. Followed then by the two human children. Arthur Ness and Teresa Smith.

She saw them. Not with her eyes, of course. Her eyes had not worked since she had stopped being Elsie Smith and started being the Dressmaker. One thing she had learned over all her lives, though, was that the eyes were easily deceived. She perceived her visitors with all her remaining faculties - and due to her connection to the Threads, that included senses most people did not have. Arthur Ness, the boy who spent most of his time being mortally scared but on whose shoulders so much rested in the next few days. And then there was Teresa.

"That is one beautiful dress," the Cat said.

"It's for a wedding on Graft," replied the Dressmaker. "The lady is very excited. It's likely to be the only dress she ever wears and I want it to be extra special."

"I thought you looked after stories," said Teresa.

"I'm afraid I've been telling them a little bit about you," said the Cat.

"May I?" the Dressmaker said, reaching out to Teresa's face. The girl nodded and the Dressmaker gingerly laid her fingers on the young girl's cheeks and forehead and nose... Sadness and joy both welled up inside the Dressmaker's heart. The joy of a mother reunited with her daughter. And the sadness that comes from a sudden and solid realisation of all those lost years. Almost an entire childhood, gone. She had missed seeing the toddler, always straining to run off and see what was happening somewhere else, now grown into this beautiful girl. She could feel it all - Teresa's strength. Her determination. Her fierceness.

It had been so long since she'd been with her daughter. The last time she had touched this face, the Dressmaker had been wearing another face of her own. So much had happened.

And so much had yet to happen.

She forced herself to step away from the girl.

"I do look after stories," she said eventually. "But I'm a dressmaker by trade. I've been doing it all my life."

Not a lie. She had been a dressmaker all of her current life.

Teresa was enchanted by the dresses. Well, not so much by the actual dresses, it was clear. More by the art and craft that went into making them. She was looking at the spindle in the centre of the room. The Dressmaker encouraged Teresa to have a go. She had been reticent at first but the Dressmaker soon guided the girl into the seat. She had started smoothly enough.

"Wow, Smithy, you're a natural!" the Cat enthused.

265

"But... I don't know what colours to do," Teresa said as she worked the machine.

"Whichever ones you feel," the Dressmaker encouraged.

"But... how do I know what to feel?" she asked. Then Arthur Ness came over and rested his hand on her shoulder.

"Just relax into it. Think of home," he said.

And that moment, something had caught in the Dressmaker's gaze. Like a splinter. She wasn't sure it was there. A familiarity between the two, even though they had only just met. A bond.

What was just a suspicion suddenly became fully manifested. Teresa started again, but this time, with Arthur by her side, her natural abilities exploded ten-fold. Suddenly, she was spinning and weaving the materials with the speed and grace of a goddess of creation.

In that moment, watching her daughter bring colour and life into being, the Dressmaker felt the connection to Teresa she had hoped for when she'd encouraged her to use the spindle. But what she had not expected, had not anticipated, was the connection between Teresa and Arthur Ness. What did that mean? It was a connection that was underlined moments later when Arthur, distracted by something on the other side of the shop, wandered away from Teresa, momentarily forgetting about her. Suddenly, the tapestry the girl was weaving lost all its shape and beauty, quickly growing twisted, jagged and dark.

The Dressmaker's senses could see what had happened. Teresa had the ability to create on her own. Together with Arthur, that ability grew exponentially. But because of this, they came to depend on each other so much that when one of them was suddenly missing, that dependency led the other to falter and fall.

All of this came from the profoundly strong bond they shared. But where did that bond come from?

As the group eventually rose from the machine, the Dressmaker comforted Teresa.

"It was when you moved away..." she was saying to Arthur. "I didn't feel the same."

That's when the Dressmaker had seen that Arthur had noticed a painting of a cottage from an English village. A picture from her previous life that would mean nothing to an Arilonian visitor. But Arthur had spotted it.

"Sorry," he stammered, "I saw a... never mind... I'm sorry."

"Never mind," the Dressmaker said to Teresa. "It was your first time and I think you did splendidly."

But the event had left the Dressmaker somewhat shaken and unsure exactly what she had seen. In that moment, her eyes passed over the Cat. And one thunderbolt was quickly followed by another. Her eyes showed her nothing, of course, but her inner eye told her this was not some ordinary talking cat. She hadn't noticed it before, but in that moment, her mind shaken by the power she'd witnessed in the minds of these two human children, the Cat suddenly appeared very different indeed.

He was like an emptiness, an explosion of anti-light. He was connected to the Life Energy of Arilon but he was the opposite of everything else that was also connected to that same energy. It reminded her of only one other being that could possibly shine like that. But surely that creature was dead? The Queen had killed him.

She barely concealed a little jump of shock when she sensed that the Cat was looking right back at her.

Could he sense her secret as she had sensed his? She had seen that he was more than he seemed. Had he seen this was also true about her?

All of that had felt like hours but only a fraction of a second had passed. And in the moment that followed, the two of them looked away from each other again.

But now, it was down to business. They had come for a specific reason and she had taken the Cat and the children to her library to utilise the special story, *The Remembered Life of Hector Smith*, to help discover the secret of Waterwhistle.

Afterwards, they had come out and - looking back on it now, it seemed incredible - but they had come out without Teresa and none of them had noticed. She had forgotten Teresa had ever existed. She knew now it was because the girl had instinctively used her unbelievable power to affect the story and had temporarily ceased to exist in the real world. After the Cat, Arthur and the two Valian knights had gone on their way - all unaware they were one person light - the Dressmaker had taken out her wooden memory box. It contained a few items that she had managed to acquire from her previous life in the Human World.

She had taken out a photograph. Her previous family. Her husband, Hector, her sons Sam and Albert. It showed the family on the day of Sam's baptism, all dressed up in their Sunday best. Usually - before that day and then a few days later - it also depicted Teresa holding onto her mother's hand. Mischievous and impatient, as always. But on that day, Teresa had been missing from the photograph.

Upon Teresa's return to the picture - and to reality - a couple of days later, the Dressmaker had a lot to think about. She had seen great power in her daughter and by all accounts, the story would have swallowed her up forever if not for her

268

bond to Arthur. Their incredible connection meant some gossamer-thin thread still remained between the two, allowing her to make her way back into reality. So, she was tempted to ask who this Arthur Ness person was? But she quickly realised the pertinent question wasn't 'who is he'...

...but actually, 'who are *they?*'

The Dressmaker knew instinctively that the fate of Arilon rested on the answer to that question.

CHAPTER TWENTY-SIX
RECOLLECTION II

- THE BLIND DRESSMAKER -

In the days that followed, the Dressmaker had continued with the responsibilities of her outward appearance. She'd made dresses, she'd helped the people of Reliance with their medical issues and even delivered a baby or two. But all the while, even while working, she had reflected on the real issue at hand.

Teresa had power. Arthur had power. They shared power. They made each other more powerful. They were each other's strongest weapon but also, as shown by the loom incident, potentially each other's most crippling weakness.

But, of course, there was another big issue that had also needed answering. Fortunately, she hadn't needed to wait long for this mystery to be solved. The day after the conflict that was already being called The Battle of Eris Island, there had been a loud and enthusiastic knock on her door. Unlike her visitor's previous visit, which she had pre-read in a story, this trip had taken the Dressmaker quite by surprise.

The Dressmaker opened the door and the Cat, sitting alone on the front stoop had simply said;

"So, you're the Beginner, right?"

The Dressmaker stiffened with the shock of the directness of the question. However, she quickly gathered her wits and replied.

"And you are the Ender."

"Good," said the Cat, walking past her into the shop. "Glad we got that out of the way. Now, let's get down to business."

The Dressmaker could barely believe it.

"When you came here before, I thought I sensed something," she said, closing the door after her visitor. "But I could barely believe it."

"Well, I suppose it is difficult to mask my magnificence in the body of this tiny creature," said the Cat.

"Same old Ender," the Dressmaker smiled. "But I thought the Queen had destroyed you when she first arrived in Arilon," she said.

"Well, she gave it a good go," said the Cat.

"So, did your family also esca-"

"No," the Cat said quickly. "No, she got them."

"Oh, Ender," the Dressmaker said, "I am so sorry."

"I'm sorry too," he said. "But I'm also grateful to you. For giving me that gift. For the spark that brought them to life and gave me a family. Long, long ago you gave me that gift and the four of us shared many happy years together. But most of all, I'm determined. I'm going to rescue them from the Queen's veins and restore them to life, one day. Somehow."

The pair were silent for a moment, their thoughts stretching back over endless aeons and forward into a future they hoped to see. The Cat took a deep breath and looked up.

"So, I survived, but what about you, Beginner? Word on the grapevine was that just before coming to destroy me, she'd already managed to destroy you."

"She did destroy me," the Dressmaker shrugged. "I got better."

"Ooh, mysterious. I can appreciate that showmanship. Fine, you can keep your secrets. Okay, so we both barely survived the Queen's arrival in Arilon. The final two Pillars of Arilon are still up and running ready to put the Queen on her behind. This is good news, Beginner-baby."

"You're a tiny cat and I'm a blind dressmaker. I wouldn't say 'up and running' is the best way of putting it. Also, she still has control of our brothers, the Thinker and the Disruptor."

"Well, we're still in the fight," said the Cat. "And as long as we're in the fight, we keep swinging."

"My thoughts precisely," said the Dressmaker. "Now, let us get down to business. We have things to discuss. I want to start with Arthur Ness and Teresa Smith."

The Dressmaker maneuvered herself easily between the various obstacles in her shop and sat down at her measuring table. She gestured for the Cat to join her and he obliged by jumping up onto the table and pacing back and forth across its surface while he spoke.

"Yes, lets," he said. "I actually just got back from the Human World. I was talking to Arthur. He's visiting his house with his parents. It got destroyed by a bomb from an aeroplane. I sense I'm filling this conversation with irrelevant information, aren't I? Okay, sorry. Please, continue."

"There's a connection between the two of them," said the Dressmaker. "Teresa and Arthur."

"Well, of course there is," said the Cat. "They are twins after all."

The Dressmaker was shocked and glad she was already sitting down. "Twins? That's… that's impossible…"

"Well, they seem pretty convinced."

"But I know it's not possible."

"How?"

"Because I'm Teresa's mother. So trust me when I say, if she had a twin brother, I would definitely have noticed."

"You're… you're what…?" The Cat stopped pacing - it was his turn to be shocked. "How…?"

"Part of those mysterious secrets you mentioned. Just know that it's true. I married Hector, I had three children - Albert, Teresa and Sam. I'm sorry, but Arthur was not there."

The Cat sat down and sank into thought. The Dressmaker did the same.

Could they be twins? She remembered the power flowing between them. That would certainly begin to explain it. But it couldn't be the entire answer. Not even twin siblings would have a connection like the one they had. There had to be something more.

Besides which, how could they even be twins in the first place? Only one child had been born that day. As she'd hinted to the Cat, giving birth to additional children was something a person tended to notice. Something very, very strange was afoot.

"Whatever's going on," said the Cat eventually, "those two have immense power. Enough to destroy the Queen and the Agency Engine. I can feel it."

The Dressmaker nodded. "Yes. I feel that too."

"So the real business," said the Cat, "is how do we make that happen? Apart from anything else, war is right around the corner. Arilon is going to fall into conflict any day now, the likes of which haven't been seen for a thousand years."

"Yes, the Idea Wars. It was bad last time and now Arilon's technology has increased, their weapons will be all the more devastating. You and I need to get to work - and quickly," said the Dressmaker. "We must find the Queen's weakness, figure out how to exploit it. And…"

The Cat nodded. "Yes. And point Arthur and Teresa at her and pull the trigger. I don't like it, either. Treating them like weapons."

"She's my daughter," said the Dressmaker. "And Arthur… it seems Arthur might be my son, though I have no idea how. I want to hold them and love them as a mother should. But my responsibility is also to Arilon. The world we created - the Thinker, the Disruptor, you and I. It has to be saved. Not to mention the Queen's inevitable follow-up target… the Human World."

She thought of Hector, her husband. The man she had loved in another life.

"So, you and I will work together," she said. "We will find her weak spot. We will find the Agency Engine. And we will destroy them both."

"You know…" the Cat said, thoughtfully, "the war may be a good thing. War has a way of highlighting weaknesses in one's enemies."

"It also has a way of ending the lives of millions of people," the Dressmaker warned.

"Well, I'm the Ender. Overseeing the end of things is my job. *But-*" the Cat held up a paw at the Dressmaker's sudden glance, "only at the proper time. I will fight tooth and claw to protect lives, you know that. I've certainly been doing that with Smithy and Arthur. Used up two of my lives saving them, not bragging, just saying."

"You… you care for them, don't you?"

The Cat stared into the Dressmaker's unseeing eyes. "As if they were my own lost children."

"Then, I need you to make me a promise, Ender. Do not bring them back to Arilon. Not until we are ready for them to strike."

"But… they've only been home five minutes and they're already desperate to return. Plus, I think there might be a problem with Teresa. I'm not sure what exactly, but…"

"They cannot be here!" The Dressmaker insisted, rising from her seat. "I will not have them in Arilon while this war is raging. On top of that, the Queen will sense their power if they are here. And we know she will not stop until she has destroyed any potential threat to her plans. They stay at home, do you understand me? Until I tell you to fetch them."

"Don't you want to see them?"

"How can you ask me that? Of course I do! But my feelings do not count! Neither do theirs! Not against the might of the enemy we face!"

The Cat nodded, admitting defeat. "Yes, I know. You're right. If we fail, all of Arilon will be forfeit. To creatures such as we, duty must always come first. So has it been since the very beginning."

"I am sorry about your family," said the Dressmaker. "But like me, you won't get to properly reunite with them until this is all over."

The Cat took a deep breath then nodded, continuing. "Fine. We'll do all the groundwork - locate the Agency Engine, work out how to strike at the Queen. Then when you're ready, I'll bring Teresa and Arthur back."

"Thank you," she said.

And that was how her partnership with the Ender had been resurrected. As the war blossomed and spread, the pair of them had met whenever possible to further their investigations. They had embarked on many missions to uncover yet more truths about the Queen and the Agency Engine.

But the entire time, the Dressmaker had simply wanted to hold her children and her husband.

CHAPTER TWENTY-SEVEN
RECOLLECTION III

- THE BLIND DRESSMAKER -

The war marched on, tearing through lives and homes and everything. The royal forces gained the upper hand, then the Arilon People's Army. Then the royals again. And all the while, people died and died and died. And all the while, the Beginner and the Ender worked.

The two Pillars of Arilon toiled endlessly, their immortal endurance put to the test. They searched tirelessly for a way to defeat the Queen. They unearthed historical texts, hoping for some clue to her origin or the source of her power. They travelled to far-flung corners of Arilon to acquire potentially crucial artifacts. They spied. They infiltrated. All they needed was one tiny chink in the Queen's armour. One small weakness. One unguarded blind spot.

But fate was not with them on their journey. Every time they were about to get their hands on something important, it was snatched away at the last moment. Each time they managed to attain some crucial piece of information, it turned out not to be the silver bullet they'd hoped for.

For the most part, the only things they discovered for sure were exactly the things they already knew - the Queen was powerful, cruel and unstoppable.

However, one day, fate, providence and the Threads smiled upon the pair's endeavours. The Cat's network of spies eventually turned up an item that would finally prove to be the game-changer they were looking for. At first, it seemed to be no more than a fable. A myth. But with extra digging and investigation, the truth behind the stories was unearthed. It was confirmed that indeed, this item was real.

"It's called the Fourth Treasure," the Cat proclaimed to the Blind Dressmer, proudly. "And it's the key to destroying the Queen."

The Dressmaker raised an eyebrow. "*Fourth* treasure?" she asked, sarcastically. "Is it not as good as the first three?"

"I don't know how it got its name," the Cat shrugged. "Maybe somebody thought it sounded cool. The point is, it's something that the Queen keeps heavily guarded under lock and key and it's rumoured to have immense power over her."

"Then we need to get our hands on it."

"I already have a group of people tracking it down. If it really exists and isn't just a late-night campfire story, they'll find it. And they'll steal it."

"Sounds like the Rogue's Run Trio," the Dressmaker joked, returning to her papers.

"That's because it's the Rogue's Run Trio," the Cat replied.

The months passed. The war had continued and the work had continued. As the conflict entered its second year, the intensity of the fighting grew and the Pillars began to find it increasingly difficult to meet. The Cat would send the Dressmaker coded letters to update her on the Rogue's Run Trio's progress. But as their other avenues of investigation began to close off and their ability to meet and discuss things was hampered by the war, the hunt for the Fourth Treasure began to turn into a basket that was definitely holding all their eggs.

In an attempt to uncover any other scraps of information about the Queen that might help them, the Dressmaker had been scouring the books in her library.

The back room of the Dressmaker's shop was no normal room. When she'd started this new life, she'd chosen this spot to build her shop because it sat on a Convergence Point. These were extremely rare places where the Threads joined together to form a junction node. From here, communion with the Threads - and the ability to peer into the past, present and future - was significantly more effective. For a person who already had the power to access the Threads, a Convergence Point was a place of massive power and potential.

The Dressmaker had placed the back room over the exact spot and, in conjunction with her own considerable abilities - reduced as they were after her defeat by the Queen - she had created a library like no other.

The books on her shelves came and went, seemingly of their own accord. The room was directly linked to the stream of life energy the Threads carried and it was this stream that brought the books into the room and swept them away again. Sometimes there were a great number of books present at once and other times, only a few. The room would change size, making itself larger or smaller to accommodate the current stock. The waters of Arilon's very soul flowed through every shelf, bringing with them the endless stories that floated around the world - stories that were designed for everyone and stories that were designed for specific people. The remembered and the long forgotten. The real and the fictional. Books that people had written and books that the Threads themselves had constructed. Stories from the past, stories that were taking place right now - and, occasionally, stories that had not yet happened. Every tale in an endless ocean of tales.

It was through these endless tomes that the Dressmaker scoured the minds, people, lives and events of Arilon - past, present and occasionally future - to try and find any and all information about the Queen she could lay her hands on.

Through meditation, the Dressmaker could let the Threads know her needs and induce them to bring forward a book that would help her meet those needs. Alternatively, she could go looking for specific stories she already knew about. However, even without her conscious intervention, the stream of life energy would constantly bring books of all kinds. Occasionally, the tide would wash up something the Dressmaker didn't even know she needed until she saw it.

It was one of these that, one day, provided the Dressmaker with a very unexpected piece of information.

Frankenstein by Mary Shelley.

She had removed it from the shelf in bewilderment. In her previous life as Elsie Smith, she had loved this book. It was rare that a book from the Human World appeared on her shelves, so the Dressmaker knew it must have been there for a specific, important reason. But what reason could it possibly be?

Deciding to put the 'whys' aside for a while, the Dressmaker had settled down that evening and read the book in a single sitting, losing herself once more in its exquisite pages. A reminder of the life and the world she missed so much but also a fascinating story. The story of a monster who killed and destroyed. Because it was evil? No. Because it was driven. Driven by the ideas it had obtained from its experiences in the often cruel world around it but mostly from its creator, Victor Frankenstein. History remembered the monster but never the being who created the monster.

And it was that moment - as the Dressmaker had closed the final page - that she had realised what the Threads were trying to tell her by bringing this book.

The Queen was not the ultimate enemy.

The revelation had stunned the Dressmaker. All this time, they had been focussed on their super-powerful aggressor but now there was the suggestion that there was something else. Something or someone driving her. Possibly, it was even responsible for her creation.

All of a sudden, the Dressmaker saw that she and the Cat faced a new danger. Something insidious and even more powerful than the Queen. She had to inform her fellow Pillar, immediately. But if it really was so powerful that it had taken this long for the Threads to be able to detect it and alert her, the Dressmaker knew she couldn't just write about it in a letter. Such a creature would have eyes and ears everywhere. It clearly put great store in remaining hidden in the shadows, undetected. Surely, it would be on the lookout for anything that mentioned its presence. No, writing to the Cat was out of the question. She would have to wait for him to return to her door.

In the meantime, she had to search for this entity. Find out anything she could about it. Perhaps the best way to destroy the Queen was, in fact, to take on this being. The Dressmaker meditated with the Threads, communing with Arilon's life force, probing the probabilities, possibilities and certainties. She searched hard for some tiny scrap of information - any clue or evidence that gave away this entity's presence. She trod carefully, as if stepping through the woods, tracking a tiger that was somewhere ahead, hidden in the dark. She had to step lightly, try not to make a sound, not even the snapping of a twig. The tiger didn't know she was onto it but the slightest mistake could turn her from hunter to hunted in an instant. She reached out through the life force, trying to find the slightest ripples that betrayed the being's presence, while also trying to avoid making any splashes of her own.

Eventually, after several days of hunting, she had opened her eyes to find a new book on her shelf, directly in front of her. It had no title on the spine and she'd picked it up with anxious trepidation. Slowly, she'd opened it up and turned to the first page. There were no words, just a drawing. A picture of a child's doll, lying on a table, its head turned slightly away and looking upwards. She turned to the next page. The same picture. The next page. The same picture again. The page after that, the picture was unchanged. Wondering at the purpose of the book, the Dressmaker had flicked patiently through every single page, looking at the same image. She eventually turned the final page to see the doll's face was now turned and looking at her.

She had immediately slammed the book shut.

No.

It had seen her.

And now, it would be coming for her.

The Dressmaker knew she had to move fast. This thing of immense power would be moving in her direction even now, this very moment. Slithering through the Threads towards her, trying to track her down. She had to leave the shop, leave Reliance. Leave the island altogether. Tonight.

She'd immediately packed some things, her clothes, her little wooden box of past-life mementoes. Quickly running to the library, she'd run her fingers over the book-spines, scanning the shelves for any last books she would need to continue her work. And it was at that moment that the library had presented her with one final gift. It was a thin book, evidently for young children. On the cover was a child's painting of a corridor - one that looked strangely familiar to the Dressmaker. It had warm beige walls with dark brown doors along it. There was a wheelchair parked to one side containing a smiling woman with a big tummy. The title was written in large, yellow, child's handwriting across the top.

Mummy's Trip to the Hospital.

Straight away, it had come to her. This was a corridor in the hospital she'd gone to in Nottingham, to give birth to Teresa. Well - she reminded herself - Teresa and, somehow, also Arthur. Quickly flipping through it, she'd seen that it was in two parts. The first part told a story of the Dressmaker seeing Arthur and Teresa here on Terminus, soon.

The Dressmaker had been shocked. Her children were back in Arilon? But the Cat had promised to keep them away..!

Her plans had needed to change, then. She had to stay on the island. But she needed to keep out of sight. She didn't know who might be an agent of the entity that was now hunting her. She had sensed something wasn't quite right with the Sheriff - might she be one of its eyes? It didn't matter, she would find someone she could trust.

The story told the future and that was rare indeed. The future was hard to see but it was just as fixed as the past. As long as you couldn't see it, you could imagine many possibilities - but once you became aware of what the future held, then there was no more 'perhaps' about it. This was what was going to happen. It was possible to try to change things but such activity was extremely dangerous and best avoided, even by one as powerful as she. Besides, this was a future she didn't want to change. As anxious as she was that her children were in harm's way, she was also excited at the prospect of seeing them again. Maybe even holding them.

282

Gathering up everything she needed into a single bag, the Dressmaker took one last look around her at her shop and home. She was possibly never going to return here and the thought made her sad. It had provided a place of stability and recovery after the trauma of her exit from the Human World. It seemed as though every time she grew comfortable in a place, she was destined to leave it.

But leave it, she would. She'd needed to find someone she trusted to help her, just for a night while she figured out a more permanent hiding place. Ordinarily, this would be pretty much anyone in Reliance. However, lately, the Dressmaker had started to get the feeling that something was a bit off with some of the townsfolk. On reflection, and combined with this latest discovery, the chilling possibility was emerging that her town was in fact being infiltrated by Needlemen. But the unsettling feeling had been happening for some time and entity had only just discovered her - could they really be linked? Or were there two sinister but separate events happening at the same time in this backwater place?

Either way, the Dressmaker had been aware of the need to pick her allies carefully. She needed someone discreet and trustworthy. She knew of one person who definitely fell into that category. Eva Torres, Reliance's only journalist. She was fearless and intrepid - too much for her own good, sometimes. But she was also kind and selfless. She had been to the shop earlier in the day and the Dressmaker had felt nothing but the woman's usual beams of truth and intelligence. Ideally, she had wanted to keep this potential danger away from everyone in town. But she'd needed help, if only for a short while and she hoped Eva would be kind enough to give it.

The Dressmaker recalled how quickly and without hesitation the journalist had agreed to help her friend, despite her appearing in the middle of the night (or, possibly, because of it - she was a journalist after all, with a journalist's nose for an interesting story).

While staying there and figuring out the best place locally she could hide for the next few days, the Dressmaker had decided she needed to alert the Cat to the presence of the entity. It had felt indescribably old and powerful and if anything happened to her, someone else needed to be aware of its existence.

Unfortunately, time was short and her options for communication were limited. Desperation had dictated an unconventional approach. It would get her in immediate communication with the Cat but it involved manipulating the Threads in a highly disruptive and even damaging manner. It was something she would normally avoid purely out of respect for the Threads and the life force that underpinned Arilon's existence. However, now the approach carried an added danger - it would potentially highlight her location to this entity. She could tell it was strongly embedded in the Threads just like herself and the Cat. It was a shark in the water and, by carrying out her plan, she would be making lots of splashes that could attract its attention to her location. The Queen might even feel ripples, drawing her here.

But desperation had robbed her of any other choice.

With a notebook and a pot of ink in front of her and a pen in her hand, the Dressmaker had entered a state of deep meditation. Very quickly, she sank her mind into the middle of the world's underlayer. The regular world was brick and stone and water and air - the Threads moved through all this and influenced it. But down here, where she now floated, was pure energy. Nothing but information and probability swirling back and forth in an endless sea of creation and destruction. This was the Threads at their purest.

As creators of Arilon, herself and the Ender had cooked up this soup of existence - along with the Thinker and Disruptor, of course, whom the Queen had enslaved. Even now, she could feel the darkness of her brothers' current prison and the guilt she felt whenever she thought about what she and the Ender had done to them at the end of the Idea Wars. But, despite the quartet's initial belief that only the four of them would ever be able to reach this place, other beings of great power - such as the Queen and this new entity - had begun to appear in Arilon and they all had the skills to get here, even if they didn't yet know it. She would need to work quickly to avoid detection.

Her mind firmly situated in the under-layer of the Threads, the Dressmaker had moved her inkpen over the page, speaking aloud as she wrote the words to help focus the raw power she was channelling.

"Cat, please hear me."

She'd waited for what felt like an eternity. Would the entity detect her right away? Would her plan fail even before it had a chance to begin. After a brief but fraught pause, she felt the ripples of a reply brush her mind, guiding her pen as it wrote down the response to her entreaty;

"Well, aren't you the naughty one, using this method? It's a good thing we don't have bosses or we'd definitely be getting a stern telling off for this. What's so urgent? I'm kind of in the middle of a massive fight but I can make a few moments for you."

Even in the beginning, during the Creation, the Ender had possessed the capacity to annoy and entertain in equal measure.

"Apparently my children are in Arilon, despite my wishes and your promises. Are they in danger?"

"To be honest, when are they not in danger? Sorry, perhaps not the best way to put your mind at ease. I am sorry but it couldn't be avoided. But safe to say they're well away from Phobos which is about the worst place to be in Arilon right now. I haven't seen battles like this since- *what was that?*"

The Dressmaker had felt it too.

They were supposed to be alone but something in the underlayer had moved.

"It's what I am here to tell you. There is an entity out there somewhere. It is the Queen's master."

No words came back from the Ender but she'd felt his extreme alarm.

"I do not know its nature or its name," the Dressmaker wrote, "but it knows of me and perhaps it knows where I am. Be warned, Ender. I believe it is our true enemy. I do not know if I will be able to keep my children safe if it comes for me. You must-"

"They have performed feats of bravery and power that will live long in the history of Arilon, Beginner. But they are still children and I will continue to protect them with however many lives I have left."

"Thank you Ender, I know you-"

The thing in the Threads had moved again, with alarming speed and savagery - both the Cat and the Dressmaker had instantly broken the connection and leapt out of the cosmic water and back into their own heads.

An intense rush of dread had immediately swept over the Dressmaker - not for herself or for Arilon, but for her children. Because of her, they had been drawn into the orbits of beings as savage as the Queen and this entity. It was her job to keep them out of danger yet all she had done was bring them into a conflict they had no knowledge of or defence against. On top of this, events continually conspired to keep her from them, unable to offer any protection or comfort. What kind of a mother was she that could bring life to an entire world but not look after her own children?

Dread had immediately turned to sorrow and for a time, all she could do was weep.

Now, sitting in the near-dark of her current hiding place, she did her best to hold back that sorrow. The tiny room that had been her home for the last several days was completely bare. In the centre was a staircase leading down to prison cells, carved into the solid earth. Her only connection to the outside world was through the metal door in front of her. She had locked it tight but it would be through that door that she would have to pass in order to see her children.

She needed to remain clear-headed and prepared. She could feel that the time foretold in the story was drawing near. Soon Teresa and Arthur would be here. She didn't know the details or what would happen. Her dearest wish was that she would be able to grab them close and never let them go, but the Threads were drip-feeding her a disturbing sense of unease. She very much doubted events were going to be so joyful.

Her head jerked up. That sound! Was it-

Silently, the Dressmaker crept to the door and placed her ear against the cold metal.

Teresa!

She was with two others. Male. But not Arthur. Where was he? The story was very specific - she would see them both together. Predictions of the future that were not followed often resulted in bad consequences as the Threads pushed back against the unnatural corruption of the timestream. The Dressmaker had to make sure the story happened as close as possible to how it was written. So, if there was no Arthur, despite her desire to immediately open the door...

...she had to wait.

CHAPTER TWENTY-EIGHT
THE MEETING

- SHERIFF GRACE -

She almost hadn't come back to the office tonight.

The Needleman with Sheriff Grace's face looked into the empty safe and thought to herself, she almost hadn't come back. She'd been so tired after the day's events, she'd planned to get home, have a quick drink and hit the hay. She'd managed to have the drink and collapse into her old, creaky, wooden bed. She'd been lying, fully clothed, too tired to even get changed, staring at the ceiling. Something had been gnawing at her but she hadn't been able to put a finger on it.

Until, suddenly, she had.

She was distracting me.

Teresa. When she'd met her standing outside the Sheriff's Office. There'd been something odd about her being there, despite her story of wanting to check up on the hunt for the Dressmaker. It had been in her expressions, her body language. The observation instincts stolen from the real Sheriff Grace had been screaming out, trying to make themselves heard. But Teresa's plan to go out into the darkness, hunting for these mysterious Dog-Men... that had been too interesting a prospect. So they'd gone and the Sheriff's instincts had been ignored.

But lying in her bed in the dark, the Sheriff had suddenly realised what her borrowed instincts had been trying to tell her.

She'd sprung up and had hurriedly started jamming her feet into her boots. Giving up after the first boot, she'd grabbed the other one, her gun holster and hat and flew from the room. She'd run across the town, hopping across the dark main street while she scrambled the other boot on before bursting into her office.

Her fears had been realised when she'd found the front door was unlocked. Things hadn't improved when she'd gone inside, checked the safe and found all the journals gone.

"Blast!" she yelled, frustration exploding out of her as she smashed a fist into the coffee cup sitting on her desk. The tin cup flew through the air, slamming into the wall by the door with a dull clang. It rebounded and zinged across the open doorway, narrowly missing the blonde-haired head of the woman suddenly standing there.

"I take it from the flying kitchenware that the journals have gone?" said Miss Sally as she stepped inside the cabin. The Sheriff looked up in surprise at her visitor and saw the saloon owner wasn't alone. Several of the others had come too. Mr. Prenderghast from the hardware store. Ozzie the blacksmith. Most of the Mormot family. A couple more.

"Sally? What are you doing here?"

"A few of us felt your distress a few minutes ago," said the saloon owner. "We came to see what was wrong."

Sheriff Grace took a deep breath, her eyes closed for a moment. When she opened them again, she was back to business. Back in control.

"I think it was the child. Teresa. Her and the young pirate," she said. "Don't worry. I'll get the journals back."

"I don't think that'll be necessary," said Sally retrieving the tin cup from the floor. "We already got everything we could out of them. Plus, I think Teresa must have already read them - Ozzie saw her, the pirate and your deputy heading up into the hills."

The Sheriff took off her hat and ran her fingers through her hair in frustration. "So not only does she know for sure there are Needlemen in the town, she's figured out where the Dressmaker's probably holed up."

Sally stepped forward and put the cup back on Sheriff Grace's desk. "But think about it. We came to Reliance because we sensed that the Dressmaker would bring to us the one we're after. That's why we didn't look too closely up in the fort. We don't need her but we do need her to be nearby - to bring us the one we really want."

"When the Dressmaker disappeared," said Ozzie the blacksmith, "we thought we'd lost the link to our true target. But we needn't have worried. Our target showed up to see the Dressmaker, just like we predicted."

The Sheriff shook her head. "Teresa? You think she's the one? The one we've been after?"

"We felt your thoughts after you spent time with her earlier," said Miss Sally, nodding. "Yeah, we think she's the one. We're going up to the fort now. All of us."

"What?" Things seemed to be moving fast all of a sudden. "Right now?"

"No time like the present," Miss Sally smiled. "I think you should stay here, though. This entity that Eva said the Dressmaker had found... I think we all know who that is. It's doubtful we're gonna get a personal visit but..."

"You want someone to keep an eye on things 'til you get back." The Sheriff removed her hat, placed it on her desk and sighed. "Makes sense. Okay. Okay, sure."

Sally smiled and the group turned to go.

"Be careful, Sally," the Sheriff said, quickly. "I got a bad feelin' about that fort."

Miss Sally stepped forward and reached out, putting a comforting hand on the Sheriff's shoulder. "We will. Don't worry, Bea. Our torment's nearly over."

The Needleman that wore the body of Sheriff Beatrice Grace nodded to the Needleman that wore the body of saloon owner Sally Powell.

And then the group was gone, soon to be joined by the other few dozen townsfolk that had been replaced. The Sheriff looked over at the empty safe.

"I hope you really are the one, Teresa," she said to herself. "And I hope you know what you're doin'."

CHAPTER TWENTY-NINE
THE FORT

- TERESA -

The old fort loomed into view, its silhouette somehow absorbing all the darkness from the night sky around it.

"Are we finally here?" Seb sighed. "We've been wilderness hiking for hours!"

"It was a ten minute walk," Teresa said. "And there was a path."

"I thought you were a big, tough pirate," Joshua glanced across at Seb, half a smile on his lips.

"I don't know if a cowboy quite understands the basics of piracy," Seb retorted, "but it tends to take place on-board a vessel. Either in the water or up in the Black. Give me a deck and some sails any day over all this..." he wrinkled his nose, distastefully, "...*nature.*"

"Boys, focus," Teresa said, even though one of the 'boys' was a fully grown man. "We don't know what might be waiting for us up here."

Night-time in Arilon was always so dark, Teresa thought. The NothingSpace closed in like a fist and the only real source of light - the Arilon sun - was nowhere to be seen. She'd learned that the islands moved. Somehow, even though they were all attached to each other, the entire system slid and spun, making the sun always above some islands and below others. At night, you could see the pinprick lights of islands or Travel Line junction points if there were any nearby.

Terminus wasn't really near any other islands, so when night fell here, it was like having a sack thrown over your head.

In the town, you had the streetlights. But up here in the hills, there was nothing.

Only darkness waited for them up here.

"You think anyone saw us leave?" Seb wondered aloud.

"Possibly," said Joshua. "People work real hard in Reliance. Aside from the odd blowout in the saloon, people go to sleep pretty early and sleep pretty heavy. But... there's always the chance that someone might be up and about."

"And if that someone happens to be a Needleman," said Teresa, "then we'll find our time and options getting really limited really quickly. Come on, let's get inside that thing."

As the group drew closer, the building's details started to become more visible. It was made of a white stone, similar to the giant boulders that peppered the hillside. Parts of the building had crumbled away but rather than make it look fragile, it just gave the impression of something that had taken everything the years had thrown at it and was still standing tall. It almost didn't look man-made at all, Teresa thought. Although it was all straight edges, it still had the feel of something that had somehow grown itself out of the rocky ground.

"Wow," Teresa said softly. "It looks really old."

"Back during the Idea Wars, it wasn't just island against island," said Joshua. "People within the islands fought against each other too. In this part of Terminus, the Devans and the Cranes fought for a real long time. This here fort's one of the Devans' places. In fact, I think the Raiders that used to live here and give the town such a hard time might have been some leftover scrap of the Devan family."

"Well, the Dressmaker sure has a taste for the classy accommodation," Seb said, sarcastically as they approached the entrance. Despite his sarcasm, Teresa suspected that Seb
294

probably liked places like this - old buildings probably had the potential for buried treasure.

Joshua removed his backpack and took out the two wooden torches they'd brought with them. Seb and Teresa unwrapped the cloth from the fuel-soaked end of each baton while Joshua produced a lighter and proceeded to ignite both torches. He took one and Teresa kept hold of the other.

The doorway was tiny for such a large building. The original door had rotted away centuries ago but the Raiders had fitted a new one which was unlocked and Seb pulled it open for the group to enter. Teresa went first, followed by Seb while Joshua, at his own insistence, covered the party's rear. The doorway was only wide enough to let one person through at a time but once they were inside, the space opened up slightly, though it was still quite claustrophobic.

With an impatient determination, Teresa led them into the corridor, plunging into the depths of the building. It was mostly a straight line but it did weave left and right ever so slightly so that you couldn't really see more than a few meters ahead at any point. As the trio progressed, they saw doorways scattered intermittently on both sides. A few of them had new doors fitted but most were just gaping holes to other rooms or else corridors that branched off into the darkness. The flickering light from the torches made the empty doorways dance and the three explorer's shadows stretched out along the floor, long and thin. Gripping her bow, Teresa had the distinct feeling of being back in the ice forest.

"Some of the rooms that come off the passageways are quite big," Joshua explained, whispering in the darkness, "but the passageways themselves are purposefully narrow. Makes the fort easier to defend from attackers."

As the trio walked down the ancient stone corridor, they ducked into each doorway they came across and checked out the room it led to for any sign of the Dressmaker. To avoid getting lost, they decided to stick to the main corridor for the time being and not follow any branching passageways. Unfortunately, the most they found in any of the rooms were remnants of the Raiders' time there - tin plates, abandoned beds and empty bottles of whiskey.

"These rooms are all too exposed for anyone to hide in," Seb said. "I think if the Dressmaker's here, she would have needed somewhere better to conceal herself. Like a room with an actual lockable-"

He didn't get the chance to finish his sentence before the corridor came to a sudden stop in the form of a small, metal door.

"Wow," Seb nodded, "talk about wish fulfillment."

"Secure-looking thing like that," Joshua said, holding his torch high, "probably leads to the cells, I'd say."

Seb cast a thief's eye over the door. "There's no bolt on this side. Not even a handle. You can see there used to be one but it probably fell off ages ago." He tried to force his fingers around the edge of the door but there was hardly any purchase to be had. He grunted as he pulled against it but the door didn't budge an inch. "Feels rusted shut. Probably hasn't been opened in decades."

Handing her torch to Seb, Teresa stepped forward and touched the metal door. Something warm seemed to vibrate into her fingers.

"She's in here," Teresa breathed softly, her heart beginning to race. "She's on the other side of this door."

"You sure?" Joshua said, sceptically.

"Dressmaker!" Teresa shouted, suddenly. "Dressmaker, it's me! Teresa! Come on out, I need to speak to you!"

There was no sound except the vanishing echo of Teresa's voice. She banged a desperate fist on the door.

"Open up, please! I know you're in there, why won't you-"

"*Teresa!*" Joshua's voice was so uncharacteristically filled with terror that it immediately snapped Teresa's attention back to him. His face was a picture of pure horror and before she turned to see what he was looking at, she already knew what she would see.

The narrow corridor was filled with Needlemen.

Seb drew his sword and Joshua - fighting his fear at the sight of every Arilonian's nightmare - drew his pistol and aimed it at the dark sea of suits and hats in front of him.

"Teresa Smith," one of the Needleman, standing front and centre, spoke in that cold, even, near-monotone voice. Teresa was well used to hearing it - and she even had the memory of speaking in that way, briefly, back on the island. But no matter your familiarity with Needlemen, Teresa knew, they always terrified you.

"What do you want?" Teresa forced herself to step forward, through her fear.

"We have come for you," said the lead Needleman. "Mother."

The word struck Teresa like a speeding train. "What...?"

The Needleman's hand reached out toward her and the others followed. "Mother." It repeated. The others suddenly came alive in an overlapping sea of voices as the entire group began to slowly step towards Teresa.

"MotMOTHERherMotherMoMOTHERherMotherM OTHERtherMoMOTHERtherMother...."

297

Teresa was totally frozen in shock.

She could hear Seb and Joshua, their weapons out, shouting at her, asking what was going on, what should they do. But their voices were muffled, as if she was under water, drowning. This was just like the Dog-Man earlier. Just like-

Suddenly, it all made sense. Teresa saw what was happening. Where the Needlemen really came from. What they really were.

There was a massive explosion at the far end of the corridor.

The corridor shook and Teresa snapped back into the moment. Sound was no longer muffled, but sharp and piercing. The Needlemen's demeanour changed in a terrifying instant. But for once, the terror wasn't being dealt out by them - it was being *felt* by them.

There was another blast and this time, Teresa could hear the unmistakable sound of Needlemen at the far end of the corridor being blasted into nothingness.

"What was that?" Joshua said. The Needlemen closest to him were beginning to turn to face this new threat coming from the rear of their ranks.

"Salvation," grinned Teresa, power beginning to run across her fingertips.

The explosions came rapidly now, like someone banging on a big, loud kettle-drum with strength and power. The Needlemen near Teresa turned to face this new threat and confidence surged into her limbs.

"Now you guys are in for it!" she cried as she began to attack the creatures from her end of the corridor, pinning them between herself and her brother. "You're facing the dream team, now!"

Needlemen were being flung and destroyed in the distance and Teresa's grin grew wider as she did the same to the ones in front of her. Her strikes of energy blew them into clouds of black ribbon that dissolved into nothingness as they slowly fell to the ground. The numbers dwindled as her other half came toward her. She was overjoyed. He'd come back to her in her darkest moment. No matter the circumstances of their separation, they were always going to come together again.

The last Needleman fell and her twin strode out of the darkness.

"Hello, Teresa," said the Queen.

CHAPTER THIRTY
THE MIRROR

- TERESA -

In the space of a single moment, everything had gone a thousand times worse.

Teresa could not tear her eyes away from the dark, sparkling figure in front of her. It was like her entire field of vision was filled with the monarch. This was how the Queen worked, Teresa knew. Something about her drew your entire attention in like a magnet. Partially, you were entranced by her beauty, and partially you were terrified that if you looked away, that would be the moment she destroyed you.

Seb and Joshua were transfixed - paralysed with terror. In the chaos with the Needlemen, they had both dropped their torches and the flaming batons lay on the ground, lighting the Queen from below, making her look even more sinister.

Teresa could feel the fear rising up off her partners like steam. She herself was scared but not in the same way. Rather than being scared of what the Queen might do to her as they were, Teresa was scared of what she herself would do to everyone else if she ever *became* the Queen. And what other reason could the Queen have for coming here, if not to try once again to convince Teresa to join her party.

"You don't give up, do you?" Teresa said through gritted teeth, trying hard to keep her nerve.

"I am only as relentless as history," the Queen said, slowly, calmly, without a hint of being in a rush. "Is it my fault history is on my side?"

"Nobody wants a Queen that would kill her own subjects," Teresa said.

"You mean the Needlemen?" the Queen seemed mildly amused. "These ones were broken."

Casually, just like that. Teresa was horrified. It was just like when the evil monarch had killed the Painted Ones and Primacy soldiers on Oblivia. It was nothing to her.

"You're a monster," she said, "to kill them like that."

"You defend the Needlemen?"

"No! I..." Teresa stumbled.

"Were you not also killing them just now?"

"Only in self-defence! They were attacking me!"

The Queen held Teresa's gaze. "Were they?"

"Yes, they-" but the words died in Teresa's throat as the memories of the last few seconds came back to her. No... they had not actually been attacking her. They'd been coming towards her, which was of course terrifying, but... but nothing else. Their facial expressions had not been hostile. More... longing? Desperate, even? And when the Queen had attacked, Teresa had assumed it was Arthur and so had joined in. But she realised with horror, now the heat of battle was over, that the Needlemen near her were actually facing the Queen - the true threat. In a wave of sickening realisation, it came to her that she had destroyed them while their backs were turned.

On top of this, she remembered what she had realised about the creatures - what they really were. And the idea of attacking them at all suddenly made her feel quite ill.

"How can you do that to them?" Teresa said. "Knowing what they are?"

The Queen's eyebrows furrowed slightly. "What do you mean?"

Teresa was shocked. The Queen didn't know what Teresa was talking about. Was it a trick, Teresa thought? But no, she could see it in the monarch's empty eyes. She was genuinely unaware of the Needlemen's true nature. But how could that be when Teresa herself had already figured it out? Wasn't the Queen a future version of her?

"I am here because it is time," the Queen said, dismissing Teresa's remark. "The Threads pointed to this moment. They told me you are ready to come with me now."

Teresa felt a tugging. Something wanted her to go with the Queen. Something deep inside, like a snake living in her heart. An evil thing made up of all her bad parts. Her impatience, her fierce, single-minded ruthlessness. The things that had made her cut down Needlemen with their backs to her. She realised with horror that one of them had probably been Sheriff Grace. At that thought, the snake in her heart seemed to grow in power. She should go with the Queen, she thought. She doesn't deserve anything else.

But with a mighty effort, she pushed down on the serpent and slammed the door on it.

"No! I told you before and I will tell you now - I will *never* join you!"

For a brief flicker of a moment, the Queen seemed genuinely taken aback. Shocked, puzzled, surprised - Teresa could see she had not been expecting that reply. She felt a glimmer of satisfaction at the Queen's momentary disarray.

But, unfortunately, it was only momentary.

Slowly, the Queen reached into the depths of her robes and produced an item that glinted and shone in the flickering gloom. Teresa gasped as she recognised it.

"I see you remember this," the Queen smiled. "My mirror. The one that Lady Eris induced your brother into stealing. The one you used to show your fellow villagers in Waterwhistle that they had nothing to fear but fear itself."

Seeing the item instantly took Teresa back. In her mind's eye, she was inside the story - *The Forgotten History of Hector Smith*. Without really understanding how or knowing exactly what she was doing, she had used the mirror to beat back the Needlemen that had been stalking towards her stricken father. Then she had jumped from that story to the linked stories of all the other inhabitants of her village, finding them in their own similar encounters with Needlemen from their past. Encounters which had sown the fear of Needlemen into the village and set the seeds for the activation of the Agency Engine years later.

"Do you remember how it works?" the Queen asked, her eyes gazing at the mirror as it twirled in her fingers. Reflected by the flames, sparkles of light emanated from it and bright dots illuminated the walls and ceiling of the dark corridor. "Your brother looked into it and saw that everyone in Arilon was covered in fear from Lady Eris' magic. You showed it to the Needlemen - encouraging your fellow villagers to do the same - and the Needlemen saw a version of themselves that was no longer feared and that knowledge destroyed them."

The Queen stopped twirling the mirror and held it still. The tiny diamonds inside her eyes flicked up to Teresa, pinning her to the spot.

"I wonder what you will see," she said.

She held the mirror out to Teresa, face down.

Teresa found her hand rising up, moving slowly toward the outstretched item, glistening in the dark.

"It will put you out of your torment," said the Queen. "It won't lie to you or try to make you feel better. It will simply tell you the truth. It will tell you who you really are."

Teresa's fingers brushed against the cold, shiny metal.

Just take it. Take it and know.

Teresa pushed the mirror down and stepped back.

"I already know who I am."

The Queen stared at Teresa, unmoving. She was frozen, like a statue, her gaze piercing Teresa to the core, trying to read every molecule of her being. She was not one to take rejection well. Eventually, she spoke.

"Do you?"

The Queen moved and suddenly Seb was crying out in pain, falling to the ground, clutching his stomach, crimson was already spreading across his white shirt. The sword was back in the Queen's hand before anyone had even seen it appear. Joshua, to his credit, reacted incredibly fast, raising his pistol and getting off a shot but the Queen deflected the bullet with the first sword while the second blade appeared from nowhere and sent the deputy spinning to the floor with an anguished yell.

The treacle that had been running through Teresa's veins was suddenly washed away in a flood of anger and she hurled everything she had at the Queen.

"Stop hurting people!"

A spiral of black lightning blasted out of Teresa's arms, straight into the Queen's outstretched hands, the swords suddenly nowhere to be seen once again. The initial force of the impact forced the monarch backwards half a step but she quickly braced herself and faced down the onslaught, deflecting it around her. When the lightning bounced off the walls and ceiling and floor, the stone turned to wood, then metal, then glass, then back to wood, then it was foliage and branches, then stone again. Reality itself began to warp around the pair as Teresa felt herself trying to rewrite it, trying to create a version where the Queen did not exist.

But the Queen was not ready to go anywhere. Through the fire and chaos, Teresa glimpsed the Queen's eyes staring at her. And she saw the corner of her mouth turn up slightly. The Queen's smile filled Teresa with terror. She had started a fight she had no way of winning. She wasn't powerful enough to get-

Another blast hit the Queen from behind, knocking her off guard and even bringing out a cry of anger.

Teresa was overjoyed - there was no mistaking it this time! She could feel it in the energy that joined and mingled with hers as it attacked the Queen. She knew without a doubt even before he stepped out of the shadows behind the Queen, his own energy blasts illuminating his face in the dark.

Arthur was here.

"Leave my sister alone!" he cried, forcing as much of himself as he could into the maelstrom.

Neither of them had the power alone to defeat the Queen, Teresa knew. But together, their power joined and grew and expanded. Teresa could already feel it surging and expanding. The very Threads themselves were becoming visible around them. The underlying fabric of Arilon, laid bare to the naked eye. Sparkling and illuminated around them, Teresa could see the endless depths of Arilon funnelling its power into her and Arthur. There was just so *much* of it...

Suddenly, faster than Teresa or Arthur could possibly react against, the Queen somehow sidestepped the forces washing over her and twisted them around, pushing them back where they'd come from. The life energy that the children had been controlling was now turned on them. It began closing in around them, darkening and hardening, trying to grab them and hold them tight. The Queen used her superior experience to act before the twins' power had grown too much to withstand. Now, it was she who had the upper hand. And the clawed fingers of that hand were closing in, irrevocably and inevitably, preparing to choke them into complete submission. Teresa could not stop it.

Suddenly, the entire corridor was lit up with a blinding white light that emanated from...

...*behind* Teresa?!

The Queen's hold was instantly broken as the light washed over the monarch.

Teresa fell backwards under the force of her own resistance against the now disappeared power. She looked up as a figure emerged from the metal doorway, striding toward the Queen, arms outstretched, smothering the monarch with a light so bright it hurt to look at. She looked like the Blind Dressmaker - but she felt like something else entirely.

"You..!" the Queen exclaimed in shock. "*You* are the fabled Blind Dressmaker? I thought I had destroyed you, Beginner!"

Teresa looked at the Dressmaker in amazement, as did Arthur.

Beginner?

CHAPTER THIRTY-ONE
THE SCRIPT

- THE BLIND DRESSMAKER -

The Dressmaker was sitting alone in the dark, hiding, as she had been doing for the last few days, when she heard voices.

Two men were speaking - wondering where she could be hiding. They had noticed her door. One of them remarked on her door's missing lock. The Dressmaker had indeed removed the bolt from the outside of the door and fixed it to this side, so she could be in control of when it opened.

It wasn't the first time she'd heard voices out there. A couple of days ago, some townspeople came up. She'd been fairly sure they were Needlemen. Hence, she had also been sure her hiding place was about to be discovered - Needlemen were nothing if not thorough. And yet, strangely, the snippets of conversation she could make out suggested that they were not especially desperate to get their hands on her. The one sentence she'd heard very clearly was 'We do not need her, we just need her to be nearby. If we leave her alone, perhaps she will leave us alone.'

That was not the normal Needleman operating practice.

Nevertheless, they had disappeared and not returned. Another mystery to add to the collection. And so, she'd been alone in the gloom, with nothing but her hand-lamp for illumination. She didn't need much food but the morsels that Eva had kindly given her had kept her going. She had spent most of her time studying the book that the Threads had virtually thrust into her hands as she'd left her home.

Mummy's Trip to the Hospital.

The first part was crystal clear. The Dressmaker would see Arthur and Teresa together here on Terminus soon. The second part was much more cryptic. It was mostly pictures, like a child's book. The pictures made sense within themselves, but their purpose was unclear.

A woman going to hospital to have a baby. The hospital looked just like the Nottingham City Hospital where she'd given birth to Teresa. Sam and Albert had been delivered at home, which had been Elsie's preference. But with Teresa, the doctors hadn't been one hundred percent happy with Elsie's blood pressure so she'd been forced to go into the hospital. And it was definitely this same hospital she could see illustrated in the pages of this book.

The pictures showed simplistic, child-friendly versions of the woman giving birth to her baby. One picture of the doctor and nurses helping her give birth. One picture of the woman's husband waiting nervously outside. Another picture of the nurses giving the woman a beautiful baby girl. And the final picture of the husband joining them - proud parents holding their new daughter.

Those events were illustrated exactly as the Dressmaker remembered them. So what was the purpose of the book? All it did was tell her what she already knew.

But wait.

Her eyes caught something on the final picture. There was a detail she hadn't noticed before. The design on the hospital floor was black and white tiles and the drawing style had put lots of shadows all over the floor and walls. But, for the first time, she noticed one of the shadows stretching across the floor was not actually being cast by anything in the room.

It almost looked like someone was standing outside, in the corrid-

"She's in here," came the voice. A girl's voice.

Teresa!

The Dressmaker's heart leaped even more than she'd anticipated. She sprang to her feet and crept to the door, putting her fingers against the cold metal. Despite the rusty, old iron trying to chill her fingertips, she nevertheless felt a glow of warm, loving energy coming through the door. It wasn't what Teresa was feeling on the surface right now - right now, she was afraid and puzzled and anxious. But that warmth and love was within Teresa, at the core of her. It was what her daughter had always had. Right from the moment she had first held her, like the picture in the book.

"Dressmaker! Dressmaker, it's me! Teresa! Come on out, I need to speak to you."

The Dressmaker's hand instinctively went to the bolt - her fingers were almost entirely closed around the handle before she stopped herself. No, it was not yet time. The book was very specific. She would see both Teresa and Arthur *together.*

When you didn't know the future, you could behave as you liked because your actions were what *made* the future. It was impossible to do anything different than what you were destined to do. But once the future was known to you then things became more tricky. What you were supposed to do in those circumstances was follow the script to the best of your ability. Most times, if you tried to do something different, the Threads (or the universe, as humans liked to say) would steer you back on course. Try to leave the house when you know you're not supposed to, maybe the door lock will be jammed or you won't be able to find your keys, or a visitor will arrive that you can't get rid of. But if you try hard enough, you will actually be able to leave the house, changing the known future. Such occurrences were never good. The Threads did not like it when the time stream was redirected and their reactions could be… extreme.

She took her fingers off the bolt, leaving them hovering there, an inch away from being able to see her daughter.

"Open up please!" Teresa was shouting now, banging on the door. The sound ripped through the Dressmaker's heart. "I know you're in there, why won't you-"

The shouting suddenly stopped.

This was not good. The Dressmaker put her ear against the thick door, trying to hear what was happening now. Hushed voices, muffled speaking. She couldn't make out exactly what was being said. But she did hear a man's voice say a particular word very clearly.

"Mother."

Needlemen. The voice was unmistakable, now. Were these the same ones living in Reliance or new ones? Was the Queen-

"MotMOTHERherMotherMoMOTHERherMotherM OTHERtherMoMOTHERtherMother…."

What was that?!

The Needlemen's voices rose up like a deathly chorus. What was going on out there?

Whatever was happening was suddenly cut short by a booming explosion that rocked the ancient fort. It was quickly followed by another and another. Teresa seemed happy - she thought it was Arthur. Unfortunately, the Dressmaker's senses told her the girl was mistaken. Moments later, the Dressmaker's blood ran cold as her worst fear was realised.

"Hello Teresa," came the Queen's voice.

The Dressmaker listened in horror as the Queen spoke words of sugar dipped in poison. She appeared to be trying to recruit Teresa..? This was disturbing beyond belief! The Dressmaker and the Cat had always assumed the Queen would want to destroy the two human children that potentially posed such a threat to her. It hadn't occurred to them that she might want to recruit them.

Again, her hand went to the door bolt as every instinct cried out for her to go out and protect her daughter from such a fate. But Teresa was steadfast.

"I will *never* join you!" she shouted from the other side of the door.

Good for you, my girl.

Then things went quiet again and the Dressmaker strained to hear what was being said. The Queen appeared to be offering Teresa the chance to look at herself. Was it the mirror, the Dressmaker wondered? That device was extremely powerful. The Queen had constructed it once upon a time and it possessed the ability to look through all lies and obstructions and show things as they truly are. However, it could also show what they have the potential to be... good or bad. Why was she offering it to Teresa? Was she trying to convince Teresa of something? If she was trying to convince the girl to join her, perhaps she was trying to show Teresa something about herself that-

The Dressmaker's head snapped up as a bloodcurdling cry rang out. One of Teresa's companions. It was quickly followed by a gunshot and then another cry as another man fell.

"*Stop hurting people!*" Teresa screamed.

And all hell broke loose.

The Dressmaker could feel the Threads tremble as they ran around her and through her. The power that Teresa was throwing at the Queen was tremendous - way beyond the level the Dressmaker expected. And yet, it was still not enough to overpower the Queen. While the monarch was initially surprised by the ferocity of the attack, she was quickly able to bear its force. Furthermore, the Dressmaker could feel the Queen marshalling her power and preparing a counter-assault of her own. The build-up of power was considerable and the Dressmaker could tell it was going to be extremely devastating.

She couldn't wait any longer. Teresa may not survive the oncoming blast - the Dressmaker had to act and damn the timeline. She gripped the door handle when suddenly the Threads went from trembling to shaking with violent intensity. A new combatant had entered the arena.

Arthur Ness.

The boy's power joined with his sister's and together they closed the energy around the Queen like a giant fist. The Dressmaker had been dazzled by Teresa's power before - but the sheer scale of the imperious might on display now was almost beyond comprehension. It froze the Dressmaker to the spot as her connection to the Threads sent shockwaves pulsing through her. In her mind's eye, she saw the Threads actually become visible as the twins instinctively drew on their limitless power. The bubble grew and grew and for a moment, the Dressmaker was actually frightened. They were amplifying the power but she wasn't sure they knew how to stop it. They would soon overwhelm the Queen, that was certain. But would they be able to stop before they overwhelmed everything else?

Arthur and Teresa were both naturally gifted in their command of the Threads but such levels of power as the Dressmaker was now witnessing should not have been possible even for them. As she'd already surmised, it was their emotional bond that made it possible. The Dressmaker could see the Threads as they swirled around the pair - similar to what she had seen when they'd come into her shop all those months ago. But a million times brighter. And suddenly, she saw what she had missed before. The source of their bond. The reason they were so close. And in that moment, the sad purpose of the pictures in the book became clear.

However, power was one thing. Experience was something else. The Queen, held fast by the mounting storm around her, was wily and much more in control of her abilities than were the children. With a crafty sidestep, the Queen flipped everything around - the mounting power was immediately halted and the energy - switched one hundred and eighty degrees - was now holding the children in place. The Queen, back in control, began to force her way through their protective shielding and slowly reached towards them, ready to crush them in the grip of her perverted version of the life force.

Except the Dressmaker knew that the Queen was out of luck - because both Arthur and Teresa were now here. And that meant the script had been fulfilled.

The Dressmaker didn't bother unlocking the door – with a thought, she blew it wide open. Her power wasn't what it once was but it was more than enough for this. Filling the corridor with the blinding light of creation, the Dressmaker stepped out, moving in front of Teresa and with a single raised hand, she turned all the Queen's power in on itself.

Instantly, the energy storm ceased, causing both children to collapse to the ground, exhausted but freed from the attack. The blowback hit the Queen full on and the monarch was forced back several steps as she tried to get her bearings.

"You…!" This was the first time the Queen laid eyes on her, the Dressmaker knew, but her power signature meant the Queen instantly recognised her true identity. "*You* are the fabled Blind Dressmaker? I thought I had destroyed you, Beginner!"

The Dressmaker could feel the confusion of her children as they learned that the person they knew as the Blind Dressmaker was in fact one of the Pillars of Arilon.

"You didn't finish the job, evil one," said the Dressmaker, the blinding light still pouring into the monarch, illuminating the hundreds of crystals embedded in her face and hands and eyes. With a shock, the Dressmaker felt the truth of what the Cat had told her - she could feel the presence of Neema and the children within those crystals that adorned the Queen's body. The horrifying cruelty of such an act just underscored the Queen's callous evil.

The Dressmaker continued to pour on the power with everything she had. She was not even a fraction as powerful as she had been twenty-seven years ago when she had been defeated and cast out of Arilon. The Queen's power significantly outstripped her own so she needed to keep surprise on her side - use the Queen's shock to mask the fact she was already at her limit.

The gambit appeared to be working. The Dressmaker felt the Queen - unable to properly see - reach out through the Threads, like a bat trying to use its other senses to navigate. Searching for a path through the Threads, feeling, probing, urgently seeking an exit. She quickly found what she was looking for - the entrance to the fort. Still disoriented from the Beginner's attack, the Queen was grateful to find that the doorway was illuminated by a pinpoint of light. A hand-held oil-lamp showed her the way out, like a lighthouse.

"I promise we will end this very soon, Beginner," she growled, her jewelled teeth glittering with rage.

Almost faster than the senses could follow, the Queen conjured a sword and sent it flying down the corridor. Locked onto the torch like a beacon, the blade weaved along the winding pathway at deadly speed. In the very next instant, it had travelled the entire length of the corridor and struck the lamp-holder instantly dead. The escape route now clear, the Queen swooped out like a great raven, catching up with her sword before disappearing out of the entrance and into the night, leaving the fort behind.

CHAPTER THIRTY-TWO
THE PRICE

- ARTHUR -

After a lonely, spooky trek through the night-time desert, Arthur, Ami and Stick were looking forward to the end of their journey and the sight of actual people. However, as they arrived in Reliance, they were greeted by a distinct lack of life.

"And I thought *Graft* wuz quiet at night," said Stick, his voice echoing down the empty main street. "We're practically a party island compared ta this place!"

"It's not like where I come from. The night's almost louder than the day, sometimes!" said Arthur. "Doesn't help us track Teresa down, though."

The three travellers had just completed a monster of a journey – from standing at Rackham's underwater table to standing in the entrance-way to Reliance. They had spent endless hours swimming, rowing, flying and finally nighttime-desert-trekking. The trip from Narrato to Terminus had been an odyssey that felt like it deserved its own reward. But the only reward had been to stand in a deserted street in the middle of the night without a clue what to do next.

Arthur had thought he'd be ready to collapse at this point, but being so close to reuniting with Teresa made him alert and nervous. On top of which, Rackham's prediction about their imminent path to the Agency Engine was more than a little unsettling. All of that was more than enough to keep a person awake.

"So, as we discussed," said Arthur, "we want to keep an eye out for anything that looks out of the ordinary."

"Like a bunch of people up and about in the middle of the night?" said Ami.

"Exactly," Arthur replied. "A sleepy town like this probably lives and dies on its routines. So, anything outside of those routines is probably a pointer to Teresa's presence."

"Like a bunch of people up and about in the middle of the night?" Ami repeated.

"Yes, that would be a-" Arthur looked at Ami and saw she was patiently pointing out a bunch of people up and about in the middle of the night. "Oh. Right. Sorry."

"Tweak those Seer powers, maybe?" Ami teased with a cheeky smile.

"Where they goin', ya think?" Stick wondered, squinting to see the distant figures in the gloom. Arthur could make out a few dozen townspeople, men and women, following a footpath which led out of town and snaked up into the hills. Not a normal night-time event for this place, surely?

"Well, we won't find out by standing here and wondering," said Ami, heading off towards the path. "Come on!"

As quickly as they could, the trio scampered across the street and towards the lonely row of buildings that marked the edge of town. Behind them, the hills rose up and away from Reliance, silent and imposing. The outline of the landscape was barely visible in the dark and the people had already disappeared from view. Stick took out an oil lamp from his pack and lit it, but he kept it turned down low so they wouldn't be so easy to spot. Their immediate surrounding now illuminated, the trio began their walk up the winding path.

"I really hope this is the final leg of this trip," Stick gasped as they walked. "We done swam, rowed, walked, ran, sailed… I might take up a sport after this is all over. Heck, after all that practice, I might take up *all* of 'em!"

Arthur and Ami both laughed, despite their brisk climb keeping them short of breath.

"You always know how to make me laugh, Stick," Ami said to her friend. "Arthur, did I ever tell you that Stick told me all about the night he first met you and Teresa in the Broken Crown?"

"No," Arthur shook his head as they walked. "I do remember that night, though. It was my first day in Arilon."

"The pub were busy that night," Stick puffed as he spoke. "Busier than usual. And then Mr. Frogham up and left me in charge while he disappeared to go an' talk with the Cat. We was runnin' outta blastberry juice and sure enough everybody wanted blastberry juice." He shrugged. "So, in the end, I had ta improvise."

"Oh no…" Arthur already felt himself smiling. "Exactly how do you improvise blastberry juice?"

"He served up a mixture of raspberry, strawberry and fizzy water," said Ami, "and when people drank it…" she had to pause, the giggles already starting to come, "…when people drank it, he'd sneak up behind them and yell-"

"BANG!" Stick shouted and stamped his foot.

The three of them collapsed into fits of exhausted laughter, impressively without breaking stride.

"I spent ages back in London wishing I had blastberry juice - at least now I know how to replicate it when I get back," Arthur grinned. The brief moment of levity passed, though, as Arthur remembered what else had happened on that trip to the

Broken Crown. "Teresa and I promised we would take on the Queen together, that night."

"I hope she's okay," said Ami. She looked up at Arthur. "I don't mind admitting, I think she's kind of amazing. She's tough, she's passionate, she's always trying to protect people. I just wish she wasn't so hard on herself."

It was interesting to hear Ami mention this, Arthur thought. He thought exactly the same thing. Rather than wade in with his views, though, he wanted to hear Ami's thoughts first - see if they matched with his.

"What do you mean, exactly?" he asked.

"Well, she's fierce, she's tough, she can be quite single-minded," said Ami, "but I get the impression she thinks those parts of her personality are bad. Things to be ignored or squashed. Our personalities aren't quite as straightforward as that - we're quite complicated creatures, really. She ought to be kinder to herself, I think. Although, I know that's not always so easy."

Arthur, as always, was impressed with Ami's insights. He supposed that people from Savis spent a lot of time observing and listening to others. Really paying attention to them. How could you be kind to people if you didn't know what they needed?

"The last time I saw her, back on Boricia, she seemed really troubled," Ami continued. "I think the first thing I'll do when I see her is give her a big hug. I just think she could use one."

Arthur realised he'd probably been overthinking things with Teresa during their last conversation. Sometimes, like Ami said, before trying to solve a complicated problem, maybe just kick things off with a little bit of kindne-

319

The sky was filled with a deafening whooshing noise. The trio looked back towards the town. They were high up now and Reliance was spread out below them. But it was no longer alone.

The *Twilight Palace* had come to visit.

"Oh, no…" Ami breathed and grabbed Arthur's hand in terror. She was probably getting flashbacks to when the Queen had attacked Savis, Arthur thought.

The royal flagship had ridden in on the single Travel Line that ran over Reliance. The flagship wasn't pulled up next to the rickety wooden platform, though. Arthur predicted that the person who'd be disembarking would not need any such device.

"Quick, get down," Arthur said, suddenly pulling Ami and Stick off the path. "Stick, turn the light off! Get into the bushes, now!"

The three of them barely got under cover when a small figure appeared on the deck of the vessel. It stood up on the gunwales, right on the edge of the ship. Far from toppling over, the person was motionless, standing there with an unearthly stillness. Their dark gown fluttered slightly in the breeze but their white hair hung down as if carved from stone. Then, without warning, the figure lifted up into the air and flew straight towards them.

"Down!" Arthur hissed and the trio pressed themselves as hard into the ground as they could, willing themselves to be invisible.

The Queen soared overhead, gown flapping in the wind like dark raven wings. She was following the path, Arthur saw, heading in the same direction as the townspeople had been going. She quickly passed over them and then swooped low towards the ground, disappearing behind a dark crag up ahead.

"Come on!" Arthur urged. The three of them scrambled to their feet and began running as quickly as they could up the path.

Where had the townspeople gone, Arthur wondered. And why was the Queen following them? This all felt like a jigsaw and the pieces were sitting there, waiting for him to put them together. How did these people fit with Teresa and why was the Queen following th-

A deafening boom suddenly cracked the air, emanating from somewhere up ahead. It was rapidly followed by several more and with each one, Arthur felt the Threads shake. And that wasn't all - each blast accompanied the unmistakable feeling of groups of life lines within the Threads just... vanishing.

"She's killing them..." Arthur exclaimed in sudden shock. He came to a stop as a tide of bleak devastation washed over him. "The Queen is killing those townspeople."

The other two gaped in horror at the unseen atrocity.

"The death," Ami said. "That's the death that Zane Rackham saw." Her eyes welled up, mirroring Arthur's own. The idea of those townspeople, whoever they were and whatever they were up to, being snuffed out like that was harrowing. "We need to get to Teresa before..."

Arthur was already running again and the other two were quickly beside him.

They almost immediately rounded the rocky crag and were met with something that they were certainly not expecting.

"Is that..." Arthur gasped, "...a fort?"

"An old Raider one, I think," Ami said.

"You think any Raiders are livin' in this one?" said Stick, re-lighting the oil-lamp. "Cuz if they was, I got a feelin' they ain't no more..."

After the initial series of blasts, the fort now sat silent and dark.

"Guys..." Arthur said as he stared at the forbidding-looking place. "I have a bad feeling about this. Maybe you should both wait out here."

Stick lowered the lamp. "And mebbe you can go find yerself a couple a' friends what are happy ta sit back and let you go inta danger all by yerself," he nudged Arthur's shoulder. "I guess 'til that happens, yer stuck with us."

"Besides, isn't there still a knight set to show up?" said Ami. "It could be Iakob or Iosef."

"Or it could be Lord Graves," Arthur countered. "We don't know what-"

An explosion of light and sound suddenly emanated from within the fort, cutting Arthur off. The initial boom tapered off into a long, deafening gushing noise laced with a dangerous crackling. It sounded kind of like a waterfall mixed with pounding electricity. Arthur knew instantly what was happening. His sister was definitely inside and she needed his help.

"Look, just..." he hurriedly instructed his companions, "...just try and keep your heads down, whatever happens, okay?"

- STICK -

Arthur sprinted into the doorway and the darkness immediately swallowed him up. The corridor's interior gaped open like a great mouth but it was intermittently illuminated

322

from within by flashes of white and yellow. The unnerving sound of lightning striking the walls echoed out.

"This is deep, old Arilon stuff, Ami," Stick said, nervously. "Stuff like my momma used ta tell me about. Pillars of Arilon stuff. I'm goin' in but Arthur's right - I'd be a lot happier if you-"

"Don't even *think* about finishing that sentence," Ami said, sternly. "Listen to that noise! I don't want to go in there, either! But guess what, neither did Arthur. And I'm pretty sure if Teresa's in there, she'd rather not be. Our friends need our help," Ami turned to Stick. "And you're not going in there alone. You and me, we look out for each other - that was the deal, remember?"

Stick nodded, remembering when the pair had first met in a devastated marketplace on Graft so many months ago.

"Yeah..." Stick sighed. "I didn't really expect you ta lissen to me. But I had ta give it a go."

He took a deep breath and raised his lamp, staring into the doorway. The noise had intensified now. Perhaps Arthur had joined in. It boggled his mind, the power being thrown about in there. But his mother had always said that, despite what people thought, it wasn't just the powerful that determined how things turned out. Everyone, right down to the meekest of people, formed a thread in the Great Tapestry. And they would all have a contribution to make to the big picture.

"Okay," he said, through gritted teeth. "Let's-"

"I'll take that," said Ami, taking the lamp from him. "And I'll go in first. I can't very well protect you from behind, can I?"

Ami was generally quite mild mannered, but Stick knew when not to argue with her. This was one of those times. "Yes, ma'am," he mock-saluted her as he followed her into the darkness.

The pair stalked slowly down the corridor. The deadly thrashing noise up ahead was louder now they were inside and it battered and reverberated off the stone walls as it raced toward them.

Suddenly, there was a wooshing noise, like a firework, Stick thought, and the corridor was instantly filled with an intense light. Stick could barely see anything for a moment, including Ami or the lamp. But very quickly, the light dimmed enough for the bartender to be able to see the corridor again - albeit, he had to peer through the spots dancing in front of his eyes. Ami's vision must have been similarly affected because Stick caught sight of her just as she was about to fall into a huge crater in the ground, probably made by the flashing destruction from before.

"Careful!" He quickly reached out and grabbed his friend's shoulder, pointing at the deep hole. "You don't wanna trip."

Ami, her vision returning, glanced down at the dark crevice and then back at her friend. "Wow, good reflexes, thanks! My knight in shining armour!"

As soon as she said those words, the pair of them froze. They froze because Stick suddenly remembered something about Rackham's predictions and it looked like Ami had remembered it too - the Knight in Shining Armour came *before* the death.

For some reason, Stick's mother came to his mind and he grabbed the lamp from Ami and threw her to the ground just as something silver and fast-moving glinted in the darkness in front of him.

CHAPTER THIRTY-THREE
THE ANSWERS

- THE BLIND DRESSMAKER -

The Dressmaker reined in her lights and breathed an exhausted sigh of relief. Somehow, against the odds, they had survived a showdown with the Queen.

She turned to Teresa. However, her daughter - having briefly checked her two companions were still alive - was now running back up the corridor towards the entrance with Arthur. The Dressmaker's heart sank for them. She had felt what had happened - one of the worst feelings the Threads could convey. The sensation of a connection to someone important being suddenly snipped as that person winked out of existence.

The sudden death of a friend.

The Dressmaker, not wanting to intrude on the group, walked slowly up the corridor toward them. The passageway's slight curve obscured the commotion from view to begin with. However, since she wasn't using her eyes, she could actually already observe what was happening even before she came around the bend into view of the tragic company.

The Threads - not to mention her ears - painted a full and sorry picture. A girl was kneeling, sobbing, over the still form of a young man. Arthur and Teresa stood over them, their hearts cracked wide open as they tried to process what they were seeing.

The Dressmaker's heart went out to them all - partly because she already knew something it would take those young people a long time to learn. That the connection to their friend wasn't really cut. It had just been changed into a different shape. They were still joined to their friend and always would be, but the nature of that connection was different now. Eventually, they would come to realise it was still there. They would realise that their friend was still with them and could still talk to them and listen to their woes and give them advice. All that would come.

For now, though, there was only emptiness and grief.

For the Dressmaker herself, her immediate future held similarly sad tidings.

While watching Teresa and Arthur attacking the Queen, their power had been so profound, it had laid bare the actual Threads around them, finally laying bare to the Dressmaker the exact nature of their bond. This was what the book had meant when it said she would see Teresa and Arthur. Not just see them physically – but see their power joined together in the Threads. See their bond and finally understand why it was so strong. And now she did finally comprehend, she realised the purpose of the second half of the book – and the sad, terrible role she had to carry out in it.

She looked in the direction of Arthur and Teresa and wished with all her might she could actually see them, not just sense them in the Threads. Or maybe that she could rush over and embrace them. But they weren't ready for the knowledge of who she was – and this sad moment was not the time to tell them. She would have to rely on the Ender to look after them, now. To help them manage their bond. To help them understand who they were as individuals as well as siblings so they could be strong together but still happy apart. His help would be invaluable because that bond *needed* to be maintained and maybe even strengthened further. Arthur and Teresa's unity was the only thing that would defeat not only the Queen but also the shadowy menace lurking behind her.

It would be the Ender's job to maintain their bond – but the Dressmaker knew now that it was her duty to go and make sure the bond was created in the first place.

She took one last look toward her children, listening to their muffled voices. With a mighty effort, she quelled her longings. Her desires were not important. Great or small, powerful or meek, everyone had to follow history's script. Even the likes of her. She had come looking for answers on how the entity and the Queen could be defeated and she had found them.

The Dressmaker turned back towards the doorway she had emerged from. She produced the book from one dress pocket and, from another, a needle and a length of string which immediately began to glow orange.

She closed the door behind her and the sound of her children was instantly cut off.

- TERESA -

Teresa couldn't believe what she was seeing. The bottom fell out of her world.

Stick…

Poor Stick…

Tears in his eyes, Arthur flung his arms around his sister. Despite her growing feeling of numbness, Teresa returned the hug. She gripped onto her brother with all her strength, hoping and searching for some small shred of solace. Some tiny bit of warmth or comfort. The slightest shard of hope that everything was going to be alright.

None of that appeared.

327

They separated.

"Ami, I'm so sorry…" Teresa started to speak but her throat somehow stopped her.

"He said we shouldn't worry…" Ami sobbed as she held Stick's head on her lap, stroking it softly. "Just now, just before he…" She took a deep breath before continuing. "He said his mother was here. She'd come for him. He wasn't scared, he was happy. Happy he saved me. Then he… he…"

Arthur, tears rolling down his cheeks, knelt down and put an arm around Ami's shoulders and rested her head against him. "He went with his mother," he said.

Ami nodded.

Teresa looked down on the scene. Her hands. Her doing. She glanced back at Seb and Joshua as they groaned softly, slowly working their way back to their feet. They needed medical attention, but they were alive. But it was Titanium all over again. Injured friends and comrades.

She looked back at Stick. No, not like Titanium. Worse.

Arthur suddenly looked back down the corridor. "Where's the Dressmaker? She's gone! Teresa, did you manage to-"

"No," Teresa said, sharply. "I didn't need to speak to her, in the end. She gave me my answer without even saying a word to me."

Arthur looked at his sister, confused. She could see his brain working hard to understand her while also processing what had happened to Stick. She was struggling with the same thing. The advantage she had was that she knew exactly what was going on and what she had to do next. And there was no time to lose.

She knelt down and kissed Stick on the forehead. She felt like she wanted to cry, like Arthur and Ami. But she

328

couldn't allow herself to. She didn't deserve to. Not when it was all her fault.

"I'm glad you're here, Teresa," Ami said, putting a hand softly on Teresa's shoulder. "I'm glad we got here in time and you're okay."

Teresa closed her eyes. Ami's touch should have brought some of that warmth and comfort she was hoping for. Instead, it felt cold as ice. "You didn't get here in time. I'm not okay."

She stood up and looked down at her friends.

"I'm really sorry, Ami," Teresa said. "I'm sorry about your island, your family and friends. I'm sorry such a kind, compassionate girl has had to soil her soul fighting in this stupid war. And I'm sorry about Stick. Because all of it is my fault."

Arthur suddenly saw where Teresa was going.

"Teresa, no-"

"I got my answers and I now know there's no hope for me," Teresa said. "My destiny is set and fixed in stone. But by accepting it now and going to her, I know she'll leave this place - so I can at least do one last good act for my friends before I go into the pit forever."

Teresa started walking away from them, towards the corridor entrance.

Towards the Queen.

"No!" Arthur suddenly leapt up and grabbed Teresa's arm. "Tee, you can't! You're not her! I'm telling you! You're not and you never will be! You're a good pers-"

"The Dog-Men were here, Arthur. On Terminus. One of them actually spoke. It called me 'mother'."

"What? But... that's..."

"I realised what they are," Teresa turned to face him. "How come they kept popping up on different islands and why only I ever saw them. It's pretty obvious, really. They're visions from my own mind. Visions I created to torment myself. They're me, Arthur. Those horrible creatures are *me*."

She started walking again but Arthur reached out to her once more.

"Teresa, I won't let you give up like this!"

But this time his hand never landed on his sister - a flash of light exploded in front of him and sent him staggering backwards.

"You don't have the power to stop me, Arthur," Teresa said, her hand raised, ready for another blast as tiny sparks ran up and down her fingers. "I don't say that to be mean. I mean literally, nothing can stop what's meant to happen. The Cat tried to gloss over it, back when I told him about being the Queen, do you remember? He said changing the future isn't easy. You know the Cat. When he says something isn't easy, he means it's impossible."

Teresa expected Arthur to argue the point but his expression betrayed his thoughts.

"You already know that, don't you?" she accused him.

"Rackham said something like that," Arthur said, haltingly. But he raced forward, trying not to let Teresa dwell on that part. "He said it's tricky, but it *is* possible!"

"No, Arthur, don't you see? Read between the lines of what they're actually saying. These guys know all about the Threads and they're telling you that changing the future is something that people just do not do. And they're right. When we connect to the Threads, you can feel it, can't you? I can. Everything's like a jigsaw - pieces, events… they fit together in a particular way. One event creates the next, which creates the next. The shape of the final piece was already determined by the first piece. The future's just history we don't know yet. And you can't change history."

But even as she spoke the words, Teresa could see Arthur wasn't going to accept it - he raised his hands and she felt invisible Threads running all around her, pulling her, holding her, keeping her in place. Before they got too strong, Teresa grabbed hold of them with her mind and flung them toward her brother. Arthur's right arm was suddenly whipped outwards, away from his body and connected to the corridor's wall, as if he were partially caught in a spider's web.

And yet, not for a single second did he give up.

"I'm not... going to let you... go to her!" Arthur growled through gritted teeth as he tried to free himself from the bindings while also hurling the same at his sister. His strength was immense and Teresa really had to concentrate to fight against it.

"There were Needlemen here, Arthur," Teresa said as she fought her brother's energy. "They didn't attack me. They called me 'mother'. Just like the Dog-Men."

Arthur stopped for just a second, as that information hit his brain. The strands of energy holding him to the wall relaxed momentarily as he stopped pulling at them. "But... the Needlemen aren't hallucinations..." he said slowly, the pieces beginning to fit together in his brain. "If the Dog-Men are yours and the Needlemen are hers... and the two of them are related, you're taking that as proof that you definitely become her?"

"More than that," Teresa said. "The Dog-Men only torment me. But once I become the Queen, the Dog-Men evolve into the Needlemen and they become the nightmare of all of Arilon. I go from tormenting myself to tormenting

331

everyone else. All these things link together to give only one outcome, Arthur, you can't keep denying it!"

"And what about the Dressmaker?" Arthur cried in desperation. "What supposed answer did she give you that led you to this conclusion?"

"A simple one, really," Teresa said, her tone flat and desolate. "She didn't come out to help until *you* showed up."

Arthur was silent for a moment and Teresa saw even he couldn't argue against that. He'd seen it for himself. But, unable to accept reality, her brother quickly shook his head, prepared to argue against even this proof.

"We don't know that's what she was-"

"*Stop*, Arthur!" Teresa suddenly cried. "You're making this so hard! I know you love me and you don't want all this to be true. I love you for trying to convince me but this is *happening.*"

The energy suddenly burst from Arthur's free hand once again but Teresa was quicker and turned it back on Arthur, holding him behind steel-hard bars of energy. He pushed himself hard against the barricade, stretching his hand out through the gaps, towards his sister with all his might.

"There's no point, Arthur," she said, tears finally starting to roll. "I'm out of your reach, now."

Teresa suddenly remembered something and reached into her trouser pocket. She took out a small piece of glossy paper and looked at it one last time.

"I won't be needing this anymore," she said, wiping the tears off her cheek and placing the photo on the ground. "You should have it."

Arthur wasn't struggling anymore. Had he given up, Teresa wondered, or was he just exhausted? He stared at her, his face a picture of failure. Ah, she realised. He blames himself. She looked down at Ami, still holding poor Stick's head in her lap. Her expression was equally clear. Shock and bewilderment. The kindest, most compassionate girl Teresa had ever come across and even she knew evil when she saw it.

She looked up at Arthur one last time. "The next time you face the Queen please, promise me... do everything in your power to defeat her. Because she..." Teresa took a deep breath, "...because *I* will be doing everything in my power to defeat you."

And with that, Teresa turned and left the fort behind her. With every step, she felt herself growing smaller and smaller - and a new version of herself was growing larger and larger. She didn't fully understand this new self or know exactly what it wanted. But she knew there was no point in fighting against it anymore. The snake in her heart had won.

As she turned the final corner of the hillside path, the town of Reliance was spread out beneath her and the sky was just beginning to turn a faint, steel grey as the sun began to peek over the distant desert horizon. And down there, still sitting on the Travel Line above the town was the *Twilight Palace*. And standing on the ground beneath the ship, staring up into the hills, right at Teresa, was a tiny cloaked figure. Her new self.

She was still far off in the distance, this new version of her, but Teresa had now decided that was the direction she was going to walk in.

So she began to walk.

EPILOGUE

- ARTHUR -

Arthur had never felt like such a failure.

He stood on the porch of the Sheriff's office, leaning against the wooden railings and looking out onto the town of Reliance going about its business as the morning sun, like the people it shone down on, slowly began its day's work.

A day had passed since their return from the fort but it felt like a week. Longer, even. Everything that had happened in that cold, dark corridor might as well have happened to someone else a million years ago.

As soon as he'd managed to free himself from Teresa's bindings, Arthur's first instinct had been to run down to Reliance after his sister. But he'd gotten as far as the fort entrance before stopping. Seb and Joshua had brought Stick out and Ami had been walking behind them, desolate and alone. In that moment, Arthur had known that there was no point in running down into town. Teresa and the Queen would already be gone. It was Ami who needed him now.

So, the five of them had trekked back down out of the hills and, sure enough, when they rounded the corner and saw Reliance stretched out below them, the *Twilight Palace* was nowhere to be seen.

Ami and Arthur had decided to bury Stick on Terminus rather than take him back to Graft. Ami said that the only thing he really cared about on his home island was his mother and they were together now anyway. It had been Arthur's first funeral - unfortunately for Ami, she'd been to quite a few after the royal attacks on her island. She'd held his hand and gotten

334

him through it, even though he felt like he should have been doing that for her. Stick was her best friend, after all.

Between giving Stick his final send-off and Joshua throwing Sheriff Grace in the holding cell of her own office, a lot seemed to have happened since he'd run into the corridor to attack the Queen. And now Arthur stood and watched horses pull carts and people go to work as if everything was the same as always. Meanwhile, all Arthur wanted to do was go home to his bed and pull the covers up over his head.

"That's a really nice picture," said Ami.

Arthur lifted his head and saw his friend approaching along the wooden shop frontages. He looked down at the object he was holding - Teresa's photo.

"It's Teresa and her family," Arthur said. "They were going out on a special day. Sam's baptism, I think. Someone from Arilon gave it to Teresa before we came here. That was the thing that kind of started this whole adventure off for us and yet we still don't know who it was, where he came from, or how come he had this picture in his possession."

"Life's full of mysteries, it seems," Ami shrugged as she perched on the railings next to Arthur. "Seems like it's up to us to do our best to make sense of them."

"And when we can't?" Arthur said bitterly. "If we don't figure out these mysteries fast enough, what then? We're just supposed to watch our friends pay the price..?"

"Arthur, it wasn't your fault. Trust me, I keep blaming myself too. He died saving me, after all. But in the end... life is complicated. We always expect ourselves to be able to keep track of everything. Be in control of everything. But the reality is we can't and that's okay, Arthur. Life... the Threads... it's all just too complex."

"But isn't that my job?" Arthur said. "I'm a Seer, aren't I? I'm supposed to see into the truth of things. Cut through the complexity of the Threads and get to what's important. Well, I did a great job of that, didn't I? I didn't *see* anything - I just *watched*. I watched Teresa running around, oblivious to the fact she was a Needleman. I watched her get sucked into the Queen's toxic darkness. I watched Stick get killed, even though I'd been warned it was going to happen!"

"We were warned there would be death, Arthur. Rackham didn't know whose or even how many. All those townspeople - well, Needlemen as we now know they were - getting killed just before we got there. That seemed to fit. We had no way of knowing that there'd be another-"

Ami's composure suddenly deserted her and her words stumbled and choked, refusing to come out of her mouth. She turned away as her eyes welled up. Arthur put his hand on top of hers and she turned her palm upwards so their fingers interlaced. They stood in silence for a little while, sharing their pain and somehow finding the pain lessened, just a tiny bit.

"This family," Arthur said eventually, looking down at the picture again. "I've always felt separate from them, even after I discovered I was one of them. It's not their fault," he said hastily. "They've always done their best to make me feel part of the family. It's just that with not knowing why I was given away or how come nobody remembered me being born… it just made it difficult to really connect with them, you know what I mean? And now Teresa's gone over to the Queen…"

"Hey, Teresa didn't go to the Queen," Ami said, sternly. "She couldn't fight anymore and the Queen was able to drag her in. That's not the same. We still have to help her. There's still time."

Arthur looked at Ami in awe. "I didn't think you would be so sympathetic after you found out about Teresa. Not after what the Queen did to Savis."

Ami took a deep breath as she looked out at the bustling high street. It was clear her eyes weren't seeing Reliance at that moment. "Let's just say, it was a bit of a shock..." She turned to Arthur. "But you and I know Teresa isn't just a good person. She's an *amazing* person. Unfortunately, all people - amazing or otherwise - lose sight of themselves from time to time. Lose sight of their own worth. And when that happens, it's up to their friends to remind them who they are."

Arthur looked away, shaking his head. "I wish I could, Ami, but I don't know if I can. I've failed her, I've failed Stick, I've failed the Cat. I feel like I'm in a deep hole and I don't know how to get out..."

"Like you're in a cave of despair," Ami whispered, wiping away a tear. Arthur suddenly looked up at her - Rackham's words. "Well, guess what? I'm in one too. And, just like you, I don't think I can get out on my own, either." She held up a hand. "So, Arthur, what do you say? If you show me the way out of my darkness, I'll show you the way out of yours."

He took her hand and grasped it, holding it tight. With her other hand Ami brought up something Arthur hadn't noticed she'd been holding the entire time. It was small and metallic and it rattled when she moved it.

Stick's badge tin.

"And I don't think Stick's quite done helping us, either," Ami grinned through her tears.

337

Arthur leaned forward and hugged his friend. She was in so much pain, he thought, and yet here she still was trying to comfort him. She was one in a million.

"Who's *that?*" she suddenly said from over his shoulder, confusion in her voice. "And why are they waving like a crazy person?"

The pair stood apart and Arthur turned around to see what Ami was looking at. He squinted against the glare of the morning sun and could just make out two figures heading up the street towards them. Just as Ami had described, one of them was indeed waving rather overenthusiastically.

"Wait…" Arthur couldn't believe it. "*Sam…?*"

Arthur jumped down the steps of the porch and sprinted across the street - dodging several carts — before eventually running into his brother, giving him the biggest hug he had the strength to give.

"*Sam!*"

"Alright, alright, I need those lungs, you know," Sam laughed. "At least leave me with a bit of air in them!"

"What are you doing here? We locked you in the cupboard!" Arthur said, standing back to look at his brother.

"Yeah, we still need to talk about that…"

"May? May Nichols?" Arthur recognised the girl next to Sam. "I am just so confused right now!"

"Yeah, well wait until we tell you what we've been up to," said May. "See how your brain likes you *then.*"

"We've been all over the place, Arthur," Sam said, excitement spilling from every word. "From one end of Arilon to the other, through time and space - the whole thing. We'll tell you all about it but first… where's Teresa?"

The glow of happiness that had briefly surrounded Arthur was immediately washed away once again. "She's... I'm sorry, Sam, but she..."

"She went with the Queen already, didn't she?" Sam nodded. He seemed to glance into the air, like he was listening to someone speaking. "No, no, I know that..." he said. "It's the closest you could get us, I understand. You did good, Guide, thanks."

May saw Arthur's confused expression.

"Don't worry, he's not mad," she said. "Well, I mean he *is* mad but not because of that. That's just the Guide. Don't worry, that's a conversation for when you're sitting down, trust me."

"Sam..." Arthur shook his head. "What's going on? Why are you here?"

"I know how Teresa becomes the Queen."

"So do I," said Arthur. The time for secrets was long gone and he decided it was best to just tell it straight. "There's no easy way to say this, Sam. She becomes the Queen when she-"

"She kills you, yes, yes, I know all that," Sam waved the words away. Arthur stared at his brother in shock. Just where *had* the pair of them been? "But that's just the trigger. I'm talking about what comes after that. It's a journey of years and years but I've seen it all, Arthur. I understand what happened. And I know how to use it to defeat the Queen and save Teresa."

"But, the future's fixed," said Arthur. "So I keep hearing, anyway."

"Well, according to the Guide, that *is* the rule," Sam admitted. "Whatever's going to happen is going to happen. *However-*" Sam raised a finger before Arthur could interrupt,

339

"...like I said, that's just the rule. And when it comes to rules, I kind of don't always completely follow them."

"He's a complete pain in the backside, basically," said May.

"Indeed I am," said Sam. "Because if you try really, really hard and if you're a big enough pain in the universe's backside..."

"Which he is."

"...then you *can* change the future. I mean, there's a slight consequence that you will kind of... break time."

"Break *time*?" Arthur exclaimed.

"Yeah, but you can probably fix it, I bet...?" Sam shrugged, hopefully. "Remember when I broke dad's flower vase with my football? We absolutely glued that thing back together, didn't we? And it doesn't leak!"

"It kind of does," said Arthur.

"And it looks exactly like it did before."

"It kind of doesn't."

"Well, we fixed it, is the point," Sam said.

"Sam," Arthur said, "the universe isn't the same as a flower vase."

"Funny, that's exactly what the Guide just said," Sam shook his head. But before Arthur could interrupt, Sam reached out and put his hands on Arthur's shoulders. "But listen. This is the only way. It's the only way to save Teresa and I think it's probably the only way to stop the Agency Engine."

As he looked at the impossible sight of Sam before him, something suddenly clicked in Arthur's mind.

"*The return of something you didn't know was lost...*" he muttered.

"I'm sorry, what?"

"We were given a series of waypoints to the Agency Engine. One of them was 'the return of something you didn't know was lost'..."

Sam cocked an eyebrow. "Should have said 'the return of someone you cruelly locked in a cupboard'..."

"Did you have any more waypoints?" May asked.

"Only one more," said Arthur. "It's 'the hand of an enemy'."

"And do you happen to have any enemy hands lying around?" Sam asked.

"We have a Needleman disguised as a Sheriff," Arthur motioned to the Sheriff's office, "locked up in a cell."

"Brilliant!" said Sam. "Come to think of it, I might have a little something to add to that..."

May snorted. "You're telling me."

Arthur glanced at her again and she raised a hand. "For when you're sitting down, remember?"

Sam put his hands on Arthur's shoulders. "So, what do you say? Does Teresa have brothers that are prepared to break the universe to give her a chance to save herself? Not to mention, give her a chance to save the rest of us by defeating the Queen?"

Arthur stared at Sam for a long while.

Then a smile crept onto his face and he put a hand on his brother's shoulder.

TO BE CONCLUDED

in

TERESA SMITH
and the
QUEEN'S REVENGE

part 3

(but before you go, just turn one more page…)

EPILOGUE II

- THE GUIDE -

"Oh, what the heck," said Sam. "I was going to wait and tell you later, but I'm just going to tell you now."

"Tell me what?" asked Arthur.

"Tell you about the Guide."

"Um...Sam," the Guide could hear May say, suddenly, "do you think that's a good idea?"

My thoughts exactly, the Guide said into Sam's brain.

"Arthur needs to know," Sam argued.

Of course, but right now?

"We've literally just walked into town," came May's voice. "What happened to waiting until he was sitting down?"

"You see," Sam said to Arthur, "she came to me some time ago..."

"Or just ignore me and have the talk now..." May said, giving up.

Sam...

"...I wanted to tell you and Teresa," Sam steamrolled on to Arthur, "but there was never a good time. Also, I would have sounded *really* crazy telling you there was a woman living inside my head..."

"Sam, what are you talking about?" The Guide could hear Arthur's confusion loud and clear. She felt sorry for him – his confusion was nothing compared to what he would be experiencing a few seconds from now.

"She talks to me in my head, you see," Sam continued, "but no-one else can hear or see her unless she makes herself visible in a reflective surface, like a mirror."

343

Sam, he is not yet ready for this...

"Or a polished surface like this one..." Sam said, raising his arm up to his brother.

From the Guide's point of view, the strange netherworld that was Sam's brain was mostly a giant, dark globe. Even though she was permanently connected to it, she could travel out at any time into a mirror or similar surface. They appeared to her like doorways of light in the dark – such a doorway appeared now. It was the polished metal plate that Sam wore on his arm which allowed the Guide to appear and speak to Sam and May together.

"What... what am I looking at, Sam?" came Arthur's voice. The Guide saw Arthur's face appear in the doorway as he peered uncertainly at the shiny metal plate that his brother was showing him. "Am I supposed to see something here?"

The Guide sighed. She supposed she couldn't put this off forever. She stepped forward into the light.

Arthur's expression didn't change at first... but then he saw the Guide's shape and form materialise in the mirror. The shock and horror that crossed his face told the Guide that, yes, he could see her.

"Sam...!" Arthur gasped. "Sam, *this* is your Guide?"

"Yep..." Sam grinned nervously.

"But that's *Lady Eris!*"

Hello, Arthur Ness. It is good to see you again, she said.

"Sam, that's Lady Eris!" Arthur exclaimed again. "Lady Eris is talking to me! How is Lady Eris talking to me, Sam?!"

"Okay, okay, Arthur, calm down..." said Sam, "...let me explain what happened..."

The Arilon Chronicles

Arthur Ness and the Secret of Waterwhistle (a two-part story)

The adventure begins as a fearful Arthur is evacuated from London to Waterwhistle.

Teresa Smith and the Queen's Revenge (a three-part story)

The story continues as Arilon erupts into war and Teresa faces the biggest challenge of her life.

Trust Me... I'm a Thief

An interactive adventure starring the Rogue's Run Trio. Will they succeed in their mission? You decide how the story unfolds...

And don't forget

www.arilon-chronicles.com

for news, book extracts and the ever-expanding *Arilon Encyclopaedia*

Tell us your thoughts on
Amazon, Goodreads, Instagram, Twitter or Facebook